"Why don't you guys come inside?" Jackson asked, holding the door.

Violet was suddenly aware of how cold it had gotten. The mountain air didn't mess around once the sun set.

"I'm sorry." Ash gestured to the door. "Please, come inside."

Violet peeked through the picture window into the cozy farmhouse. If she walked in the front door, she'd be tempted to never leave.

"I should get going. I've already taken up too much of your time." Violet stood and began gathering up her things.

"It's no problem. This was...fun."

Violet met his gaze. It had been fun. While Outcrop was challenging, and Hacker's behavior an off-brand imitation of Laurent's bullying, an evening with Ash had her feeling up to the challenge. Working together was freeing, like the play of children, when there are no limits.

She just needed to remember the hard limit. Ash was a friend, nothing more.

Dear Reader,

I'm thrilled you've returned to Outcrop, Oregon, for Ash's story! He may be the bossy older brother of the Wallace clan, but his romantic side is revealed in *The Cowboy and the Coach*.

Violet Fareas has her work cut out for her, convincing Outcrop that a new-to-town female football coach can bring home a winning season. Ash tries to keep his distance from the beautiful, brilliant Violet, but when half her coaching staff quits, the former quarterback has to step up. Can this cowboy keep his heart on the sidelines?

My husband is a legendary high school coach. My son was a multisport athlete, always up for the next challenge. Watching their experiences, I saw how a good coach could shape more than just a season, but a lifetime. This book explores the pressure and privilege of working with high school athletes in a small community.

I'd love to hear what you think of Love, Oregon! You can find me on social media and at my website, anna-grace-author.com.

Happy reading!

Anna

HEARTWARMING

The Cowboy and the Coach

—

Anna Grace

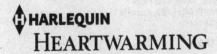

HARLEQUIN

HEARTWARMING

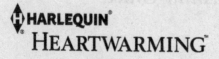

HARLEQUIN®
HEARTWARMING™

ISBN-13: 978-1-335-47549-7

The Cowboy and the Coach

For questions and comments about the quality of this book, please contact us at CustomerService@Harlequin.com.

Harlequin Enterprises ULC
22 Adelaide St. West, 41st Floor
Toronto, Ontario M5H 4E3, Canada
www.Harlequin.com

Printed in U.S.A.

Recycling programs for this product may not exist in your area.

Anna Grace justifies her espresso addiction by writing fun, modern romance novels in the early morning hours. Once the sun comes up, you can find her teaching high school history, or outside with her adventure-loving husband. Anna is a mediocre rock climber, award-winning author, mom of two fun kids and snack enthusiast. She lives rurally in Oregon, and travels to big cities whenever she gets the chance. Anna loves connecting with readers, and you can find her on social media and at her website, anna-grace-author.com.

Twitter: @AnnaEmilyGrace
IG: @annagraceauthor
Facebook: Anna Grace Author

Books by Anna Grace

Harlequin Heartwarming

Love, Oregon

A Rancher Worth Remembering
The Firefighter's Rescue

Visit the Author Profile page
at Harlequin.com for more titles.

To my son Owen,
thank you for all the summer river walks where
you helped me with the details of this novel.

CHAPTER ONE

ASH WALLACE STOPPED right in the middle of his determined, well-planned tracks. Yes, he was staring. It was technically impolite, but who wouldn't stare? For the first time in a decade, he didn't know what to do.

Stunning was the only word for the woman. Ash wasn't much of a wordsmith, but since he was frozen on the spot, he was pretty sure he'd been stunned. He was like a deer on the highway, mesmerized by oncoming head-lights. As such, he should move out of her way before he was flattened, leaving his kid fatherless.

But she needed help. The woman was jug-gling a binder, several notebooks, two differ-ent bags and a ball cap. Her car had California license plates, and by the way she was scan-ning the parking lot, this was her first time in Outcrop. Ash's well-honed sense of chivalry couldn't let anyone carry that load on their own, especially not a guest in the community.

The cool autumn breeze picked up a lock

of her dark hair, pushing it against the soft curve of her face. She shook the errant wave out of her eyes, then reached back in her car and somehow balanced a jacket and a clipboard on top of her pile.

That was the final straw, or clipboard, as it were. The tower wobbled precariously to the left.

"You need some help?" Ash gave in to instinct and jogged toward the beautiful, overloaded stranger.

She glanced up, as though shocked at the common courtesy. Deep brown eyes met his, and Ash smiled. The facial expression felt out of place and completely unexpected. A brief, capable nod was his general greeting to everyone, even his own parents. The greeting said, *I acknowledge you but have no time for any nonsense.* When was the last time he'd smiled at a stranger?

She studied him, then smiled back, becoming even more beautiful. "I've got it. Thank you."

It must have been the reverberation of her speech that did it. The jacket slipped off her pile. She attempted to pin it down with her chin, sending the rest of the stack sliding out of her arms.

Ash caught the first notebook and the ball

cap. She lunged for the clipboard, upsetting the binders. Ash reacted quickly, and between the two of them not an item hit the gravel parking lot.

"Or not," she admitted, laughing at herself. Her gaze connected with his. "You've got quick reflexes."

He nodded. It had been over twenty years since he'd captained the football team, but he still called upon the skills he'd honed playing quarterback as a teenager. Intelligence and planning helped him as head of his family's ranching operation. Physical strength was needed for working with the horses. Leadership and teamwork were essential for raising a son. Agility came in handy when evading his matchmaking sisters' attempts to set him up.

"Happy to lend a hand."

"I always underestimate the amount of stuff I'm carrying." The woman walked to the back of the car and balanced her pile on the trunk. "Someday I'll learn to get a bigger bag."

"Or maybe a dogsled?" Ash turned her ball cap in his hands, then glanced at her from under his Stetson to see if the joke had landed.

She grinned back at him. It had.

"I don't think I could afford to feed that many huskies."

Ash fought to tamp down the warm feeling rising within him, but some kind of happiness lunged in his chest, like a pack of joyful sled dogs. He had a hundred things he should be doing this afternoon and joking around with a gorgeous woman was *not* on the list.

"Where are you headed?" he asked.

She glanced over his shoulder to Eighty Local. "Here."

"Good choice. My brother owns this place. Best restaurant you'll find in central Oregon according to most folks."

"And according to you?"

"Best restaurant period." Ash clamped his mouth shut before he offered to buy her a late lunch.

What is wrong with you, man?

She pulled her hair up off her neck and wound a rubber band around the thick, dark waves. "Good to know."

Ash was disappointed she'd trapped her beautiful hair in a knot at the back of her neck, but she was still gorgeous. And he was still staring.

"My brother is a gifted chef. He's also over-extended and exhausted, but the guy can run a kitchen." Ash gestured toward the addition his brother was attaching to Eighty Local. "I've got a meeting here too."

She shook out a bright red track jacket. "Popular place."

Ash glanced around at the parking lot, packed like always, but today was different. He, and half the town, was here to deal with an emergency. Hunter had kindly offered the use of the events center, even though it was only half-finished and there was no seating. "Our football coach had to step out unexpectedly. Everybody's here to check out the new guy."

"Oh yeah?" She slipped her arms into the jacket. "Are you part of the coaching staff?"

Ash let out a dry laugh. "No, ma'am. But my son plays. He's pretty excited about it, and I'm just here to make sure he gets a good high school experience."

Why was he babbling like this? And to a woman with California plates?

"Hmm." She gazed at him. Ash couldn't tell if she was actually interested in his small-town drama, or just amused. "What do you hear about the new coach?"

"Not much. He's got some big shoes to fill."

That was putting it mildly. Coach Kessler's shoes were unfillable, and this was a tense meeting he was heading into. The legendary coach had unexpectedly and unapologetically quit. He'd been telling the town for years that he wouldn't leave until he found a suitable replacement. Kessler was irreplaceable, so no one bothered to take him seriously. Then a week ago he'd told the booster club he was retiring, said the new coach was better than he'd ever been. When Ash had tried to argue with him, Kessler had slapped him on the back and told him his son would be in good hands, then cut out on a camping trip.

She shrugged, then glanced down at her feet. "Maybe this coach will bring some new shoes?"

He chuckled. "Maybe."

She zipped up the jacket, and Ash was somehow reminded of a knight donning armor for a battle.

A really beautiful knight with long eyelashes, a dry sense of humor and a softly curving face that forced him to clench his fists so he didn't accidentally reach out to touch her cheeks.

Ash attempted to clear his thoughts, like he'd been trained to during his years in the National Guard. He needed to get away from this woman. Priority one was his son, and he was here to make sure Jackson had a positive football experience. He wouldn't let anyone hurt his son ever again. Until he'd finished raising Jackson, there was no space for a woman. Standing around bantering with an out-of-towner made no sense. Ash was nothing if not sensible.

He opened his mouth to say good-bye, but instead found himself blurting out, "Let me help you with all this."

"Sure. Since I seem to have left the dog-sled at home, and the dogs." She grabbed the ball cap from his hands. Ash moved to pick up the two binders and small pile of books. "And since we're going to the same meeting."

The words filtered through his brain. He looked at the books and clipboards, words slowly coming into focus.

Coaching manuals. Playbooks. Team rosters.

He glanced at the woman, who was now settling an Outcrop Eagles ball cap over her hair. She smiled at him.

"I'm Coach Violet Fareas."

THE COWBOY'S GAZE ran from her face to her coaching materials and back again on repeat like a sprint drill. Violet repressed a laugh. She loved upending other people's expectations. Which was fortunate because as a woman in football, she'd been doing it her entire life.

He gave up on the books and just stared,

his green-brown eyes connecting with hers, sending a jolt of anticipation through her. Violet had been excited about coming to Outcrop, and relieved to walk away from the program at Taft, but pure, giddy anticipation? She hadn't felt that since walking onto the field in college. Just what was it she was anticipating?

When his shock finally dissipated, he pulled off his Stetson and held out a hand, like he'd been trained to politely greet out-of-state female coaches since infancy. "Welcome to Outcrop. I'm Ash Wallace."

Violet slipped her hand against his large, warm, calloused palm, and it became clear that *this* was what she'd been anticipating. She'd be happy to stand here shaking his hand all day long. For the first time in her life, she wished she were European, so the handshake could be followed by a polite kiss on the cheek.

His eyes crinkled at the corners as he smiled, and she realized she'd been shaking his hand for a *lot* longer than was strictly necessary.

Get a grip, Vi.

Her hand suggested this was *exactly* what it was trying to do. Violet forced herself to step back and turned to her massive pile, still smiling despite herself. She was here to get her first head coaching experience, not flirt with handsome cowboy dads.

There would be no flirting with anyone. She was in Outcrop for one year, two at the most. This was an important step in meeting her ultimate goal—head coach at a NCAA Division III college. She needed to get a head coaching position at a bigger, more competitive school next year, then get herself on the staff of a college program. That would take a winning season, and a good showing in the playoffs.

"You settling in all right?" he asked.

"I am. My uncle runs a store here—"

"Outcrop Hardware, Tack and Feed, right?" Ash nodded at the old wooden building her uncle Mel kept in pristine condition. "We all know Mr. Fareas."

Violet glanced back at the adorable little town. Brick buildings lined a main street opening onto a town square and park at the far end. She'd rented an apartment above a chocolate shop, down the street from her uncle's store.

"Can I help you carry these books into the meeting?" Ash offered again.

He's going to carry my books? As far as she knew, no one had ever offered to carry anyone's books since 1957. Violet glanced around, wondering if she'd been transported to some alternate universe where chivalrous cowboys welcomed female football coaches without question.

"Sure. You're not as fluffy as a sled dog, but I guess you'll have to do."

He built himself a large, well-constructed pile of her stuff, a little grin playing on his lips. "What you need is a pack mule. Easier to train than a big group of dogs, and a mule can go anywhere."

"Yes!" Violet laughed. She'd give herself another twenty seconds to flirt with this guy. But that was it, twenty seconds. Then it was all business from here until November. "But wait, mules are stubborn, right?"

"They are."

Violet shook her head. "So am I. That might be a problem."

Ash pressed his lips together, clearly holding back a smile. "Maybe a llama then?"

"Or a camel? Camels are fun."

He shook his head, mock serious. "I hear camels can get pretty competitive."

"Me too!" She threw her hands up and sighed. "Guess I'll just have to keep hauling my own stuff around."

"Hmm…stubborn, competitive, willing

to pull her weight." He smiled down at her. "Sounds like the perfect coach."

Okay, she *had* been transported to an alternate universe. Or she was dreaming. In which case she should flirt as much as possible before she woke up or was transported back to the real world.

"I plan to do my best," she said, with way more eye contact than anyone had ever used uttering that sentence. "I'm not perfect, but what you see is what you get."

"Then I'm glad we got you. I won't lie, though—Kessler's departure was a real shock."

Violet nodded. She was expecting a bumpy start, but it wasn't anything she couldn't handle. She was more than ready for this.

"If you run into any problems, don't hesitate to call on me for help," he said.

Violet finally gave in to the overwhelming urge to glance at his ring finger. Then she fought a second urge to raise her hands in victory, shouting *Yes!* when she saw there was no ring.

She forced her gaze off Ash's unmarried hand and cleared her throat. "You said your brother owns this place? Must be nice." She picked up her stack and headed toward Eighty Local.

"One of my brothers," he said, then nodded to a side door. "We're meeting in the events center."

Violet followed him to the correct entrance. "How many siblings do you have?"

She was going to stop flirting the minute they walked through the door. That was the hard cutoff. The first impression this community had of her would *not* include getting cozy with the parent of a player. Coaches were always the object of scrutiny, and few things would tank her credibility faster than accusations of favoritism toward the son of a good-looking, unmarried cowboy. She knew firsthand how quickly rumors could spread.

He raised his brow, dipping his head toward hers as he said, "Only four, but it feels like more most days."

"You're the oldest?" she guessed.

He nodded, lips twisting in a wry smile. "They're a lot to keep in line."

Violet laughed. His eyes lit up, and he seemed as surprised by their connection as she was. She glanced at the door to the events center. It was beyond time to shut this down... whatever it was. She wasn't getting involved with a guy in Outcrop, and certainly not the parent of one of her players. Period. Exclamation point. Full stop, end of story, no sequel.

To remind herself that he was off-limits, she asked, "And your son will be one of my athletes?"

His expression shifted, and sobered. He stopped before the entrance, his green-brown eyes muddying with something between sorrow and regret. "He will. This was going to be his first year playing for Kessler."

Violet held eye contact. "But instead, it's his first year playing for Fareas."

He rubbed his left hand, his fingers pinching the spot where a wedding ring might have rested once.

She'd stepped into something here. It was like the two of them had been playing in the sandy shoals of a lake, then she'd inadvertently swum out too far, the solid ground beneath her feet giving way to a murky expanse of cold water.

Ash shook his head, as though he could clear his thoughts like an Etch A Sketch. "Right. I'm glad you're here. I just want my son to have a good experience."

"Perfect. I want the exact same thing."

He smiled again, but this time his smile was tinged with worry. He was probably concerned about his son. Football dads were always concerned, wanting their kids in the starting lineup, convinced their offspring should play quarterback.

Ash opened the door, then held it with his foot.

"It's gonna go well," he stated, as though he had the ability to decide such things.

Violet glanced through the door. People milled around, voices rumbling in concerned annoyance. Unfinished pine walls glowed in the September sunlight pouring through the high windows. The room was devoid of furniture, save for one folding table set up on a small dais.

"Of course, it's gonna go well. It's a meeting with the booster club. What could go wrong?"

At her words, a man glanced up from his conversation. He took in her hat, and arms full of coaching manuals, then stepped back. The other occupants of the room followed suit, and a path cleared between her and the folding table.

Violet relaxed her shoulders, and walked into the room.

TWENTY MINUTES LATER, Violet knew all too well what could go wrong. *Everything.*

She might love upending other people's expectations, but the Outcrop Eagle Booster

Club didn't want anything upended. The only things they seemed to want were her resignation, Coach Kessler's reinstatement and free range to wear as much plaid as humanly possible.

Questions started flying the minute she claimed the table, and only grudgingly stopped as she began her speech. Their silence was even more threatening than the interrogation.

Violet scanned the crowd, then took a deep breath and smiled as she finished up her rehearsed speech. "I know change is hard, and unexpected change can be frustrating. I bring fifteen years of experience in football, as well as the belief that there is no better way for kids to learn valuable, lifelong lessons. I look forward to working with you as we create the future for the Outcrop Eagles." She inclined her head, like her dad used to do when speaking to team parents—a signal that he was finished, and they could begin applauding.

The room was silent. So quiet you could have heard a pin drop, only no one here was dropping anything. She suspected these folks would keep a tight hold on all their pins and any other sharp objects, so they could impale her the minute she stepped from behind the folding table. She cleared her throat, absently scanning the room for pitchforks.

The Eagle Booster Club was not happy.

For the most part, anyway. Her parking lot cowboy gave her an encouraging nod, then glanced at another man standing near the back of the crowd, who smiled at her too.

Ash had been shocked when she introduced herself as the new coach. He'd recovered well enough, his gorgeous smile and subtle humor cracking as he carried her books into the meeting. She'd been tricked into thinking this was the type of person she'd be dealing with. Had her one concern walking in here really been that she might get too attached?

If the Outcrop Eagle Booster Club had their way, she wouldn't have time to attach to anything. Ash would be politely carrying her coaching materials right back outside and helping her into her car. She could imagine his gentlemanly wave as she headed back down I-5 to California.

But she wasn't budging. While Violet had never gotten the chance to play on the line, she'd watched enough tough linemen in her day to know how it was done.

She was new, and new was hard.

Also hard? She was only here for a year or two. She needed to get the players on board, coach a winning season, then move on to a larger high school if she was going to reach her goal of coaching D III. She could just imagine the look on her parents' faces as they sat in the stands watching their daughter's college team play. She could anticipate David Laurent's reaction when he learned she'd risen above him in the coaching world. Laurent might be head coach of one of the biggest high school programs in Southern California, but Taft High wasn't college ball.

But first she had to get through this season, and it would sure help to have the parents on her side.

"Let me get this straight." A man wearing a mustache leftover from the last time such things were in style crossed his arms and glared at her. "You've never been a head coach before."

"This is my first head coaching position." She'd led with that. There wasn't much to get straight.

The man glanced at his compatriots. He seemed to be repressing a laugh.

"You've never been head coach, and you're from *California*." He said the state's name as though it was a den of evil and vice. "And we're supposed to trust you with our boys?"

Violet gazed politely at the man. She'd met his kind before.

"I hope my actions earn your trust." She took her eyes off the troll and scanned the room for friendlier faces. Mostly men, but a strong contingent of women glared at her from the crowd. It was one big, angry, plaid-covered mass of humanity.

Not a lot of love coming from Outcrop today.

She glanced up at the rafters, then around the unfinished events center. Tools had been neatly stacked in a corner, and the room was clean and bright, like someone had abruptly stopped working and done everything he could to get the space ready for the meeting.

Her eyes dropped back to the crowd. This meeting mattered to these people. She wasn't what they were expecting. Their kids had been practicing all summer with Coach Kessler. Most of the men in the room had probably played for the legendary coach when they were in high school.

Trust takes time, her father loved to say. Violet rested both hands on the folding table and let herself feel her dad's support. She'd learned a lot watching him handle players and parents; it was time to put that knowledge to work.

A woman in steel-toed work boots and a brown canvas jacket raised her hand and asked, "Did you play football?"

Violet nodded. "I did. I played for my father's team in Miner's Creek, California. Go Diggers!" No one chuckled at her continued sense of school pride. Time to pull out the experience. Violet straightened to her full five feet nine inches. "I was a three time, all-state cornerback in high school, and I kicked for Mount Union in college. I worked in recruiting for the university for five years, but wanted to get into coaching, like my dad."

Murmurs of respect burbled in some pockets of the room. "You plan on recruiting some girls for our team?" the same woman asked.

"I plan on recruiting anyone who wants to play. Football is a complex game of intelligence and athleticism. There's nothing like it in the world. There are a lot of good lessons to be learned on the field, and I hope to offer that learning opportunity to anyone who wants it."

A few heads nodded. The woman in the work boots was satisfied. Maybe the tide was turning?

"Janice, I don't see why that would matter," Mustache-man barked. "We don't need a team. We've already got our crew. We need a coach."

Violet widened her stance and addressed the man. "I have seven years of coaching experience, and eight years of playing. After I graduated, I stayed on at Mount Union as a recruiter for the team. Then I moved home and started a business as a personal speed and power coach for elite high school athletes, which is lucrative work in Southern California. That allowed me the freedom to assistant coach with my dad, for my old high school. From there, I was asked to join the team at Taft in San Jose, one of the biggest programs in the state. For the last four years, I've been the quarterback coach there. Now I'm here, and I'm excited to get started." Violet gave a firm nod this time, the one *she* used to signal to her players that her word was final, and she wasn't at all interested in discussing things further.

But something was off. Violet scanned the crowd, trying to figure out what it was. They were disappointed to lose Kessler, naturally. They weren't expecting a woman, fine. It wasn't like this was the first time she was the only woman involved in a program. But there was something else at play, and she needed to figure it out. A little compassion might go a long way.

Hopefully, because a *little* compassion was about all she had left.

"I understand this change in leadership is unexpected and—"

"You don't understand anything," her challenger barked. "You're not from Outcrop. You're not even from Oregon—"

"Settle down, Hacker," Ash's voice resonated from the back of the crowd, firm, but not adversarial. "Let the lady—" He stopped, cleared his throat, then continued, "Let the coach speak."

"I don't think this is the time to settle, Wallace. My boy's a senior this year." He turned accusingly on Violet. "I know my son's got a good shot at a Division One scholarship."

You and every other overly invested football parent in America.

Violet took a deep breath. "I've helped a lot of kids navigate the NCAA Clearinghouse over the last few years. As a former college athlete—"

Hacker swatted her words away. "You were a *kicker.*"

Wow. This guy could win a national championship in getting under someone's skin. Violet had been proud, thrilled to kick for

Mount Union in Ohio. It was an incredible experience, and her jersey was preserved, framed and would go on the wall of her office when she eventually settled into a head coaching position at a Division III school.

But she'd wanted to play cornerback. She was fast and had the hops and hands to turn the ball. No college coach would even consider her. *A woman as fast as you should be a track athlete*, she'd been told by every program she approached. But Violet didn't want to run on an oval. Football was her passion. If she had to use her power and coordination to kick the ball rather than catch it, so be it.

And if she was still a little salty about not playing cornerback after all these years, it was what it was. Her experience would help her change the world and provide opportunities to other girls with similar goals.

This plaid-encrusted, smirking, caterpillar-faced alpha dad was getting in her way. She nodded, then did the one thing her father had warned her to never, ever do. She intentionally humiliated a parent in public.

"What position did you play? In college."

His face went blank. She knew a hundred parents like this, men who were probably pretty good in high school, or not. Men who'd built a story for themselves about a bad knee, or a disinterested coach that kept them from playing in college. As the years passed between their high school experience and the present, people could convince themselves they'd possessed the skills and work ethic at eighteen that most people didn't develop over a lifetime. Very few people had the drive, ability and interest to sacrifice their youth for the opportunity to play at a higher level. And that was completely reasonable—there were a lot of great things to do with the teenage years. Most athletes understood logically and at a gut level that college play would never lead to a professional career. But they did it anyway, just to stay in the game a little longer.

The majority of folks who liked to pretend they'd walked away from a college career were harmless, but not all. The worst of those people took their broken dreams out on their kids, forcing them to realize a goal they'd never been in danger of reaching in the first place.

Hacker's stunned expression flashed to anger. "If you're such a hotshot, what are you doing here?"

Saving my soul from being crushed by my former boss, she was tempted to yell. But this man didn't look like he had much of a soul left himself, and certainly didn't care about hers.

Coach Kessler had a private reason for stepping down, and he'd explicitly asked Violet not to say anything until the doctors had a better sense of what they were dealing with. "Coach Kessler contacted me a few weeks ago—"

"How'd he even find you?"

"My uncle, Mel Fareas, runs a store here in town, Outcrop Hardware, Tack and Feed."

"We all know OHTAF," a woman said impatiently.

"Yes, well, Uncle Mel put Kessler in touch with me a few weeks ago, and he asked if I was interested in making a move. I heard about the program here in Outcrop and—"

"That makes no sense," Hacker barked. "Why would Kessler quit? I've coached offense for him for the last three years and he never said a word to me."

Did the guy think she had the former coach tied up in her trunk so she could take over his team?

"I can't speak for Coach's decision, only—"

"And why'd he pick you? If you're the type of coach who walks away from one team, how do we know you're not going to walk away from this one?"

Violet made her second mistake with Hacker. She looked straight into his eyes. The anger and frustration she saw there clarified everything.

He'd been under the impression that he was next in line for the throne.

Mr. Hacker had been planning on filling Kessler's shoes, and if Kessler hadn't offered the position to one of his assistants, it was because he didn't think those shoes would fit.

She had *a lot* to learn about the ins and outs of this community. But she'd given Coach Kessler her word. He loved this program, and it would break his heart to see it disintegrate. She had to work with these guys. And as upset as they seemed to be at the moment, they couldn't be worse than David Laurent. Nothing could be worse than Laurent.

Her worst trait was a stubborn inability to listen to others when she was angry. Most people were wired for fight, flight or freeze under stress—Violet was all fight. She tended to get her back up and go on the offensive before she had all the information.

Willingness to fight made her an excellent football player, but as a coach she needed to learn to listen, and talk things out, particularly in a tight community like this one.

Violet drew in a breath and scanned the back of the crowd. Ash's gaze connected with hers, and he gave her an encouraging nod.

She had one supporter. And somehow, Ash felt like enough.

"My initial words must not have made it clear. I love this game, and working with high school players has been the most rewarding endeavor of my life so far. I'm competitive. The fastest way to win is to build respect and cohesion in a team. That's what I'm here to do, and I look forward to working with you all to get it done."

The crowd shifted with her words. A few people nodded. They'd been shocked by Kessler's retirement, and it would take some time to get over it. It was her job to help them. Violet breathed in with relief. *Everything is going to be okay.*

Or so she thought for .067 seconds.

"You can love this game all you want," Hacker spat. "But I'm not going to stand by and watch you ruin my son's senior season. I quit."

Another man moved to stand next to Hacker. "I will also be resigning from my assistant position. No offense, but I signed on to work with Kessler."

The rush of humiliation hit her, a cold slimy fear that felt like slowly slipping down a crevasse filled with Jell-O. It seemed as if she should be able to stop the fall, and she didn't want to die of suffocation by gelatin, but she had no clear options.

She swallowed and picked up her clipboard. Her hands shook as she crossed Hacker's name off the list as offensive coordinator. She glanced at his compatriot. "What's your name?"

"Ramirez."

She drew a line through the name of what had been her receivers coach. She gave the men a wry smile. "Literally no offense, then. Good thing that's my coaching specialty." She glanced out at the crowd, her heart pounding, ready for a fight. "Anyone else?" She took a quick look at the list. "Looks like I've still got a little help left. Then there's snack coordinators, gear check out. If you want to quit, quit now. Makes it easier in the long run."

"Larsabal," one man muttered.

"Greg Larsabal," she read loudly, and drew a line through his name. These people were awful, but she'd coach this team straight to state playoffs with nothing more than a chalkboard and a bullhorn if she had to. After a few others had spoken up, she scanned the piece of paper. There was one name remaining. "Looks like I still have a Jet Broughman on the list." She looked around the room, angry and unconcerned about showing it. "You gonna bail? Because now's the time."

A tall, dark-haired man in his early thirties startled. He glanced at her cowboy, and a world of information passed between the two men. Jet's eyes darted to the unfinished floor, his jaw working as he formulated a response. Then he raised his chin and spoke loudly, "No, ma'am. I'd like to stick with the defensive players if you'll let me." The quitters in the front row mumbled disapprovingly. He cleared his throat. "I'm ready to get to work, Ms. Fareas."

She let her gaze connect with his, and smiled as she said, "I go by Coach Vi."

He touched his fingers to his forehead in a salute. "Coach Vi, welcome to Outcrop. I'm here to help."

Her slow, cold descent into humiliation Jell-O halted. She was buoyed, ever so slightly.

"I think this concludes our general meeting. Coaching staff," she looked at the one man left on that staff, "please remain behind."

The crowd mumbled as it broke apart, heading toward the exits. Some people glanced apologetically in her direction, others intentionally turned their backs on her. Violet's gelatinous free fall resumed.

"Wait," a deep, resonant voice commanded.

Ash held out a hand in front of Hacker. "Hold up. This isn't right and you boys know it."

"It's *not* right," Ramirez challenged. "Kessler can't just leave like this."

"Kessler's given his time and talents to this town for over thirty-five years." Ash's voice dropped dangerously. "He can do whatever he wants."

People's feet stilled at the authority in his voice. *Who is Ash Wallace? The mayor? The sheriff? The only reliable dentist in a hundred miles?*

"Let's all come back together." Ash gestured. "I don't like the way this ended."

"I don't like the way it started, Wallace," Hacker said.

For once, something we can agree on.

"This is Brayson's senior year, Joe. You can't leave the lady without an offensive coaching staff."

"You're one to talk." Hacker gave Ash a once-over. "You haven't stepped up for the program once since you've been back."

Ash widened his stance and glowered at Hacker. "I have a lot on my plate."

Hacker scoffed. "We've all got a lot going on, Wallace. You had four years as quarterback on this team, and you haven't so much as stopped by a practice since you returned to town."

The cowboy gave Hacker a long, hard look, then dropped his gaze. He seemed to be wrestling with something as he studied the Stetson he held in his hands. Finally he nodded, as though to himself.

"You're right. It's time to step up." He glanced at Violet. "Coach Vi, if you'd like my help with offense, I'm at your service."

CHAPTER TWO

JOE HACKER, ED RAMIREZ and everyone else in the booster club stared. Ash glared at Joe, then Ed, then anyone else who was still looking.

What are these guys thinking, being so rude to the new coach?

And more importantly, what was he doing?

The minute he'd seen Violet he'd been drawn to her, like a mule deer to a prize-winning rosebush. He had a son to raise, a ranch to run, the family's herd of Canadian Horses and four siblings to keep in line. He didn't have space in his life for a woman, and certainly not one who made him feel like tripping over his own feet.

And now he'd committed to spending six afternoons a week with her.

Nice work, Wallace.

Hacker had his hands in his pockets, poking his head forward like a self-satisfied rooster. "Now you're stepping up? Kessler's been asking for your help for the last five years, and now you throw your hat in the ring?"

"Kessler didn't need my help. He had a full staff." Or that was the reason Ash had clung to, anyway.

Hacker shook his head. "You want to help row this sinking boat, be my guest. No one else is gonna work with *Coach Vi*." He spat out her name, sending a frisson of anger down Ash's spine. Hacker was harmless for the most part, but he had a mean streak. As seemed to be the way of such things, Hacker had married an incredibly nice woman and had a couple of good kids. Back in high school, Hacker knew how far he could push the limits and still get away with bad behavior. That hadn't changed.

It was time someone called him out.

"You're out of line, here. You haven't even seen her on the field." Hacker opened his mouth to speak, but Ash spoke over him. "Now, I know you're upset. We're all going to miss Kessler. I can only assume he has his reasons for leaving."

"And what did she have to do with his decision? That's what I'd like to know."

"No one knows why Coach retired, but I'll remind you he's been talking about it for years. He's just started dating Christy Jones. Maybe, after years of giving his heart to this team, he's ready for a break."

Hacker seemed to consider this, then anger flashed across his face. "Why'd he choose her?"

Ash glanced at Violet. *Because he wanted to test my resolve by dropping a beautiful, talented woman into my path?*

He refocused on Hacker. "This is *our* team. We all want the same thing—great experiences for our boys, the same lessons we learned playing for the Eagles. If we want the legacy to survive, we need to carry it."

Ash looked into each man's face and could almost see their resolve wavering. These were essentially good men, reacting to the situation out of fear. They could come around. There was still time to salvage this.

Then Hacker sneered. "I want a full ride for Brayson at the University of Oregon, playing for the Ducks." He pointed to Violet but couldn't bring himself to look at her. "There's no way she's gonna get him there."

Waves of anger rose off Hacker, nearly visible in the cool air of the unfinished events center. His fury seemed all-consuming, until it was interrupted with a calm, almost irreverent, "Yo. Wallace."

Ash looked over to see Violet addressing him. She seemed completely unperturbed as she said, "We've got a coaches meeting now. You can chat with your friends later."

A tiny smile bent her lips as she beckoned with her head.

Okay, the woman knows how to cut her losses.

Ash glared at Hacker and his cohort in disgust. What was happening to this town?

As the booster club filtered out through the doors, Ash moved against the crowd, toward Violet. He couldn't speak as his thoughts pinballed from post to post.

He couldn't help out right now; he was too busy with the ranch.

He had to step up, or Jackson wouldn't have a season.

He should get out of this woman's path ASAP before he did something he might regret.

All the while his steady steps brought him closer to Violet as the last of the booster club left the room. The unfinished events center his brother was adding on to Eighty Local was silent, save the sound of Jet flipping pages in a manual.

Violet held eye contact with Ash. "I can handle it," she answered his question before he asked.

Ash nodded. "I see that. It's just these guys—"

"Read this tonight." She handed him a playbook. "I've been over your offense and it's solid, but we need to mix things up."

Ash let out a breath, then looked into her eyes. *Is she going to pretend like nothing happened?*

"I'm interested in working through our size, rather than in spite of it. I went over the roster, and while we have a few big guys, there's no use pretending we have brawn where we don't."

Apparently, she is.

Jet cleared his throat, then looked up from the manual. "We do have some real big egos. Will that make up for our lack of size?"

Violet laughed, a beautiful lilting sound, rising, filling the room to the exposed rafters and unfinished walls. Ash laid a hand on his almost-brother-in-law's back. He'd always appreciated Jet, and today just confirmed what a legitimately good guy he was.

Violet drew in a breath and wiped tears from her eyes. "Bigger egos than the ones barely managing to squeeze out the door earlier?"

"Not possible," Jet said, sobering. "These are good kids. And this is a great town. I'm real sorry this was your introduction."

The door into the kitchen opened, and Hunter came trotting in. "What happened?"

Ash looked at his brother and slowly shook his head. "Hacker happened. Then Ramirez and Larsabal felt the need to join in."

"Is that why Kessler quit?" Hunter looked to Violet for answers. "Did he finally get sick of Hacker?"

Violet locked her lips together. If she knew why Coach resigned, she wasn't saying anything.

"The dining room is buzzing. I'm sorry it all went down at the first meeting," Hunter said to Violet.

"I'm not," she responded calmly. "It's better to know what I'm dealing with."

Hunter nodded to Ash, impressed, then reached out to shake Violet's hand. "I'm Hunter Wallace. Welcome to Outcrop."

"Thanks. Want a coaching job?"

Ash chuckled, but Hunter didn't seem to realize it was a joke. He hesitated, as though he was actually considering it. Ash took a step in front of his exhausted, overextended brother and spoke for him.

"No. Hunter runs a restaurant, and he's under a deadline to finish this events center." Hunter started to interrupt. Ash spoke over him. "You're working twelve-hour days as it is. Jet and I can keep things afloat until the old staff returns."

Violet raised her brow. "You really think those guys will be coming back?"

"I expect they will."

"And you think I'm going to let them?"

"Valid point." He gave her a wry smile to mask his apprehension. "When you find out I'm not very good at coaching, you may re-evaluate."

She looked him straight in the eye and said, "You're not very good at coaching, *yet*."

Hunter laughed out loud. "Man, she dropped a *yet* on you. There's no backing out now."

"Growth mindset," Violet explained, setting Hunter laughing even harder. "You can get better at anything, no matter how bad you might be right now."

Ash had used those exact same words on each of his siblings numerous times. In this family, he was the one pulling out the *yet*.

"Besides, you couldn't be worse than the guys who just quit," she said. "I'd pick you over them any day."

And that's when Ash got worried. She *had* to let the old coaches return. He was happy to fill in the gaps, but he wasn't a coach. Jackson should have the chance to play football without his dad's legacy looming over him. People would expect Jackson to play quarterback, and Ash didn't want that kind of pressure for his kid. Jackson had a stressful enough childhood, thanks to Ash's bad decision-making. The kid should be able to enjoy his teenage years. If Jackson got shunted into the position of quarterback, his high school experience would be weighed down with responsibility and expectation, like Ash's had been. He didn't want his son to wind up like him, exhausted by the weight of the world he carried.

"Let's keep an open mind. Hacker and those guys might come around." Violet gave him a look. Ash continued, "I'll be honest, this isn't a great time for me to be coaching." He gestured to the unfinished room. "Hunter needs help finishing this place up. Our other brother Bowman's off fighting the Fallen Ridge fire in eastern Oregon, so I've got double duty on the horses, along with helping the new doctor get her clinic in order."

"Maisy's doing great," Hunter said, heading over to where he'd piled his tools. "And I can help with the horses."

"No," Ash snapped. Hadn't he just reminded Hunter how busy he was? Even now, Hunter was back at work on the events center, while running his restaurant. Ash rubbed his forehead. Everything would be so much easier if his siblings would do what he told them to. "You're busy here. Mom and Dad are home for a few months. We're fine with the horses. But the Ranching Federation is starting to mobilize with this county commissioner situation." He finally found a real smile and slapped Jet on the back. "And my sister's getting married to this guy, on my ranch."

Jet grinned, a flush rising up his neck. There was a lot going on right now, and Ash was determined to do everything necessary to make his sister's wedding perfect. Clara and Jet deserved to have everything run smoothly on their big day, considering it had taken the two of them a long, bumpy decade to get there.

"Are those all your excuses?" Violet asked.

Ash shifted. "They're not excuses…"

She glanced up at him. "Your son's on the team?"

He nodded.

"So, your excuses are weddings and horses and county commissioners." She eyed him. "But your *reason* is that your son is on the team, and you don't want to get in his way. Am I right?"

Ash took a step back, as though her insight had a two-foot radius, and he could escape it physically.

"It's admirable. It's rare, actually. I respect it." She reached back and pulled the rubber band from her hair, freeing the dark waves. "I wish I didn't have to take advantage of your kindness."

"It's okay," Ash said. "I'm happy to—"

"Sure," she interrupted him, a little smile playing on her lips. "There was nothing but pure joy on your face when you volunteered."

Ash clenched his jaw to keep from smiling back. He'd always had a weakness for women who understood the power of well-timed sarcasm.

"Now, what have I got here?" She gestured between the three of them. "Who are you guys? And why didn't you two quit like everyone else?"

"Personally, I'm not much for quitting," Jet said. "And Ash here is incapable of letting down his community. Neither of us played one minute of football after high school, unless you count a backyard pickup game."

Violet studied them—dusty work boots, worn-in jeans, calloused hands. "You're ranchers?"

"Yes, ma'am," Ash said. "Wallace Ranch is a horse-breeding operation. Jet runs cattle."

"And you've both lived here all of your lives?" she guessed.

The men looked at each other and chuckled. "Actually, no. Jet just returned to Outcrop last winter."

"I was in Seattle." He shuddered. "Tech industry."

Violet cracked a smile at his reaction, then turned to Ash. "And you?"

"I, uh, I was with the National Guard."

"Can't you be in the National Guard and still live in your hometown?"

"You can." He turned his hat in his hands, studying the rim.

"I thought that was the point of the National Guard."

"The point of the National Guard is to serve your country."

"Right." *Way to offend one of the two people in town interested in helping out, Vi.* "Sorry."

He rolled his shoulders, then looked up at the ceiling. "There are a number of ways to serve with the Guard. I was career and worked full-time. I returned to Outcrop after I retired." Ash had a finality to his voice that allowed for no further questions.

Yes, sir...

"I'm happy to help out where I can with the team," he continued. "My son's been looking forward to football season all summer long. First game is on Friday, and I'm not about to let it fall apart now."

"Thank you," she said. "I'm not about to let it fall apart, either."

She glanced up at him and he held eye contact. It was a nice, long, heart-rate-increasing gaze. Like running a hill workout, only fun.

Violet forced herself to look away. She knew better. If embarrassing the parent of one player was a bad idea, developing a crush on the parent of another was worse. But his eyes were bright and crinkled around the edges with laugh and worry lines. His lips curved up when he made a joke. And the whole boots, jeans and Stetson situation? She was officially a fan.

Jet cleared his throat. "You, uh, been over the equipment lists yet?"

Okay, Vi. Time to get it together.

"Yeah. No." She shook her head. "Let's talk equipment."

Jet handed her a list. Violet focused on the brands, condition, purchase dates.

Not good.

She scanned the equipment list a second time. "You're still using this stuff?"

"I guess so. This is my first season coaching." Jet took the list from her hand, then pulled his head back. "These helmets are pretty old."

"These helmets are ancient."

Ash and Jet exchanged a look. "Kessler's been trying to raise money for new equipment, but the booster club has the final say on spending, and they earmarked most of it to pay the assistant coaches," Jet said.

"Well, that's not much of a problem anymore."

The men chuckled.

"To be clear, I'm volunteering. I haven't had, and don't want, a salary," Jet said.

"Same here," Ash concurred.

"Thank you both. Still, new helmets are expensive." The men were incredibly kind to donate their time, but the salaries would only be a drop in the bucket for new gear. Their first game was Friday. There was no way they could get helmets in time, even if they had the money, which they did not.

This was a mess. An angry community, only two assistant coaches, one with three months' experience and the other with none, old equipment, unsafe helmets.

What's next?

The back door banged open, answering her question. A tangle of boys tripped over themselves as they came crashing into the room.

"Coach Broughman!" one of them yelled, holding up his hands for a double high five. Jet turned to the kid and started a complicated

handshake routine while the other kids jab-
bered about escaped emus and painting the
interior of a cabin.

Violet crossed her arms as she observed
the interaction. The boys were good friends,
full of rowdy energy. The one in the midst
of the handshake choreography was big, and
still unaware of how his body filled the space
around him. She heard Jet refer to him as
Manuel, and he was clearly the joker of the
pack. Off to one side was a quieter kid, the
sort who never called attention to himself but
was the glue keeping these guys together. All
the boys were good-sized. Not the huge high
school linemen you might find at Taft, but big
enough to determine this must be the defensive line she'd heard about.

Only one boy looked more like a receiver
than a lineman. Closing the door and catching
up to the pack was a young man that had to be
Ash's son. His hair was lighter and partially
covered with a ball cap rather than a Stetson.
His eyes were blue as opposed to Ash's hazel,
but his shoulders, the shape of his face, and
even the way he walked were uncanny repli-
cas of the cowboy.

Then there was also the way he bounded
across the room and said, "Hey, Dad!"

Ash nodded at his son the way he had at

Jet, at his brother and everyone else. But Violet could see the pride in his eyes.

"Jackson, boys, meet your new coach."

The enthusiasm immediately turned on her.

"You're the new coach?" Jackson asked, as Manuel said, "Dude! You're a woman!"

"I am."

"That's cool. Is it true you played for Mount Union?"

Violet grinned. These boys had whipped past the obvious and were on to the important stuff.

"I did. It was a great experience."

"I wanna go to a school like that," Manuel said, as another boy chimed in, "I'm gonna play in college, if I can."

Jet nodded at the quiet one, saying, "It's got a business administration program, Aaron. You might look into it."

"And Mount Union's the best D Three in the country," Aaron replied.

She nodded. "I think so. You guys must be the famous Outcrop Defense."

The boys turned to each other and held their hands up in a way that looked like they were imitating a bird's beak, then they all yelled, "Larry!"

Of all the bizarre things she'd seen since arriving in Outcrop, this had to be the weirdest. Ash kneaded his fingertips against his forehead and sighed. Then he glanced at Violet. "You'll meet Larry eventually."

"He can't be worse than Joe Hacker."

Ash's lips quirked in a smile. "You say that because you haven't met Larry...*yet*."

Jet stepped forward. "This is the defense. We've been working hard all summer and look forward to hitting the field."

"We heard Hacker lost it and all the other coaches quit," one of the boys said, with no sensitivity or tact. As one would expect of a seventeen year old.

"News travels fast," Violet muttered.

"It's okay," Manuel said. "All those guys did was stand around and bark at us. You're better off with just Coach Broughman."

Ash laid a hand on his son's shoulder. "It's, uh, not just Coach Broughman." He looked down at Jackson. "I volunteered to help out, until Coach Vi can find someone more qualified."

If Ash was expecting Jackson to balk at this, he was sorely disappointed. "You are? Dad, that's awesome."

Ash shook his head as though the statement was debatable.

"Tomorrow's practice is going to be a real

change for everyone," Violet said. "Can you boys take the lead, show the others what hard work and flexibility look like?"

The boys glanced at one another.

"Yes, Coach," Jackson said.

"I'm counting on you." Violet made eye contact with each player, eliciting their silent promises.

Of course, with Manuel, as she was learning, few things were ever silent. "We gotcha, Coach!"

"Hey, Dad, can I get a soda?" Jackson asked.

"You can have one soda, but don't spoil your dinner."

Jackson shook his head and looked at Jet, then over to Hunter, who was fitting in a piece of trim along one of the windows. "I don't even know what that means. Like I've ever not been hungry at dinner."

Ash gave him a begrudging smile, then said, "Go get a soda with your friends. We'll head home in a half an hour."

"Let's go!" Jackson headed toward the main restaurant. "It's my turn. I'm buying."

"Hey…" Hunter's voice stopped the boys in their tracks. "Outcrop Eagles Defense doesn't pay for soda in this establishment. Your money's no good here."

The cheer rising from the boys was cut off abruptly by Ash. "You pay for your soda, Jackson."

Hunter turned on his brother. "I'll give these kids free drinks if I want."

"I'm trying to establish a work ethic in my son."

"And I'm trying to spoil my nephew."

Ash scoffed as Hunter held up his hands in innocence. "What's the point of owning a restaurant if I can't use it to bribe Jackson into thinking I'm his favorite uncle?"

"You're one of my two favorite uncles," Jackson said.

"For now." Hunter pointed a thumb at Jet. "In a few weeks Jet's gonna be married to your aunt Clara, and then where do I stand?"

"Uncle Coach Jet Broughman, the favorite." Jet crossed his arms as he considered the title. "That has a nice ring to it."

"No, it doesn't," Hunter said. "By the time he gets finished saying it, our other sister, Piper, will marry someone even cooler than you and bam! There's another uncle to compete with."

"Go get your soda." Ash addressed the boys, while shutting down the banter with a glare. "Then we need to get back to the ranch.

It's cold tonight so we'll close up the turn out pens."

"Coach Vi, would you like a soda?" Jackson asked.

She was startled. The kid put no thought into offering her a drink, just as Ash hadn't hesitated to help her in the parking lot.

And honestly, some carbonation and sugar sounded great after this long afternoon.

"I'd love a soda. Thank you."

"Have you ever had an Italian soda?" he asked. "It's where you take fizzy water—"

"Sparkling water," Hunter corrected.

"Then you add a flavor, like lemon or strawberry. I'm getting pretty good at making them."

"Lemon is my favorite. Thank you, Jackson."

"We're on it!" Manuel yelled, lunging for the door. The other boys waved and jostled their way toward the restaurant. Jackson grinned at her and touched his fingers to the rim of his ball cap, just like his father did his Stetson. The noisy pack rolled out of the events center as Hunter trotted after them, yelling, "Wash your hands!"

The room stilled as the boys and their energy swirled out into the restaurant. Violet glanced up to see Ash studying her. He held her gaze for a moment, searching for something. Approval? A guarantee that she was going to do right by these boys?

He must have found…whatever it was, because he refocused on the hat in his hands and grinned, giving her a glimpse of the anticipation he must have felt toward football season when he was their age. "Think you can do something with this crew?"

Violet's heart beat with the challenge of showing Ash what she was capable of, and giving these players the best high school athletic experience possible.

"Absolutely."

There was nothing in the world like student athletes. Their excitement, energy and raw potential were precious, like a handful of uncut diamonds. Her father always said it was a privilege to be entrusted with young people's time.

She was going to give these kids everything she had and make this a season to remember.

New helmets. New ideas. High expectations.

All of it would be next to impossible with the support of only three community members so far.

The parents were going to make it diffi-

cult to stay. But if these kids were any indicator, leaving the team at the end of the season
might be even harder than getting through it.

CHAPTER THREE

"CIRCLE UP." Violet widened her stance and blew the whistle, gesturing for the team to gather around her at the end of their first practice. It was a brilliant September afternoon, with the occasional cool breeze coming off the Cascade Mountains.

A steady, colder breeze blasted out of the stands, where dozens of parents sat, arms crossed, judging her.

Not that she blamed them. The first practice had been a little rocky.

Or maybe a lot rocky.

Violet tried to focus on the positive. The boys she'd met the day before at Eighty Local were a solid, hardworking, functional crew committed to the team. They thought of themselves as defensive players, but with their energy and work ethic, she'd need them filling in gaps on offense as well.

Currently, Manuel, Aaron, Jackson and the rest stood together, with Jet right behind them. They all wore T-shirts with a devious-looking bird on the front and one word splashed across the back, Larry!

So Larry was an emu, and her defense was weird. She'd take it.

A larger concern were the boys slowly ambling over to the team meeting: her quarterback, the running backs and the receivers. The starting team was made up of seniors, and not surprisingly, the sons of her recently resigned coaching staff. These boys had been dragging their cleats all practice long, grumbling about everything from warm-ups to cooldowns. The second string was taking their lead from the first. And because this was a tiny town in the middle of nowhere, there was no third string.

Violet had started practice with her best rousing speech, and a couple of new plays she wanted them to have ready for Friday. All afternoon the boys had steadfastly refused to run the new plays correctly, clowning around in the field, then looking to the stands for approval from their fathers. There was no outward defiance she could easily deal with. They just pulled the team down being slow, unmotivated and right on the edge of sabotage. She was engaged in battle with a powerful, leisurely mudslide. But now that she knew, she could shore up her sandbags and dig in.

VIOLET RAISED HER chin and paced in front of her players. Some looked interested. Others were nervous. A few looked downright defiant.

It wasn't an unusual set of facial expressions for any team practice. But her quarterback, Brayson, turning toward the stands and exchanging a slow smile with Hacker? That made her skin prickle, alert to trouble.

"That was interesting," Violet said, giving the players a wry smile. "I saw a lot of things I liked." She nodded to the players who had really gotten after it in practice. "And a few I didn't. I know you all signed up to play for Kessler, and this is a big change. But I'm confident we can work together for a winning season."

Some smiles, some grimaces.

An encouraging nod from Ash, along with a thumbs-up from Jet buoyed her confidence.

"Our first game is Friday night. For the most part, we'll keep things steady until I see where we are. But we *will* be running the new plays."

More grumbling came from the back of the group. Violet continued over them. "I've gone over the rosters from Bend and Redmond—those teams are our biggest opposition. Literally. They have some huge guys. We need to work through our size, and to do that I've dipped into strategies making use of speed and agility."

The grumbling got louder. One kid in the back said something about not needing to learn anything new about football.

"What was that?" she asked.

The group silenced.

"I thought I heard someone express a concern about learning something new." She scanned their faces, giving the boy who'd spoken a long, awkward amount of time to express himself. "No? Good. Because one of the many ways we're going to outsmart the opposition is by keeping them on their toes. Expect new plays regularly."

A voice of dissent came from the parents in the bleachers behind her. Violet refused to turn around to acknowledge it, but she was pretty sure it was Hacker. She noticed Ash shift and glare into the stands.

Yeah, definitely Hacker.

"I learned a lot about the Outcrop Eagles today," Violet said. "There's solid skill and athleticism in this group. We've got some rough patches to smooth out, but there's nothing we can't work with. Friday night I'd like to see—"

"You can't expect the team to learn new

plays four days before the game," Brayson interrupted her.

Violet gazed steadily at him. Her fingers twitched, and she forced air through her lungs to fuel her patience. *Never argue with a teenager*, her father always said. *They have nothing to lose, and you have everything to lose.*

"I can't?" Violet mugged a thoughtful expression, then glanced around at the rest of the team. "Tell me none of you have ever crammed for a test before?" A few kids chuckled. "I learned a semester's worth of algebra one weekend my sophomore year."

Brayson tried to interrupt her again, but Violet kept speaking. "I went over your academic records this morning. You're a hard-working team." She paced, keeping her eyes on the kids. "No one is on academic probation. Not one of you. That's almost unheard of on a team this size. Several of you are four-point students." Her eyes landed on Brayson. "Including you. So yeah, I've got some high expectations." She glanced at her watch. "Now, it's almost six o'clock. How about you all get out of here and get your homework done? I'll see you tomorrow."

Violet hesitated briefly before trotting ahead of the players to the exit gate, where she stopped before the line of kids filing out.

Her dad ended every practice by high-fiving each kid and giving them a specific compliment on something they'd done that day. She'd been looking forward to having her own team, and ending practice this way, for as long as she could remember.

"Nice work, Kaellen." She held up her hand for a high five. Kaellen slapped it back, without excitement, but not disrespectfully. She noticed Ash glowering at the next kid, Joaquin. His high five was a little more enthusiastic.

She'd studied the roster and knew everyone's name, and for a lot of the kids she gave a specific comment on at least one thing they'd done right today. On she went, getting a lukewarm but not cold reaction.

Then she got to the receivers. She held her hand up. "Good work, Soren. Your sprint drills were impressive. I'm guessing you run the one hundred in track, right?"

Soren Larsabal looked trapped. Brayson and the others stood behind him, and his father glowered in the stands. The kid was a talented player. Violet guessed he was the type who lived for Friday nights, and this whole situation couldn't be anything he wanted to deal with his senior year. Soren stared at the green turf beneath his cleats, anger coloring his cheeks. Her eyes flickered to the stands. The expression on Greg Larsabal's face suggested there would be consequences if he so much as offered her a smile. Soren looked up and glared at Violet, as though it was her fault he had to be rude, then he pushed past without acknowledging her.

Violet, for the first time since arriving in town, gave in to a glimmer of uncertainty. She took a slight step back.

The next two boys followed suit, pushing past her to the gate.

Ash ran in her direction, ready to swoop in and save her. Violet saw his approach and gave him the slightest shake of her head. She had to handle this on her own if she wanted to prove to herself, or at least that David Laurent had been wrong about her.

Brayson squared his shoulders and strode toward her. Violet kept her hand up, like they were playing a game of high-five chicken.

"Nice job on the sprint ladder," she said, naming the one time in practice he'd given his all as he raced his friends. "I like that competitive spirit."

Brayson stopped and glared at her, then stalked toward the exit.

The next several players followed Brayson's lead. Violet had half a mind to kick each non-high-fiver off the team. There might not be enough kids left to actually play at that point, but whatever.

Toward the back of the group, she noticed Jackson had his hands on his hips as he spoke to the other linemen. Manuel nodded, then broke away and cut to the front of the line. He stepped up to Violet, expression serious.

Her heart caught in her throat. She was not going to take it well if this happy, gregarious kid followed Brayson's lead.

Then Manuel grinned, offering both hands for a double high five. "Coach Vi, up high!"

Relief washed through her. Violet's smile broke out as she slapped him five.

"Down low!" Manuel held his hands down and Violet followed. "Now the elbows!" He bumped one of her elbows with his, then the other. Manuel was always loud; Violet suspected he'd been loud since birth. But right now, he was extra vocal for the benefit of others. Brayson watched from the edge of the field, annoyed with the challenge to his leadership. "And squawk!" Manuel held his hand up like an emu beak.

Violet followed suit and let out a squawk to be heard in three counties. Manuel whooped with excitement. "Coach's got it!"

He did something that could be considered

a victory dance, if one were very generous in their definition of dance. He didn't exit the gate but stood back and crossed his arms over his chest. Aaron was up next in line and went through the entire high-five routine again. Tears pricked the backs of Violet's eyes as he planted himself on the other side of her, crossed his arms and waited as the next in line came up. And soon enough, she was exchanging high fives with everyone on the way out, as the defensive line stood watch.

At one point, she glanced up to see Jackson, a big grin on his face as he gave his dad a thumbs-up. Ash looked surprised and humbled. This must have been Jackson's idea.

What an incredible kid.

As the last player exited the field, Ash trotted over to Violet. He stopped in front of her, and any words she had evaporated. His hazel eyes met hers, a mix of respect and concern, relief and fear in his gaze. Violet closed her eyes slowly and let out a sigh.

"We need to come up with a plan," she said quietly.

Ash's deep, resonant voice set off tremors in her belly as he said, "I'm here to help. Any time."

Parents trickled out of the stands, passing them on their way to the exit.

"That wasn't too bad," she overheard one mom say.

Violet mugged an exasperated expression and Ash's lips twisted in a smile.

"She did okay," another answered back. "But Coach Kessler left some pretty big shoes to fill."

Ash drew his eyes away from Violet and called after the women, "I think Coach Vi brought her own shoes."

She chuckled. Ash gazed down at her, his rare smile slipping out. "You were amazing today. I don't know how you did it."

Violet basked in his words. She wasn't sure how she'd done it, either. The practice had been intense, but she'd kept her cool, kept focused on the positive and made it through day one still in charge of the team.

Ash rested his hand on her shoulder, giving it a friendly squeeze. Hope ignited in her chest. She had friends in Ash and Jet. She had seven years of coaching experience. She could do this.

That hope was quickly extinguished with the bucket of cold water that was Joe Hacker's voice.

"Ash Wallace, nice to see you finally stepping up." He glanced at Greg Larsabal, then

Ed Ramirez. "'Course she is a lot prettier than Kessler."

Ash dropped his hand instantly, turning on the men.

Familiar humiliation shot through her. Every ugly whisper she'd endured working at Taft came back to her like wind howling through a canyon.

"I'm here because you left her in the lurch, Joe," Ash said. "And if you're going to hang out in the stands heckling, you may as well get back on the field and help out."

Violet opened her mouth to remind Ash that Hacker would *never* be welcome on her coaching staff. But Hacker turned to the exit, followed by his friends, speaking loudly, "I intend to be coaching on this field again. Any day now, I expect a vacancy will come up."

CHAPTER FOUR

ASH SANK INTO the porch swing after dinner, exhausted. The sun hung low over the mountains, but stars were already emerging in the fading blue September sky. It was going to be another cold night. Ash pulled the collar of his jacket tighter, then picked up his guitar, strumming absently. A tune could form or not, and no one was listening, so it didn't really matter.

Light and laughter poured out of the big red barn—Clara and her friends were getting it ready for the wedding. Behind him, a lamp glowed through the front window. Jackson was sprawled out on the sofa, with his homework on the coffee table before him. Ash's parents were home for the next few months, living in the apartment they'd built over the garage. Hunter would be back soon. Bowman had called that morning, and Piper was coming into town for Jackson's game Friday night.

His family was okay.

His town, on the other hand, was not.

Ash picked at the strings of the guitar, as though he could pluck out the disrespectful players, the arrogant parents, and send them off like music into the night. Joe Hacker had made one good point in all his nonsense, though. Ash had waited way too long to step up and help out with the team.

Ash had his reasons—or *excuses*, as Violet had called them. The divorce had knocked Ash's world out of alignment. Everything true and sacred had shattered, leaving dangerous shards rather than solid bedrock. It was all he could do at the time to salvage a relationship with his son and come limping back home.

Ash glanced at the apartment over the garage. He could see the backlit silhouettes of his parents at the window. Mom was laughing as Dad read something out loud from a book. The little-known problem with having happily married parents was it led him to think marriage made people happy. He'd thought the loving couple who raised him was the norm, not the exception. Ash had been judgmental of divorce as a young man. He'd always thought, 'You get married, you treat your spouse well, you fight for each other when things get hard, you work it out.'

He hadn't realized there were people who

weren't interested in sticking around when things got hard, or situations got so dire you couldn't fight your way back.

Ash shuddered, then twisted around on the porch swing to make sure his son was still in the living room, still okay, still *here*.

Jackson balanced a textbook on his knee, leaning over the book to fill out a worksheet on the table. His face was changing so fast, his jaw filling out, his child's giggle turning into a man's laugh. Sometimes Ash saw a reflection of Piper in the quirk of Jackson's brow. Other times his son's focus reminded him of Bowman. But the blue eyes came straight from Jackson's mom, a daily reminder of the worst decision of his life. Ash hadn't had to take the deployment to Djibouti. He'd just looked at the numbers, the money, and made the choice with the expectation that Kerri would have everything covered back home.

Ash turned back, gazing out at the creamy gravel drive winding away from the house, up to Wallace Creek Road. He wasn't ever going to make another decision that could hurt his son. Until Jackson graduated, he was the first and only real priority. Ash had to work to keep this football program running, even if he had to play all the other positions himself.

Even if he had to spend the next three months

in the company of a woman so beautiful he could hardly think of anything else.

Hacker's insinuation about Ash's interest in Violet couldn't have been clearer. Ash was going to have to double down on his emotions and not give anyone an excuse to think there was anything going on between him and the coach. Because there wasn't, and there wouldn't be.

Ash refocused on the guitar. A song unfolded into the cool, darkening night. "Something," by George Harrison. He leaned back in the porch swing, relaxing into the music.

Headlights flashed on the driveway. Hunter must be coming home early. Nice to see his brother making a sensible move for once. He'd been working way too hard of late.

Ash strummed a few more chords, then looked up again. The headlights were too low for Hunter's truck.

A red car with California plates pulled up in front of the house. Ash's hand froze midstrum, his heart picking up the tune where he left off. The car door opened, and Violet stepped out.

Violet, out of her coaching gear/battle armor, wearing blue jeans and a soft white sweater, her hair falling in waves around her shoulders.

"Hey!" She kept two hands on the top of her car door, like she might jump back in and speed off at any minute. "I don't have your number. Is this a good time?"

Ash couldn't speak. A good time to sit with his jaw hanging open as he stared at a beautiful woman?

Good a time as any.

"I need someone to brainstorm all this out with." Her gaze connected with his and her smile faltered. "I hope that's okay. You said anytime."

"Of course. Welcome." Ash set his guitar aside and trotted down the steps to help her. "How'd you find me?"

She opened the back door of her car and pulled out several clipboards, then loaded a number of coaching manuals onto the pile as she spoke. "It was tough. I looked up a map of Outcrop on my phone, found Wallace Creek, took a left off Wallace Creek Road, then turned in when I saw a huge sign that said Wallace Ranch." She gave him a dry look over her pile. "It was a major challenge, but I'm a navigational genius that way."

Ash laughed, reaching for the pile in her arms. "Let me get this."

"I hope I'm not disturbing you."

"No. Not at all." She'd been disturbing him

since she rolled into town, but they didn't have to go over that now.

She paused, gazing at him for a long moment. Finally, she said, "You're helping me out so Jackson can have a good football season, right?"

Ash nodded. "That's right."

She pressed her lips together. "And Hacker's a jerk."

"He is. I could tell you stories."

She gave him a wry smile acknowledging this. Then she drew in another breath, as though it were hard for her to get out the next sentence. "And he just said that thing about you helping out because I'm prettier than Kessler to make us angry, and to make me feel incompetent."

Ash gazed down at her. Violet was so beautiful, she must have been dealing with unwanted interest from the men she worked and played with her whole life. He wasn't going to be that guy.

"Yeah, he was just spouting off." He studied this stunning woman in her soft sweater, hair brushing against her face. Then his lips twisted in a grin. "There's no way you're prettier than Kessler."

She laughed at the unexpected joke, and while Ash knew the last thing he should be doing under the circumstances was trying to make her laugh, he couldn't help but add, "I mean, you're not bad looking, but you're no match for a fifty-five-year-old American history teacher."

Violet laughed harder, then snorted to get in a breath.

It was the cutest thing humanly possible. Ash was impressed that he didn't take her face in his hands right then and tell her so. He focused, instead, on the big pond in the distance and tried to distract himself with thoughts of mowing the overlong grass around it.

Mowing had to be the least romantic activity in human history.

"Lucky for me, it's not a beauty competition," Violet said.

"Lucky for all of us." Ash gave an exaggerated shudder. "He might be a natural beauty, but I *don't* really want to see Coach in a bikini."

Violet laughed again, ending with another snort that made him laugh. She finally drew in a breath and wiped her eyes. Ash was helping with the team *despite* how beautiful she was, not because of it.

"Hacker's always been like this, pushing limits as far as he's able to get away with. Kessler's absence is just an excuse for bad behavior." Ash gazed at Violet for a moment, then asked, "Is he okay?"

"Kessler?"

Ash nodded, half afraid to hear the answer.

She took a moment, then said, "He's in good hands."

"You'd let me know if I could help?"

She unloaded several clipboards into his arms and looked up at him. "You *are* helping. And I can't thank you enough."

Ash let her words seep in. He was helping. It was hard—the kids at practice were frustrating, and Violet's intelligence and bravery were unfairly appealing to him, but this probably was the best way he could support Coach Kessler.

She glanced around the property, observing the stables, the barn, the fields and ponds stretching out behind them. "This is gorgeous." She leaned back against her car, taking it in. "It's breathtaking."

Ash warmed. But breathtaking wasn't quite right. Breath-giving was a better phrase. When he was here, and his family was here, he could finally relax and breathe.

"We're lucky." Ash gestured toward the porch, and she headed up the steps. He glanced at the barn where Clara and her friends were now blasting music, hoping his matchmaking sister wouldn't smell a visitor and come swarming around the new coach.

Then he looked up at the front porch. With the swing and his guitar, it looked a lot more romantic than he could handle at the moment.

Movement from his parents' apartment caught his eye. Mom had spotted Violet and was pointing her out to Dad.

In the military, he'd learned to assess his surroundings and make fast decisions regarding his own safety. Right now, it was clear the front porch was a hot spot for trouble.

"Hey, I was about to check on the horses. Do you want to drop your clipboards and come with me?" She looked shocked, so he quickly added, "We can talk out the problems as we walk."

"Okay," she said. "Yeah. I'd love to."

Violet dumped her coaching materials in a chair, then trotted back down the steps. She looked so *at home*, in front of his home.

So, it was time to get away from the house. He'd take her to the stables. She'd probably be a little spooked by the horses, and definitely wouldn't like the smell. Proof that there was no future for him with Violet Fareas.

He fell in beside her and started walking toward the stables, feeling his parents' eyes on them.

Violet scanned the property. "How'd you wind up here?"

"I was lucky enough to start out here. This is where I grew up." The sun dipped another notch below the mountains, sending pink rays across the property, cooling the air another degree. "My parents bought this place and fixed it up over the years, piece by piece, all while teaching full-time."

"Wow. And they breed horses too?"

"Yep. Canadian Horses were on the verge of going extinct. My parents saw potential for the breed as a good family horse." He opened the bypass door into the stables. "We raise pets. You won't find Canadians at an elite dressage competition, or at the Kentucky Derby, but they're lovable, hearty and full of personality."

"Like our boys on the defensive line?"

Ash laughed, enjoying the way the right side of her mouth curved when she made a joke. He gestured for her to walk ahead of him, but she paused before entering, spun back and looked out across the property.

"There is *nothing* like this in Southern California." Her gaze connected with his. "Or if there is, it costs forty million dollars and is owned by a teenage pop star."

He laughed. "I feel for that pop star, then. Canadians are a handful."

Ash flipped on the soft strings of party lights Clara had hung in the barn. When there was serious work to do, the bright overhead floodlights were called for, but he just needed to check water and feed. And show his son's coach the not-forty-million-dollar stables.

"Wow." Violet's face lit up as she moved down the snug line of stalls. "They're so pretty."

The glossy, dark brown horses, alert to a new presence, came to the fronts on their stalls. Their breaths came out in gentle huffs, ears twitching with curiosity as they got a look at the new human. In the festive lights, with the sunset's glow coming in the windows, it really was magical.

"They're a pretty breed."

Stan, the oldest horse in the herd, chewed placidly as he eyed her. Violet reached out a tentative hand. "Can I pet him?"

"He won't forgive you if you don't," Ash told her.

Violet ran her hand down the horse's nose, a smile lighting her face.

"He's a good boy." Ash came to stand next to her and scratched his ears.

Bella, his mom's horse, eyed Violet coolly but didn't turn away: a high compliment from the aggressive lead mare. Bowman's horse,

Jorge, inclined his head to Violet, like a medieval knight. So much for Violet not getting along with the horses.

"You really can tell their personalities, can't you?" She moved to gaze at Cricket, the friendly, curious trail horse who never met a human she didn't love. "How do you not spend every moment of every day in here?"

Ash laughed. "A lot of days, I do. We breed and train horses, give lessons, sometimes rent out for trail rides."

"But you were gone for a long time, in the National Guard, right?"

Ash ducked into Pepper's stall to refill the water, keeping his face away from Violet. "Yeah. I joined the National Guard, did ROTC in college and served for eighteen years. I came home just as my parents retired from teaching. They offered me and Jackson the house if I'd take over the ranch so they could travel."

"Eighteen years?"

Ash dug his thumb and forefinger into the base of the ring finger on his left hand. He knew exactly how suspicious eighteen years sounded in a profession with a twenty-year buy-in for pension. And he was not interested in explaining that choice to anyone.

"Yep. Eighteen years. It's great to be back in Outcrop."

She gazed at him, clearly aware she wasn't getting the whole story. He gazed back, letting her know she wasn't going to get that story.

"You were incredible today." He changed the subject. "I was ready to knock heads together two minutes into practice. You didn't get riled or mad, you just ran that practice like…" Ash fished around for the right image. "Like a symphony conductor."

"A poorly behaved symphony," she added. Ash chuckled. "*You* did great," she continued. "Most of our trouble comes from the kids on offense, the ones you're working with, and you handled it well."

Ash furrowed his brow. The National Guard had very clear strategies for dealing with indolent, disrespectful men. None of those were appropriate, or possibly even legal, in a high school setting.

"How do you keep so calm?" he asked.

"I work at it." Violet let out a puff of breath. "I have a lot of big feelings—too big, according to some people. Over time I've learned to channel my emotions to help my players."

"Was it hard to keep your emotions in check when you were still playing?"

Violet laughed. "No, big emotions are an

asset in football. Caring too much about the outcome of a game allowed me to push further and harder, finding deeper levels to my own grit. When I get mad, I'm all fight, full throttle, no gloves. When I love something, I'm all in. I laugh easily. I cry at the drop of a hat."

"You cry?" he asked. She'd been so stoic through the tense meeting and practice, with only occasional glimmers of emotion skittering across her face.

"Mostly when I'm happy. Somebody makes a great play on the field. We win against a worthy opponent." She mugged a thoughtful expression, then admitted, "If I'm watching a particularly well-done dog food commercial. I'm a crier."

Ash laughed, then stilled as he felt her eyes on him. "What about you? What makes you cry?"

Nothing. Ash had become a master at stuffing down his emotions. Not too happy, not too sad, steady down the middle as chaos spun all around him. It was what everyone needed from him.

He couldn't remember the last time he'd cried. And he'd laughed more with Violet in forty-eight hours than he had in the last year.

He looked up to find her gazing at him,

waiting. What could he tell her? It wasn't that he didn't *have* big emotions. He just did his best to pretend they weren't there.

"I...uh...don't get to see a lot of dog food commercials these days."

Violet raised her brow, waiting for the real answer. Ash stepped into Midnight's stall. The gentle, intuitive horse seemed to know he was in there to avoid Violet's questions, but he was sweet enough not to bring it up.

Then Clara's laughter rang out from the barn on the other side of the riding arena, shifting the mood. The music blaring out of the barn bumped up a notch louder.

Violet's steady gaze gave way to confusion. "Is there a Taylor Swift festival happening here?"

"Every time Maisy and Joanna come over to help Clara get ready for the wedding."

She nodded approvingly. "I hear that. I'm a little more old-school when it comes to music, but there's nothing wrong with TSwift." She gestured with her chin back at the house. "I saw the guitar back there. You play?"

"Poorly, and erratically, but yes."

She bit her lip as she studied him, then asked, "Johnny Cash or John Denver?"

"Both."

"Hmm."

"What kind of music do you listen to?" he asked, trying to dodge her line of inquiry.

She stared him down, alert to his attempt to refocus the conversation.

Ash finally realized how tactical her conversation had been since arriving, designed to offer him just enough information about herself to get him to keep talking. He'd been spilling his guts over here while the only new piece of information he had about her was that she teared up at the occasional advertisement.

He let his eyes connect with hers, clarifying that he knew what she was up to, and letting her get away with it because she was a guest. Her half smile turned into a full grin, and Ash realized he had no control over what she did or did not get away with.

Then the right side of her mouth curved. "I love a good high school pep band playing a fight song."

He shook his head and smiled back. "Fine. If you like a good pep band, you've come to the right town. You ready to head back up to the house? Figure out what we need to do before they fire up the band on Friday night?"

She nodded, then took one last look around. "Thank you for showing me this. I love it. These horses are amazing."

The sun sank lower over the mountains, brightening the stars as they headed back up to the house. The cool breeze stirred something in his chest that it took him a moment to identify as anticipation. As a kid, this time of year had held nothing but anticipation—Friday night lights, school activities, upcoming holidays. Over the years, the feeling of anticipation had faded to a persistent, overarching worry. Concern for his siblings, his parents, his son and a deep, terrifying knowledge that he couldn't really protect any of them.

He knew he should utilize his ability to stuff that feeling deep down inside him, but right now, with Violet, he felt excited about the future.

THIS MAN WAS...*WOW*.

She'd known that before hopping in her car and heading over, but she hadn't imagined how much more appealing he would be here in his natural habitat.

It had been a mistake to drive out to brainstorm with Ash. They *did* have problems, and he could help. But did she need to put herself in a position to meditate on his cowboy skills, on top of everything else?

Because those big emotions never had confined themselves to football.

Violet settled back on the porch swing, then bit her lip and gazed at him, specifically imagining where she would fit under his arm—his soft flannel shirt against her cheek, the slight scruff on his chin against her hair. If he were to sit next to her on this porch swing, they could snuggle *and* strategize.

But no. That would only open up a whole new batch of problems. He was the parent of one of her players and an assistant coach. Off-limits. Bad idea.

She snuck another glance at him.

A really good-looking bad idea.

Violet turned her attention to the ranch, trying not to focus on the gentle, authoritative, guitar-playing cowboy. But then she was gazing at his picture-perfect property.

He cleared his throat. *Time to get your head back in the game, Vi.* She needed to keep on offense with this one, and not let her guard down.

She laid out three clipboards on the low table before her and pointed as she spoke, "Players, parents and money. Big questions to start. How can we inspire the players we already have, while recruiting more? How can we raise over twenty-five thousand dollars in the next few weeks to replace the helmets and pads as quickly as possible? And what are we going to do about the parents who don't want me to succeed at the first two goals?"

Ash nodded, reaching for a clipboard with his strong, calloused hand. "Let's start with money. Parents and players might be a lot less oppositional when confronted with new helmets and gear."

"Sounds good. But I don't want players to have to sell candy bars or raffle tickets. It's not their job to go begging for money. They've got school and football—that's enough."

"You should be able to rely on your booster club for fundraising." She gave him a flat look and Ash chuckled. "Yeah. Probably not your best bet right now."

He paced a few feet, and Violet resisted patting the seat next to her on the swing.

"What if we asked local businesses to each sponsor a helmet?" he suggested. "It's one thing to support the vague idea of a football program, but if I knew I was buying a helmet for a specific player, that's a concrete contribution."

"I love the idea." Violet considered, then said, "We could give each donor business a sign with a player's number on it to place in their window. So, my uncle's store could buy a helmet specifically for Aaron, then he gets a sign saying something like, 'Thank you, from number 78.'"

"Yes." Ash nodded. "Brilliant. Put Wallace Ranch down for two helmets."

Violet grinned. "You got it."

"Once the signs go up, everyone's going to want in on it. Great idea." He moved toward her. Violet's heart sped up when he held out his knuckles for a fist bump.

Because a fist bump is some surefire sign of romantic interest?

"It was your idea," she reminded him.

He shook his head, and kept his fist extended. "Our idea."

Violet bumped back, feeling supported for the first time in years. At Taft, she'd had a lot of great ideas that Laurent would shut down privately, then claim as his own in public.

"How does fundraising go in this town?" Violet asked. "Can we do this?"

"It's a supportive community. We can raise the money. And I'd like to get the kids in new helmets as soon as possible."

"Me too. Okay, let's start with the individual helmet donations and see how far we get." Violet made a few notes on her clipboard, then set it aside. Ash leaned down and picked up a second clipboard.

Violet tried to grab it from him, but he

pulled it out of her reach, then laughed out loud when he saw what she'd written under the title Recruitment.

Get some more kids to play football...or something.

Violet cradled her face in her hands and groaned. "I've never had to convince anyone to play before."

Ash laughed even harder.

"I was the quarterback coach at one of the biggest programs in Southern California. Everyone wanted to be on our team, and specifically in the position I was coaching."

Ash hesitated, then sat down beside her on the swing, and awkwardly patted her back.

"We'll figure it out," he said, humor in his voice. "I'm sure there's a way to convince kids to play the greatest game on earth."

Violet glanced up at him. His hand stilled on her back, warmth radiating from his palm through her entire frame. His scent, leather and pine, wrapped around her like a strong, solid, snuggly shield against the world at large.

Ash pulled his hand back, then shuffled through the materials she'd piled on the chair. "Why did you leave the program at Taft?"

The question was perfectly innocent. Ash had no idea how loaded it was.

Violet still couldn't forgive her younger, overly confident self for walking into the trap at Taft. She was on the rise as a coach, so why shouldn't she work for one of the most successful programs in the state? She'd be running it in no time.

It had never occurred to Violet that the position at Taft would be a dead end. The head coach ran a toxic, rat-infested ship, but that ship was a juggernaut. State championship banners hung throughout the school. Poisonous gossip kept the territorial coaches constantly looking over their shoulders. Kids were wrung out, putting their all in for high school glory, many injured and unable to keep playing in college. And in the captain's chair of this rotting keel was David Laurent.

Laurent had her as quarterback coach, a small, specialized part of the program where he could keep her away from big decisions and ensure she connected with as few of the players as possible. Her job was to produce able quarterbacks and keep her mouth shut. He needed her in the position. And to keep her there, he bullied and belittled her, making her feel like she was the one who was deluded for thinking she could do more. Logically she knew it was wrong, and intuitively Violet was a fighter. When she called him on his behavior, Laurent just smiled, reminding her his word had weight in California football. No one would hire her without a recommendation from him.

Then the rumors had started, ludicrous whispers coming out of nowhere. There had always been gossip about Laurent, a married man, getting cozy with the moms of some of his players. And if those players got more time on the field than the others, well, that was David for you. But then her name got thrown into the mix. Other coaches and parents suggested that she kept her coaching job by secretly dating David. The rumors did nothing to his reputation, but as a woman in football, those same rumors defined her.

Getting as far away as possible was the only option.

Now she was here, in Oregon, and head of her own ship. A chaotic, midsize craft that was currently under torpedo attack, but her own ship nonetheless.

Violet shrugged. "This opened up. Kessler needed someone to step in, and I'd had my eye out for a head coaching position. Plus, I've always been curious about Oregon, so it was a good opportunity to check out the state."

Ash leaned back, crossing one ankle over

his knee, and rested his arm along the back of the swing. He held her gaze. "I'm glad you landed here." He grabbed a pen and propped the clipboard on his knee, grinning at her. "Now, let's figure out how to get more kids to play football, or something."

Time spun away from them as they sat together, strategizing for the season. Violet had forgotten how good it felt to laugh, cold rushing into her lungs as she gulped for breath. Her embarrassing tic of snorting in air while laughing was admittedly funny, and gave Ash a measurable goal for his jokes. At some point the sun set completely, and the brightest stars blanketed the sky. She had no idea how late it was when she heard the front door open behind them.

"Hey, Dad?"

They were both startled to see Jackson. Ash sprang up from the porch swing, as though Jackson was the parent and he and Violet were the ones getting into unsupervised trouble.

"Coach Vi?" Jackson stepped fully onto the porch, wearing a T-shirt with his jeans, and no shoes. "What are you doing here?"

"Go grab a coat," Ash told him.

"Why don't you guys come inside?" Jackson asked, holding the door.

Violet was suddenly aware of how cold

it had gotten. The mountain air didn't mess around once the sun set.

"I'm sorry." Ash gestured to the door. "Please, come inside."

Violet peeked through the picture window into the cozy farmhouse. If she walked in the front door, she'd be tempted to never leave.

"I should get going. I've already taken up too much of your time." Violet stood and began gathering up her things.

"It's no problem. This was…fun."

Violet met his gaze. It had been fun. While Outcrop was challenging, and Hacker's behavior an off-brand imitation of Laurent's bullying, an evening with Ash had her feeling up to the challenge. Working together was freeing, like the play of children, when there are no limits.

She just needed to remember the hard limit. Ash was a friend, nothing more.

"I really appreciate it," she said. Then she turned to Jackson. "We're trying to come up with recruitment strategies. Can you think of any way to get more kids on the team?"

Jackson shrugged. "Most of the athletic guys already play."

"And the athletic girls?"

"We have a really good volleyball team."

"Right." Volleyball was her nemesis, a lot of tough girls with no time for football.

"There could be kids who want to play sports but never did. Like Kessler asked Coach Broughman to play when he was a freshman, and he turned out to be an Outcrop legend."

"Excellent. That's who we're looking for."

"Okay." He furrowed his brow and glanced at the ground, looking like a miniature copy of his dad. "We've got Club Day Wednesday. Do you have a table?"

"Club Day?"

"It's after school," Jackson said. "All the clubs set up tables and advertise."

Ash's gaze met hers. This was the opportunity they needed.

"I'll get the table," Ash said.

Violet grinned at him. "I'll make a sign."

Ash reached over to give her a fist bump and Violet tapped back.

Get your team straight, was one of her father's favorite sayings. Violet may have made bad decisions about who to ally herself with in the past, but if there was a team to be on in this town, Ash Wallace was the captain.

CHAPTER FIVE

"WELCOME TO THE TEAM, CJ!" Violet's arm brushed Ash's as she reached forward to hand out yet another T-shirt. "See you at practice this afternoon."

Ash enjoyed watching Violet grin as she made another note on her clipboard. The woman liked winning, and if the club fair were a competition, they'd be dominating. Their table had been the busiest one all afternoon. A new-to-town, female coach was quite the draw, as were the BBQ sliders provided by Eighty Local.

But once everyone had satisfied their curiosity, and hunger, Violet's calm, straight talk about the game had intrigued a lot of kids. She was good at this. Maybe a little too good, given the kid who trotted away from the table to show off the T-shirt to his friends.

"You sure about him?" Ash asked.

"That guy?" She pointed to the student, who was now gesturing back at her. "Absolutely. He's enthusiastic, open-minded—"

"He weighs a hundred pounds at best."

"And he's a sophomore. Those things grow like duckweed."

Ash laughed, but Violet shook her head seriously. "A sophomore boy can grow a whole foot in a weekend. I've seen it happen."

"That's fair." Ash glanced over to where Jackson and his friends were talking to their Spanish teacher. There were days when Jackson seemed to grow taller between dinner and dessert.

The school courtyard was buzzing with activity. Clubs and sports had elaborately decorated tables, representing every possible interest. Even the pep band was setting up.

"This your first time at a club fair?" Violet asked. She was back in her red track jacket with an Eagles ball cap covering her hair, looking every bit the coach. "We didn't have this type of thing at my high school."

"This *is* my high school, actually," Ash said.

"Oh, right." Violet shook her head. "You went here."

"I grew up here. Mom taught geography and Dad taught science. I was at Club Day every year for the first eighteen years of my life. When I was little, I made a habit of joining every club, every year. Didn't matter

what they were into—science, cheer, chess—
I signed up."

Violet laughed. "That must have been adorable."

Ash could still feel the childish excitement of running from table to table, where
there was usually at least one teenager willing to patiently explain the club's mission to
an eager five-year-old, then help him scrawl
his name on the list.

"Or annoying," Ash admitted.

She gave him a long look. "I doubt it. What
about when you were in high school?"

Ash glanced around the courtyard. He'd
taken high school so seriously. His parents
had never told him he needed to represent
the family and be a good role model for his
siblings, but he'd been driven to do it all
the same. Academic achievement, athletics,
school leadership, he'd taken it all on like a
sacred duty. Dad used to joke that Ash took
school more seriously than most of his teachers, and in some cases it was true.

He could remember his first Club Day as a
high school student. He'd come prepared with
his own pen and the decision to join two clubs
in addition to football. Nervous excitement
and the earnest desire to make the right decisions were his memories from that day. By

the time he was a junior, he was in charge of Club Day, barking at underclassmen if they didn't have their tables set up on time.

"Well, if you ask my siblings, they'll tell you I'm still annoying."

She nodded. "And if I ask your parents, they'd say you're still adorable."

Ash laughed. "Parents probably never get over that, do they?"

"I doubt it. My mom's gonna think I'm the cutest when I'm sixty."

Ash glanced at Violet, imaging the gray in her hair, the laugh lines forming around her eyes. She was going to be adorable at sixty.

"Hey there!" Violet called to three girls eyeing the table. "Want to come check it out?"

Two of the girls waved their hands, as though to ward off the sport, laughing. The third wasn't quite so enthusiastic in her rejection. She was tall and looked strong. Ash glanced at Violet who was also tall and strong. She was built like the elite sprinters or long jumpers he'd seen at the Olympics, strong and curvy in a fierce, feminine combination.

Great, he was staring at Violet again.

"Sandwiches are for everyone," he told the girls.

That got a stronger reception. The three swept in and grabbed burgers, the third lingering a moment to read one of the fliers. Violet held an information packet out but didn't say anything more. The girl grabbed it and walked away.

Violet pressed her lips together in a smile as she watched the girls.

"How did you start playing?" Ash asked.

"I've always played. My dad is a legendary high school coach. He's incredible."

"Like Kessler?"

"Right. Everyone respects my dad. Everyone wanted to play for him. Including me."

"Was it hard for him? To see his daughter on the field?"

"I don't know. I think he was more proud than anything else." She glanced up at him, a little smile playing on her lips. "I was good."

"Of course." He held out his hands, as though he could push his own awkward words out of the conversation. "I know. I just meant—"

"I get it. You don't need to tell me there aren't a lot of women in this sport. But my dad and I had been playing football in the backyard my whole life. He fought for me to be able to join a middle school team. By the time I got to high school, I was good enough that I was an asset."

Ash gazed down at her. "You must have been fierce."

"I was." She nodded, then glanced up at him. "I still am."

The pep band started up. Violet moved to the beat, then sighed happily. "I love this song. I don't ever get tired of it."

"'Eye of the Tiger'?"

"Always a classic."

Ash laughed. "How about 'We Will Rock You'?"

"I'll probably have it played at my wedding."

Ash opened his mouth to ask if she ever had been married but stopped himself. She had to be about his age, so maybe? Then again, she probably hadn't made the same humiliating mistakes in her youth as he had.

No, with a woman as smart, beautiful and ambitious as Violet, there were broken hearts and unaccepted marriage proposals scattered across the country in her wake.

"What about that kid?" she asked, pointing at the tuba player in the pep band.

"For the football team?"

"Yeah. He looks strong. Or should be, anyway, after carrying a tuba around."

"Yeah. But then what would the pep band do for a tuba player?"

"Sounds like a band director problem to me."

Ash shook his head. "You want to tangle

with Mr. Katz, be my guest. I'm staying neutral."

As though he could hear them, which was impossible over the racket of classic eighties rock, Mr. Katz turned around and glared at Violet.

"Yeah, he looks like the type to get sore over a poached tuba player." She refocused her attention on the kids milling past their table. "Want to check out the program? Everyone's welcome."

A young man started to respond but a commotion on the other side of the courtyard drew his attention.

"What's that?" Violet asked.

Ash looked over Violet's head to a group of kids clustering around something across the courtyard. He'd been nervous all day that Hacker or Larsabal or one of the players might try something this afternoon. He was prepared to head off any trouble before Violet knew it was happening.

But he was not prepared for the real problem that reared its head in the courtyard that day. Or reared its beak, as it were.

Ash groaned. "Larry."

A massive, flightless, brainless bird trotted into the courtyard. Ash didn't need to look to know his sister Clara held the leash attached to the harness she'd rigged up for Jet's favorite emu.

The bird strutted into the courtyard, a devious smile splitting his beak as his head swiveled on an ungainly neck. Kids exclaimed and laughed as the bird moved across the courtyard.

Jet came jogging behind Clara and the emu.

"Seriously, Broughman?" Ash asked.

"Just trying to stir up some interest in defense," he told him, raising his hands in innocence.

"It was my idea," Clara said. "Save your lectures for me."

"I'm not planning on saving this lecture." Ash shook his head. "Is it even legal to have that bird in here?"

"What, does the high school have some kind of anti-avian policy I'm not aware of?" Clara tucked her hair behind her ear, pretending to look uninterested.

"You can't just bring huge birds into public spaces."

"Tell that to the creators of Sesame Street."

Larry bent down and pulled up a tuft of grass, then shuffled his beak over to a bed of late-blooming mums.

Ash turned to Violet, who was staring at the bird in horrified curiosity. She was going to have to meet his sisters sooner or later. "Violet, this is my sister Clara. Clara, this is Coach Vi."

Clara's trademark charm was so strong it was almost tangible. She turned her dimpled smile on Violet.

"I'm so super excited to meet you! Jet told me all about you, and while I'm one hundred percent worried about Coach Kessler—I'm glad you're here. Are you single?"

"Stop it," Ash commanded.

"What? It's a question."

Violet sputtered, whether because of the bird or Clara's line of questioning he didn't know.

Jackson came running over to greet Larry, along with Manuel, Aaron and the rest of the guys. The bird, by this point, knew the players well. The boys on defense had spent a good part of the summer working to renovate a cabin on Jet's ranch to earn money for their college funds. Which also meant they'd spent a good part of the summer rounding up escaped emus and getting them back into the pen.

Activity and noise around the football table ratcheted up. The defense team joked with each other and the bird. Other kids came to see what was going on.

Larry, as though sensing Ash's mistrust, raised his head and focused his amber eyes on him. Ash picked up one of Violet's ubiquitous clipboards and began flipping pages. He really did not want to commune with the bird.

But Larry *really* wanted to commune with him. As Ash turned away, the bird shuffled around and looked into his face. Ash spun in the other direction. Larry dipped his neck around so he was beak to nose with Ash. Ash tried to turn in the other direction, but Larry, now sensing a game was afoot, swiveled around, his beak open in delight at finding himself staring into Ash's eyes, again.

"Clara!" Ash snapped. "Get it out of here."

Clara's laugh rang out, joined by Violet. Ash shook his head but could see how funny it was. The emu took a long step toward the table, then snapped his head out to grab a slider, making Violet laugh even harder, leading to an adorable snort.

It was hard to forgive his sister for showing up with this ridiculous bird, but watching Violet laugh went a long way toward helping him do just that.

VIOLET COULD NOW call the football booth a zoo. Literally. The boys on defense helped with recruiting, and with eating the sliders.

Clara chatted amiably to Violet, to her fiancé and with the kids checking out the table. The bird was absolutely besotted with Ash and wanted nothing more than to gaze into his eyes with that smile on its face.

Not that she blamed the emu.

Ash was a true gentleman: strong, fair, kind, helpful. He was gruff, for sure, like he didn't have time for nonsense.

But nonsense was all he was getting at the moment, and it was adorable.

"Jet, get this bird away from me."

"I'm sorry, man." Jet tried to redirect the emu's attention with a handful of feed. The bird gave Jet's palm a cursory peck, then got distracted by the pearl snap buttons on Ash's shirt. Violet tried not to laugh again.

She glanced out at the crowd and sobered immediately. Brayson and his friends stood a few feet back from the table, arms crossed as they smirked at the mayhem. Violet straightened her shoulders, then waved. "Hi," she called out. "Want a sandwich?"

"Naw. You need them to bribe people to join the team, right?"

The challenge shot through her, and she held eye contact with Brayson as she reached for a BBQ slider. "Not really. Hunter just wanted to make a donation."

She took a bite of the mini burger, and everything around her, the snide boys, the issues she faced with the team, even the emu disappeared. The slider was incredible. A perfect, savory combination of flavors in a light, doughy bun. She looked down at the burger in surprise, then glanced at Ash, who didn't seem to think there was anything out of the ordinary about serving the world's best burger to kids for free at a recruiting table. These burgers could change the world. She'd sign up for the Scrabble team if these were on offer.

She glanced back at her quarterback and held up the burger. "It's really good."

The boys wavered. She was almost tempted to call a truce so they could come try one, because…*wow*. But calling a truce meant admitting they were at war, and that wasn't going to happen.

"I'm good." Brayson tossed the football he was carrying and caught it easily.

"Bet they don't have to bribe kids to join the team in Bend," Soren said, loud enough so she could hear. West Bend High School was about a half an hour away, and from her research, Violet understood they were favored to win the league title again this year.

"Everyone wants to play for the Swarm," Brayson said.

Violet took a purposefully casual bite of the burger, chewing and swallowing before she said, "The Bend Swarm is a good team, but right now I feel sorry for anyone who's not in on these sliders."

She redirected her attention to a boy talking with Manuel, grabbing a T-shirt for him and letting him know he was welcome to check out practice for a few days to see if football was for him.

But as she spoke, she continued to watch the boys out of the corner of her eye. Were these boys thinking of transferring to Bend and joining the Swarm? While life in the short run would be easier without them, she needed their skill and leadership on this team. She had to coach a winning season if she had any hope of moving up as head coach of another, more competitive team. Brayson was smart; he was a strong leader and a solid player. If she could funnel his leadership into the success of, rather than the sabotage of, the team, it would be powerful.

But he'd signed up to play for Coach Kessler and probably thought his dad was the logical next choice for coach. It was going to take a lot more than an emu and some seriously good BBQ to turn him.

"Hi."

Violet looked up from her thoughts to see the young woman who'd approached the table earlier with her friends.

"Hey. Welcome back."

"I have a few questions," the girl said.

"Shoot." Violet glanced around. Ash was quibbling with Clara. Jet kept the emu occupied while Jackson, Manuel and Aaron signed kids up to play and handed out T-shirts.

"What position could I realistically play?"

Violet looked at the girl's sturdy, muscular frame. "Are you fast?"

The girl nodded. "I'm a sprinter. And a powerlifter."

Violet widened her eyes. "Wow."

"My mom manages a gym in Redmond."

Violet kept calm as she spoke. This girl was easily the most athletic student she'd talked with all day. "Cool. Depending on your skills, maybe a receiver. I played cornerback in high school."

"Would I honestly have playing time? Or would it just be, like, *look there's a girl on the team*."

Violet raised her brow. "You're asking me that question?"

The girl seemed to realize her mistake, then nodded, a smile growing.

"You'll get as much playing time as you earn. You're a first-time player, I'm assuming, so don't expect to start until you earn a spot. But if you're good, you'll play."

The girl considered this. Violet grabbed the sign-up clipboard from Manuel's hands and held it out. Manuel's mouth dropped open when he saw who Violet was talking to, then he nudged Jackson with his arm. The girl still didn't take the pen.

"Where would I shower?"

"In the girls' locker room. All my team meetings are held on the field or in a classroom. I'll expect everyone to change and shower quickly, then meet as a team outside of the locker rooms."

The girl considered her words, then glanced at the boys on defense.

"You should do it, Carley," Jackson said.

"You think Mom's gonna freak?" she asked Aaron. For the first time Violet noticed the similarities between the two. This was Aaron's sister.

Aaron shrugged. "Probably."

"I have a question for you." Violet paused, picking up the football on the table and examining it, before tossing it to Carley. The girl caught it easily. "Do you want to play?"

Carley's face lit up. She kept her eyes on the ball as she said, "I want to play." Then she looked up at Violet. "I *really* want to play."

Violet pushed the clipboard toward her. "Then let's do it!"

Carley grinned and signed her name. The boys on defense whooped. Manuel whooped louder than the rest, and continued whooping until Carley acknowledged him by saying, "It's not a big deal."

Violet's heart beat fast with excitement. For years at Taft, she'd tried to get Laurent to encourage girls to play, but that was shot down along with all her other ideas. Now she was here, head coach and making space for everyone who wanted to get on the field. If this girl was as good as Violet suspected she could be, this was the first step at payback. The first step on a path that would lead her to coaching a college team in a few years. She might always miss coaching high school kids, but she could learn to love coaching college players, couldn't she? It would all be worthwhile when she surpassed Laurent, coaching at a level he'd never reach.

CHAPTER SIX

"THANKS FOR MAKING the time to stop by practice," Violet addressed the new parents in the bleachers. "I'm so glad your kids have chosen to join the team."

Behind her, Ash and Jet ran drills with the help of this week's team leaders.

"Nice hustle, CJ!" she heard Ash yell. She glanced back at the field in time to see CJ beaming at the compliment before he tripped over his own feet. Hustling seemed to be CJ's one athletic gift, and they were going to celebrate whatever they could.

Violet turned back to the assembled parents. Most of them were blissfully unfamiliar, with the exception of Joe Hacker, Ed Ramirez and Greg Larsabal.

Don't these guys have jobs?

Then she remembered they'd all had part-time jobs as assistant coaches. Jobs they'd quit a few days prior. Apparently, their afternoons were free.

Violet continued, aiming her remarks at

the new parents. "I love this game, and I hope your kids will too. Please don't hesitate to come to me with any questions or concerns. Life as a football parent can be pretty daunting."

The new parents chuckled, glancing at one another as if they all felt a little out of place here.

"Your kids are new to this game, and it takes time to learn. Don't expect them to be star players right out of the gate. My goal is to get every player on the field, every game. I won't always make that goal, but I keep track of the minutes played and do my best to make sure everyone gets time on the field. It's the only way anyone gets better."

"So, if my parents drive over from Eugene on Friday, they'll get to see Ben play?"

"I can't make any promises, but I'll do my best to make it happen."

On the field behind her she heard a kid yell, "Oops!" and something crashed onto the ground. Ash let out a sigh, then called out, "Let's give it another shot."

Violet smiled brightly in the face of chaos. "The players have a responsibility in this too. There's a lot to learn in football, and if they don't have the plays down, we're not sending them out to trip others up. Also, if anyone is late to practice, they don't play in the first half of the game. They miss practice, they don't play at all."

The parents nodded. She heard one mom murmur to another that it had been a similar situation with Suzuki violin lessons.

"On the other hand, each week we choose four leaders who stand out during games and practice. These kids will act as team captains for the week and represent the team in the coin toss at the start of the game."

"What about the boys who'd already been chosen as team captains before you got here?"

Violet didn't bother to look at Joe Hacker as she responded. "Those players are welcome to join the weekly captains as leaders at any time. In fact, I'd love to see Brayson and Joaquin step up."

"Is my son going to get a concussion?" a man asked.

"That's what I want to know," a mom joined in. "How safe is this?"

"Excellent questions," Violet said. "I know there's been a lot in the news about the safety of high school football. Fortunately, there's also been a lot of research, so we know how to mitigate injury. That said, kids can get hurt playing high school sports."

"Kids can get hurt getting up off the sofa,"

a man wearing an old-school Metallica T-shirt said, setting the group chuckling. "I know from experience."

Violet used all her self-control not to ask if he was CJ's dad.

"One safety precaution I'm working on is getting new helmets for the team. Coach Kessler had been trying to earmark money for helmets. Manufacturers have made great strides in technology, and my goal is to raise enough in the next few weeks to get us outfitted with first-rate helmets as soon as possible."

Greg Larsabal spoke, "Yeah. You know the booster club decides how all the funds are spent, and there are a few other considerations."

"The booster club decides how to spend all the money the booster club has raised. I, Violet Fareas, decide how to spend all the money *I* raise. And I am raising money to buy new helmets." Then she turned to the rest of the parents and smiled. "And if you haven't considered joining the booster club, you should look into it. They could use some fresh voices."

"Where are you going to get the money so quickly?" Hacker asked.

Violet smiled at him. "I've got an incredible fundraising team behind me. And it turns out this town is interested in protecting teenage brains."

"I'd be happy if my teenager could find his brain," one dad mumbled.

Violet laughed along with everyone else.

"Can I make a donation?" the mom who'd compared football to violin lessons asked.

"Anonymous donations can be made to the school. Just make sure you include a note saying it's expressly for helmets."

Her dad had taught her a long time ago it was best not to know who donated and who didn't. It sent a clear message that playing time wasn't up for sale.

Violet checked her watch. "I'd better get down on the field. Any last questions?"

"Yeah. I got a question." A muscular, tattooed woman stepped up from the back. "Are you really gonna let my daughter do this?"

Violet took a moment to study the woman who must be Carley and Aaron's mom. She was strong and looked like she could handle herself in a fight. The scar above her left eye suggested she *had* handled herself in a fight.

"I'm very excited to have Carley on the team."

"Yeah, you don't know her attitude."

Violet looked down at the field where Carley was getting after it in drills, fierce and focused.

"The same rules will apply to Carley as everyone else. So far, she's been pretty motivated." Violet took a few steps toward the field and waved at the parents. "Thank you all for coming. Don't hesitate to ask if you have more questions."

The group broke up, but Carley's mom remained, arms folded over her chest.

"I flat-out told her I didn't want her to play, but you can't tell that girl anything."

"Are you afraid she'll get hurt?" Violet asked. The mom seemed as tough as they come, and Carley wasn't far behind.

"No. It's just, that coach—" she pointed to Jet "—the rich one. He's got Aaron's head all filled with dreams about college or whatever. I told 'em there's no money to pay for them to go party with rich kids for four years. But that guy keeps telling Aaron there's ways to do it for free."

Violet didn't know much about Jet, only that Ash's parents had helped him secure a scholarship to the University of Washington, and now he was determined to give back to the community. "Jet's a man of his word," Violet assured her. "He went to college on a full ride, and I'm sure he wants to help others do the same."

The woman shrugged, her scar making the furrow in her brow more dramatic. "I don't want someone gettin' her hopes up. Life's hard. I don't want her dreaming about some fantasy college we can't afford."

Violet gazed at the woman, wondering what her dreams had been.

"Let's see how this week goes. High school football is supposed to be fun. We can start there and worry about college in the future."

The woman rolled her eyes and walked away, but she didn't leave the bleachers. She parked herself in the stands to watch practice.

Violet trotted down to the field with her surly star players and enthusiastic recruits, the bleachers packed with parents waiting to see what she could do. Carley glanced over, eyes flickering between her mom and Violet.

Determination swept through Violet. This was a challenge, and she wasn't going to let anyone on this team down. She scanned the field, eyes coming to rest on her assistant coach, who looked very good in a worn-in pair of blue jeans and an Outcrop Eagles sweatshirt left over from his own days on the field. He grinned at her, a spark lighting up his face, then he looked down briefly, returned his gaze to her and waved. She paused a second, then waved back.

Ash Wallace was in this with her, and with him everything felt possible.

PRACTICE WAS MAYHEM. Adding the new players went about as well as setting a few dozen squirrels loose in a ballet. The hardworking, middle-of-the-road athletes were worried about their playing time, the arrogant first-string players were confusing the new kids on purpose, and no one seemed to know what a whistle meant. The only thing that would make this practice worse was an emu.

Ash froze at the thought, then slowly looked around, just in case there actually was an emu here.

He let out a breath in relief. This could sincerely be worse.

"Coach Wallace, my arm kinda hurts." Brayson bent and unbent his elbow in an unconvincing show of pain. If the kid were one of Ash's siblings, or his own son, he'd suggest the time-tested medical practice of toughening up.

But he wasn't a blood relation, and they didn't have time to argue. "Take a break then. Gabe?" he called to the second-string quarterback.

Gabe looked at Brayson, then moved his arm in the exact same way. "Mine too."

Ash flashed on a memory of his drill sergeants at basic training. Every repercussion for laziness he'd learned there was completely inappropriate for a school environment. Tempting, but inappropriate.

Violet had laid down the protocol, and he just needed to follow it. Don't lose your cool; don't let anyone get to you. Give your focus to the kids who are working hard.

This is football, she'd said. *Come Friday night, the boys will either step up or they won't. We need to prepare the kids who are willing to play.*

"Can I try, Coach?" CJ materialized eagerly at his side, already reaching for the ball.

Ash called on all the patience he'd ever cultivated, then dropped a hand on CJ's shoulder. "I love the enthusiasm. Since this is a drill for the receivers as well, I'll take over the throws. But if you're interested in learning, this is a great opportunity. Come over here with Gabe and Brayson." Ash lined up the two seniors and the enthusiastic sophomore. "I want you three to watch me. Brayson, you have good accuracy, but you need to work on power this season."

The quarterback looked shocked, as though

no one had commented on this one fairly substantial flaw in his throws. Since his dad was the main offensive coach, it was a little weird they hadn't been over it. Then again, Joe Hacker had never played quarterback.

Ash had worked on his passing tirelessly in high school, forcing Bowman and Hunter to catch his throws for hours on weekend afternoons. In the end it was a net gain for Outcrop football, as both Hunter and Bowman wound up playing receiver. In the National Guard, there was always someone up for a pickup game in their downtime. And when he returned to Outcrop, there were family football games in the field out behind the house. If you could call it football, the way his siblings bent and battered the rules to suit their whims. That said, they played frequently. Ash had cultivated a strong throwing arm in high school and kept it up with the practice.

All in all, he still had it.

"Joaquin, you're up."

Joaquin ran, and Ash enjoyed letting the well-practiced movement flow. He launched the ball at the perfect height and speed for the athlete to catch it easily.

"You boys see that? It's in the release." He mimed the final movement of his throw.

"Brayson, when your arm is better you need to work on it."

Brayson's face lost color, but he kept his expression neutral.

"Soren, ready to go?" Ash looked at the first-string receiver and running back. Soren looked at Ash, then at the stands where his father stood with Joe and Ed.

Ash tossed the ball and caught it. He felt for the kid. Soren didn't want the drama, but his friends and his dad were bringing it full force. Ash offered him a temporary out. "Take some time to think about it. Blake? Let's go."

One of the new recruits was up next, and he came nowhere near to catching the ball. Another one of the first-string players came down with a mysterious injury and stepped out of practice. Some kids were too slow. Some kids were literally running in the wrong direction. Some kids couldn't catch the ball if it were covered in superglue and contained a million dollars.

"Carley?" Ash called out.

The young woman clenched and unclenched her fists, then walked to the line of scrimmage.

"Ready?"

She nodded, tensed her muscles in preparation to run, and at his command took off like a hawk. Ash launched the ball into the air. Carley sprinted down the field then hopped up easily and snatched the ball. She landed lightly on her feet, as though instinctively knowing this was the moment she'd run for the end zone.

Everyone at practice had seen it. She was a natural, and the huge grin on her face suggested she could feel it too.

Then her brother came barreling out of defensive practice and tackled her.

The fight between siblings was brief, ending up with Carley pancaking her brother and reclaiming the ball before heading back to Ash.

"This is fun," she said.

Ash offered her a high five. "It is. That's why we play. Greatest game on earth."

"Can I go again?"

"Coach?" Soren stepped forward, interrupting the phenomenally talented girl who had the ability to take his position as first-string receiver. "I'm ready."

Ash cleared his throat. "Sure thing. Carley, watch how Soren tracks the ball as he's running. I want you to try that next time."

Soren straightened at the compliment, then got ready to run.

Ash glanced over to where Violet was working with Jet and the defense. She grinned, looking meaningfully at Soren.

This was why she'd recruited so many new kids. The competition lit a fire under the more experienced players. But Carley was going to be more than just a motivation to this team. She was an asset.

He nodded back to Violet, keeping a straight face as his insides celebrated the small win. Then he drew back and threw a perfect pass just in case Coach Vi was still watching.

"WALLACE, CAN I talk to you for a second?" Violet was reluctant to interrupt his throwing. That man, sending passes down the field, was absolutely her type of catnip. She'd be happy to stand there watching him until he threw his shoulder out.

But that wouldn't do anyone any good.

"Sure." He smiled. "Brayson, you ready to take over?"

Brayson glared at him, then Violet, flexing his uninjured arm.

"What's wrong with him?" Violet asked. "Besides…" She gestured to the stands where Joe Hacker was glaring at them.

"I think that's all. And his condition appeared to be catching because Gabe's not throwing either."

Violet let out a breath. "I need a quarterback. I need three quarterbacks."

Ash nodded. "I know."

"See if you can get him to take at least a couple of throws today. I need him to play on Friday, and I can't put him in if he's saying he's injured."

"I'll do my best."

"Is there anyone who can throw for a couple of minutes? I need your help figuring out where to funnel a couple of kids."

Ash shook his head. "All the kids trained up for quarterback are following Brayson's lead."

Violet sighed as she scanned the field. Then her eyes landed on Jackson.

There was no way that kid hadn't thrown the ball around with his dad a time or two.

"Can Jackson throw?"

"He's got a decent arm. He's not interested in playing offense, though."

Violet furrowed her brow. They were desperate, and what one kid did or didn't want to play wasn't real high on her priority list.

"But he's all in on helping you out," Ash quickly amended. He turned to where his son was lining up for drills with Jet. "Jackson? Can you throw passes for a minute while I talk to Coach Vi?"

Jackson nodded, then trotted over and took the ball. Ash explained the drill, then followed Violet as she strode away. "Talk to me about Carley," she said.

"Have you been watching her?"

"Everybody's watching her. The girl has speed and good hands."

"Did you see the way Soren stepped back in after Carley's first catch?"

"Nothing like a little competition." Violet glanced over Ash's shoulder to see Jackson launch the ball at Joaquin. A nice straight pass into the receiver's hands. "Anyone else showing any promise?"

Ash blew out a breath. "Maybe on kickoff team? If we were twenty points up."

Violet nodded. It was going to be hard to find everyone a place on the field Friday night.

Jackson threw another pass, using the technique he'd obviously learned from his dad. Soren ran this time. He caught it easily, then tried to look like he was bored.

"Carley, see if you can catch this one," Jackson yelled.

"Let's see if you can throw it," she challenged.

Violet and Ash turned to watch the action. Carley, once again, sprinted down the field.

Jackson put a little more power on the ball, sending a near-perfect throw to his friend. Carley kept an eye up for the ball, then reached up and plucked it from the air like she was taking it off a Walmart shelf.

Violet's insides leaped. The girl was going to do this; she'd play and be good.

Also impressive? Jackson's throw. There was potential there she could work with. Violet glanced up at Ash to see if he was thinking what she was thinking.

He wasn't.

"You can put Brayson in on Friday night. He still thinks he's going to play in college, so when we come down to the wire, he'll perform."

Violet nodded. "Okay. But I'm on the hunt for a backup." She gestured meaningfully at Jackson.

"I'll keep looking." Ash finally glanced at Jackson, then his head whipped back around to Violet. "Probably not Jackson, though. He's a defense guy. You need him on defense."

Violet needed her good players on defense, offense, and probably the cheer team and marching band with the way all this was going. But she and Ash didn't need to hash that out now.

Jackson launched another throw, this one

for Soren. Violet listened to Ash but watched out of the corner of her eye as the close-but-not-quite-perfect throw spiraled into Soren's hands.

Then the strangest interaction of the day took place.

Brayson checked to make sure she wasn't looking, then trotted over to Jackson and helped him adjust his hold on the ball. Jackson gave him a nod, like Ash tended to when learning a new piece of information. The interaction lasted less than twenty seconds. The quarterback hustled back to the sidelines and resumed his bored expression. Jackson launched another throw, this one even better than the last.

Hacker's kid wasn't all in on the sabotage. Interesting.

Violet looked up at Ash, his eyes more green than brown in the afternoon sunlight. Words she'd been holding back since the moment he approached her in the parking lot pushed up in her throat. They were light and unstoppable like a clasp of balloons, flying out before she could retain her grasp on them.

"I am *so* glad you're here. Thank you."

He startled at her words. "Happy to help out." He shifted, holding her gaze. "I'm glad you're here too."

Her heart expanded fast, taking over any available space for breath or thought. Could she just stand here forever, basking in Ash's words?

Something solid and squirming hit her shoulder and Violet stumbled.

"Sorry, Coach!" CJ yelled, recovering after bowling into her. "Sorry! This is fun."

"It's okay. Get back out there." She gestured toward Jet. Jet saw CJ coming and shuddered, then got a hold of himself. Violet looked past Ash to where Brayson was now sulking on the sidelines again. "We better get back to work."

Ash tipped his head in acceptance of this, then sighed as he looked at the growing crew of "injured" players on the sidelines of his drill.

She raised her brows, then headed straight for Brayson and Gabe. "I hear you two have been having trouble with your arms. Or is it your shoulders?"

Brayson dramatically rubbed his shoulder. "I'm a little sore."

"Too sore to play on Friday night?" She raised her clipboard and pen, hoping the kid didn't call her bluff.

He glanced into the stands at his dad, then back at her. "No, it's just sore."

"Oh. Well, I hope you can jump back in before the end of practice. I'd hate to have you miss the game."

"I'm good—" Violet turned to walk away but stopped dead in her tracks when Brayson finished the sentence with "—Miss Violet."

Miss Violet? Where'd that come from?

"I go by Coach Vi."

"I'm sorry Miss Vio—I mean, Coach Vi."

Violet crossed her arms over her chest and stepped up to Brayson. "Don't make that mistake again."

Gabe feigned innocence. "It's a pretty easy mistake to make. What if we mess up?"

"Then you're sitting out Friday's game."

Brayson scoffed. "You'd seriously bench a first-string player for calling you by the wrong name?"

Violet took another step toward the boys. "I'd bench my first and second string for blatant disrespect." She made eye contact with each player. "Any questions?"

She walked away but could hear Gabe mumble something about quitting. Her heart constricted. She needed to push these boys, but just hard enough that they came through as better players, and better people.

She glanced up at the stands where the ever-growing number of parents watched her, some out of general curiosity, some out of spite.

The phenomenon of parents hanging out to watch practice had developed over the last ten years, and Violet both understood it and didn't.

For many, particularly in the traffic-choked city of San Diego, it just made sense. They'd pull out their laptops and cell phones, finishing up a business day as the kids ran drills. Others used the time to pursue a passion project, like writing a novel. One dad had started a cooking blog when his son played on the freshman team, which was quite popular by the time the kid reached varsity.

But for other parents, their child's sport *was* their calling. They watched practice with a critical eye, wrote up lists of suggestions for the coaches, took note of whose kid was on first team and whose wasn't, and listed reasons why their child should be at the center of the game.

And in Outcrop, they seemed as interested in her failure as they were in their kids' success.

The afternoon soldiered on. Violet kept her cool with the difficult players and their parents. How these practices managed to last a thousand lifetimes, Violet did not understand.

According to her watch they'd only been there a few hours, but she could swear empires had risen and fallen since three that afternoon.

Finally, Violet blew her whistle and ran her hand in a circle around her head.

"Let's go!" Manuel bellowed, ushering everyone in his path toward Violet like a jovial snowplow.

She glanced at Ash, who looked as exhausted as she was. Gorgeous, but really tired.

"Nice work today. I've got the starting lineup for tomorrow. Before I get into this, my word on Thursday afternoon is final. You don't like where you are, or where you aren't, that's a conversation for Monday. I've thought long and hard about where I need everyone." She held up her clipboard. "This represents our starting point. As the game continues, I'll shuffle players in and out. It's my decision and mine alone, understood?"

Kids nodded. Violet swallowed and glanced at the list.

"Starting offensive line: Aaron, Left tackle, Jackson, Left guard, Manuel, Center—"

Manuel spoke before she could get any further. "Coach Vi, we play defense."

She glared over her clipboard. "Didn't I just get through saying this isn't up for discussion?"

"Oh. Right. No disrespect, Coach. But we're defense."

"I understand that, but I need you on both sides of the ball. Outcrop graduated four starting linemen last year."

"But we're defense," Aaron said, as though this point had not been made abundantly clear.

Violet raised her brow. "Are you complaining about getting too much playing time?"

"No."

"Are you questioning my decisions?"

"No, ma'am."

"Good."

"Alex, you're a right guard, Jamison, right tackle."

Brayson tensed, then exhaled when she read his name as starting quarterback. When she added Soren to the list of starters, the two boys looked at each other, a glimmer of uncertainty passing between them.

This was hard for the kids too. They were getting pressure from home that had to be pretty intense.

The difference was she chose to step into this position. The kids didn't. And for all this community knew, Kessler had abandoned them to go have fun, which couldn't be further from the truth. Uncle Mel had heard from

Kessler yesterday. He'd started treatment on Wednesday and was optimistic. But from what she knew about the legendary coach, he was always optimistic, no matter the odds.

She needed a little of his optimism right now, and to have patience and grace with her players.

A low laugh drew her attention. Brayson had said something that had Soren smirking. She needed to have patience with these kids, but she also needed to watch her back.

As the circle broke up, Ash's hand came to rest on her shoulder, signifying that he'd be watching her back too. She looked up at him and smiled.

"Nice work, Wallace!" Larsabal called from the stands. Ash turned to him, confusion clear on his face. Larsabal gestured between him and Violet, saying, "That's one way to get your kid in the starting lineup."

CHAPTER SEVEN

THE SKY DARKENED and stars seemed to flip on at the same moment stadium lights flooded the field. Evening air chilled as the sun fell behind the mountains. The home field at Outcrop sat on a plateau, one side giving way to the rocky crevasse of the Crooked River, the other running to the Cascade Mountains in the west. This small, old stadium in the middle of Oregon seemed to hold everyone on earth, and certainly everyone in Outcrop.

As the players ran onto the field, breaking through a paper banner, the entire population rose to their feet, cheering. Violet and her tiny coaching staff of two followed.

At Taft, the stadium was four times this size and always packed. But somehow this crowd seemed larger. In a rural community, she knew some people had traveled for over an hour to get here. These games were where they connected with, and celebrated, their community. Other sports gathered large crowds as well, but there was nothing compared to Friday Night Lights.

Violet gazed into the stands as she, Ash and Jet walked silently across the field. She saw her Uncle Mel and Aunt Rose. Jet's fiancée, Clara, sat with a whole passel of people, who Violet assumed were the rest of the Wallace clan. Joe Hacker, Ed Ramirez and Greg Larsabal had front row seats.

Her heart pounded. She had no idea what was going to happen tonight. She'd done everything she could to ensure success, but she couldn't control what her players chose to do.

By the time they reached the sidelines, Violet's heart beat so loudly it nearly overpowered the pep band. She hadn't felt such intense pressure and anticipation since she'd been on the field in college.

"You ready for this?"

Violet spun around to see Ash. He was out of his usual canvas work jacket and Stetson, and instead wore a coach's jacket and a ball cap. Still gorgeous. Still off-limits.

She smiled up at him. "I've just got to stand here barking at people." She gestured toward the team with her chin. "It's these guys we should be asking."

He cleared his throat, then glanced at the turf between them. "It occurred to me this morning, this is your first game as head coach."

It *was* a big day. She'd called her parents earlier. They were thrilled, but of course, Dad had his own game to coach and so they couldn't be here. "It is. I'm excited about it."

His hazel eyes connected with hers. "We should have done something to celebrate."

Violet let herself get lost in those eyes, which felt like a pretty nice celebration all on its own. "How 'bout we win this game?"

He nodded. "Sounds good. Let's do it."

The announcer went over the starting lineup, then asked the audience to stand for "The Star Spangled Banner." A cool breeze stirred her anticipation as she took off her ball cap. She could feel the crowd watching her as she kept her eyes on the flag. This week's team captains ran onto the field for the coin toss, then took their places.

Then the horn blew, and the game started.

THE SHRILL WHISTLE blew again, the ref clearly irritated. Violet took three steps out onto the field before Ash's hand landed on her left shoulder and Jet's landed on her right. Her assistant coaches held her back, again.

"What is Brayson doing out there?" she demanded.

Her quarterback stood doe-eyed before the ref, acting like he didn't know he'd broken a rule. Soren paced behind him, smirking.

"We're not losing," Jet reminded her.

"Because your defense hasn't let the other team score." She gestured in frustration, then realized she was making a frustrated gesture to the one functioning part of her team. "Thank you. Madras hasn't been able to score, and that's the only thing we have going for us."

"Doesn't seem like our side wants to score," Ash muttered.

"Or is allowed to score," she added, glancing to where Hacker and his cohort sat in the stands.

The three coaches turned back to the field, crossing their arms over their chests as they watched Brayson smirking his way through another lecture from the ref. The crowd in the stands behind them was frustrated too. They'd been waiting since last November for this game and nothing much was happening. Nothing much good, anyway.

"What time is it?" Larsabal called loudly in the stands behind her. Something about his tone set off a warning in her gut.

"Time for a new coach!" Hacker called back.

Fear and anger ricocheted through Violet, intensified when a number of people in the crowd chuckled. Ash laid his hand on her shoulder, eyes straight ahead. She focused on the warmth of Ash's hand, soaking up his strength.

On the field, Brayson was still talking to the ref, gesturing at her and feigning confusion. He was blaming this on her. Jet lowered his head to Violet's and said quietly, "He's doing this on purpose."

"The kid wants to play D One and he's sabotaging this game on purpose?" Violet shook her head. "I get that he doesn't respect me, but he's throwing away his own chances here."

"What time is it?" Larsabal called again.

"Time for a new coach!" several other community members joined in with Hacker this time.

Jet glared into the stands, then spoke quietly to her, "They're trying to get you to quit."

"Yeah. I picked up on that vibe."

"And if you don't, Brayson and some of the others are going to transfer to Bend." Jet looked as angry and offended as she'd ever seen him when he continued with, "to play for *the Swarm*."

So that was their plan. A cool, determined sense of power flooded through her. These boys were a lost cause. It was a bummer—

she didn't like losing causes, but it was good to know where she stood.

Violet signaled for a time-out. The boys came trotting off the field and Violet asked the first string to circle up around her. The linemen were furious, while the backfield sauntered over slowly, smiling.

That was all she needed.

"What happened out there?" she asked.

"I just couldn't remember the play." Brayson was grinning. "I told you we didn't have enough time to learn it, *Miss Violet.*"

"You're on the bench," she said simply.

The color drained from his face. He glanced at the stands, then back at her. "You can't bench me."

Violet stared at him, way past trying to understand. "You're on the bench."

He looked panicked. "We still have two quarters to go."

"I am aware of the clock."

He glanced at the stands again. The plan had been for him to bumble out here like a clown during this three-ring circus, making her look like a fool.

Confusion, then anger flooded his face. He'd been told, *convinced* that this was all okay. And she'd bet good money he was beginning to understand it wasn't. "Gabe's not going to go in for me."

Violet glanced slowly behind her to where Gabe stood at the sidelines, looking very nervous, then back at her players. Soren crossed his arms over his chest. "You should quit," he muttered.

Manuel pulled off his helmet and stepped into Soren's face. "Say that again," he demanded. "Say it again and I'll flatten you."

Violet stepped between the boys. "Neither of those scenarios are going to happen." She gestured to Brayson. "You're out for the game. Soren, you too."

Brayson pulled off the helmet Violet had personally inspected and refurbished so it was safe for tonight's game and dropped it at his feet before storming off to the bench. He looked so vulnerable and upset Violet was tempted to give the kid a hug. His dad's plan sorely underestimated her strength, and Brayson was the one bearing the public humiliation for it.

Violet remained calm as she said, "Jackson, you're in at quarterback. Let's go get this done."

ASH WATCHED AS Jackson glanced first at Violet, then at his buddies on the line. She said something else to him, then called out, "Carley, you're in as receiver."

Carley shot onto the field. The guys, minus Brayson and Soren, followed to the line of scrimmage. Jackson didn't take his normal position but moved to the center of the line, behind Manuel. Ash was confused for a moment, until he saw Violet's face as she returned to the sidelines.

Ash was desperate to ask Violet what she was doing but knew she wouldn't take well to being questioned right now.

The crowd murmured behind them.

"Everybody's going to be so shocked a girl is receiving, they won't focus on Jackson as QB," she explained. "That should give him some breathing room."

Ash nodded calmly, while his insides were strung tight, as though he'd sat twisting a tuning peg mindlessly, readying the strings to snap.

"You boys better shape up if you expect to go back in," he said to Brayson and Soren.

"They're not going back in," Violet stated coolly.

Ash closed his eyes as she confirmed his fear.

He'd done his time as starting quarterback his junior and senior years at Outcrop, but he didn't want that kind of pressure for Jackson. There were also the repercussions from Brayson and the other seniors to consider. Gabe was on the bench right now because he didn't want to cross them and become the target of bullying. But Jackson would do the right thing. Violet knew that and was using him to win this game. She had no business putting him in at quarterback.

As though reading his thoughts, Violet looked up at him and held eye contact.

Right. She was using *all* the players to win this game; that was her job. And Ash had no business questioning her decisions.

He refocused in the field. Jackson seemed nervous as he barked out the cadence. Manuel hiked the ball. Ash nearly whooped out in relief when Jackson caught it.

Then he stepped back and prepared to pass to Carley as she launched down the field. He hesitated a second too long. The line broke and a massive left tackle threw himself at Jackson, flattening him on the field.

The crowd let out a groan. Ash started to race onto the turf when he saw Jackson pop up, grinning. He continued toward his son, but Jet had a hold of the back of his jacket.

The team set up again. The ref's whistle split the air, and the number sequence was called again. Jackson took the snap and this time managed to pass it off to Joaquin, who promptly got tackled.

"What time is it?" Larsabal called out.

Ash was ready to take the men out himself, but his sister Clara beat him to it. Hacker and his crew didn't have a chance to respond with their taunt because a small blonde matchmaker flew down the stands and got in their faces. Clara didn't get angry often, but when she did, watch out.

Jet grinned as he watched the altercation. "She's gonna be my *wife*."

Ash couldn't help but smile. There was some good left in this world.

Before the final down they managed to move the ball in the right direction. Jackson headed to his defensive position for the next play, but Violet tapped him out. "I need you fresh for the final quarter," she told him.

Jackson trotted off the field and came to stand next to Ash. Ash dropped a hand on his shoulder. "I'm proud of you."

"I never got a good throw in."

Ash shook his head. "I'm proud of you for stepping up." He glanced behind him to where Brayson and the others were sulking on the bench. "It's not easy to stand up against your peers."

Jackson looked shocked. "I'm not going to

sabotage Coach Vi." He glanced back at the boys. "I'm glad they're out. This is fun."

Ash stared down at his son. *Fun?*

"You've been tackled three times."

Jackson shrugged. "The line isn't used to working without me. They'll figure it out. Manuel's on it."

The whistle blew and defense quickly intercepted the ball, sending Jackson in again as quarterback. The crowd, now caught up in the drama, was rooting for Jackson as he stepped up. *And* when he was summarily flattened. By the end of the fourth quarter they still hadn't scored, but Jackson did hold the record for the most sacks of a quarterback in one game.

"Please lie still for another moment." Maisy, the new doctor in town, hovered over Jackson near the end of the fourth quarter.

"I'm fine," he said, pushing up on his elbows.

"You do what the doctor tells you to," Ash snapped. He glanced over at Violet. Hadn't this gone on long enough? The guys must have learned their lesson by now. Or they might not have, but it didn't seem like Jackson's health was worth trading for their need to shape up.

"Dad, I'm fine."

"I'd like to hear that from Dr. Maisy."

Dr. Maisy, or Doc Martin as his brother

Bowman referred to his girlfriend, could be counted on to worry about any given situation appropriately.

Maisy rocked back on her heels and glanced up at Ash. "He's fine. Just got the wind knocked out of him."

Jackson sat up.

"He's a human bouncy ball, just like his uncle Bowman." Maisy grinned at Jackson as he did, indeed, bounce up. The crowd cheered.

Violet signaled to the refs to keep playing.

"There are two minutes left in this interminable game, and overtime is looking more likely by the minute," she muttered as she headed back to the sidelines. "Joaquin, you're in."

"Does Jackson have to stay in?" Ash asked.

Frustrated confusion flashed in Violet's eyes. "The doctor said he's fine."

Ash stared down at the turf. Maisy had cleared him, but...

But this was a lot. Playing a new position. Standing up to the senior players. Getting sacked five times in two quarters.

"He can handle it," she said.

Ash glanced at his son. Sure, Jackson might be able to handle it. But could he?

The whistle blew. Jackson was more confident as he called out the cadence. The line was learning to function without him and held tighter this time.

Jackson readjusted his grip on the ball and watched as Joaquin flew down the field. He pulled back and threw.

The defensive backfield on the opposing team were as surprised as anyone, and not ready for a completed pass. Joaquin easily snatched the ball and glided into the end zone. The crowd was on their feet, roaring with approval. Even the opposing team's fans were impressed by the pass.

But no one was more excited than the guys on the line. Manuel, Aaron and the others rushed Jackson, and honestly were in more danger of hurting him in their excitement than the opposing team ever was.

Overwhelming relief flooded Ash. Jackson had stepped up. With any luck, the first-string players would come around. And he'd never have to watch his son get repeatedly knocked down by large linemen again.

Ash turned to Violet, exhausted as the adrenaline drained from his body.

Violet, after an entire game of taking the high road, looked ready to fight.

CHAPTER EIGHT

BOISTEROUS CELEBRATION WITH an undertone
of grumbling rippled out of the team room.
Conflicted emotions—along with the strong
scent of dirty sneakers and Axe body spray—
had Violet hesitating at the door. Most of the
time, a team had a clear feel after a game:
excited, lethargic, joyful, frustrated, cocky.
Most of the time a coach knew what she was
walking into.

Tonight, the team room held all the feels.

Instinctively, Violet wanted to celebrate.
She wanted to high-five anyone within a ten-
mile radius. They'd won despite everything;
they'd gotten to the horn with six more points
than the opposing team.

She was also furious, as angry as she'd
ever been in her coaching career. Working for
Laurent had been a daily exercise in keeping
her frustration at bay. But through it all, she'd
always had the respect of her players. No matter what happened with the head coach, or
what rumors were circulating, the boys she

worked with knew and valued her. If any of her old players saw what had gone down tonight, they'd be shocked and furious.

The Eagles had won, leaving her both sighing with relief and gasping for breath. She hadn't failed...yet. Violet moved toward the door, still not sure how to address her team.

"Coach Vi," Ash called, jogging to catch up with her. She stopped, relieved to have an excuse to take another minute before entering.

He took her arm and steered her away from the door, lowering his voice so he wouldn't be heard. "We need to put a stop to this."

"You think?"

Ash's gaze connected with hers; his jaw clenched in frustration. "Those boys cannot be allowed to treat you like this."

Violet glanced into the room. The boys she'd benched sat sullenly in the back, but they were still here. They wanted to play football. They were angry, confused and rude beyond comprehension, but they were still kids. They could have walked off the field and off her team at any point, but they hadn't.

"I agree."

Ash's fingers ran absently along her arm. Then he nodded with confirmation and let go of her. "I'm going to go in there to knock some heads together."

Violet stepped in front of him. "No heads will be knocked, and I will defend myself."

"Violet, let me help. You don't understand the way this town works."

Violet pressed her lips together. She knew all she needed to about the way this town worked. "Outcrop is small-minded and petty. I can handle it."

Ash stepped back. The buzz of fluorescent lights overhead filled the space between them. "I wouldn't say that."

"You wouldn't?"

He honestly looked confused, like a lost puppy. "Outcrop is a great town. Three men are behaving badly, but the town's not all bad."

"Three men, their sons and everyone who supports them."

He reached his hands out, paused, then placed his palms against her shoulders. "I hate that you have this impression of our town. I hate that this has been your experience." His fingers wrapped around her arms. He bent his head to look into her eyes. "Please believe me when I say this is a good place, and most people support you."

She let his words wash through her. She was tough. She didn't want to care what others thought of her, but she cared all the same.

"Once we get these guys straightened out, you'll see. Outcrop's a good place."

Violet leaned her head toward Ash, imagining the solid embrace of his arms. It had to feel so good, snuggled against his chest, his deep voice reverberating through her.

"And I don't want Jackson to have to play quarterback again."

Violet jerked her head back. "Jackson was incredible at QB."

"He was sacked five times."

Was he being serious? Because if so, he was the only man in America who didn't want his son playing quarterback. "That's not his fault. The line needs to readjust."

"The line is stronger with Jackson on it."

"You do understand that a hundred-seventy-pound lineman is not optimal? Jackson shouldn't be on the line. Safety or cornerback, sure. But the line? He'd do much better at quarterback."

Ash shook his head, like *she* didn't understand. "How can you say that? He was sacked more times than any quarterback in Outcrop history."

"Again, not his fault."

"Okay, it's not his fault, but he was the one being hammered with the consequences."

Violet thought back through the game. Jackson seemed to be having a fantastic time.

Yes, he spent a lot of time at the bottom of a large pile of boys, which could not have smelled pleasant. But he was grinning, and gunning to get back in the game, every time he popped up.

"Ash, he's our best bet for a backup. If Gabe and Brayson pull this again, I want Jackson ready. And both boys are graduating. Jackson is an excellent choice to fill the hole."

Ash rubbed his forehead, clearly ready to argue. But Violet had plenty of conflict ahead and wasn't interested in one drop of it coming from her assistant coach.

"Quarterback is a lot of pressure," Ash said.

"Pressure makes us stronger," Violet countered.

"Coach Vi!" Manuel called out into the hallway.

Violet stepped away from Ash as he said, "Just, please, consider my request."

She didn't like this feeling. Jackson had been the brightest spot of a grim game. She wasn't interested in promising to hold him back at his dad's request. That said, Ash was one of her two pillars of support. She couldn't hold up her end of this circus tent without him.

"I'm always open to constructive feedback from my staff," she forced herself to say.

Violet turned away from the conversation and strode into the team room, crossing her arms as she observed the players. *Where to start?*

The players she'd benched sat sulkily in the back, ready to fight. But if they were willing to fight, it meant they were still attached to the team.

The new players were bouncing off the cinder block walls, still high off their first game. It wouldn't have mattered if the Eagles won, or lost, or broke out into a flash mob singing songs from *Glee*—they were just excited to be here.

Manuel, Aaron and the gang were elated. Violet glanced at Ash. Was he worried Brayson and his crew might take their anger out on Jackson and pick a fight? It was the only legitimate reason she could think of for his hesitation. But the kid was literally surrounded by linemen and would be for the foreseeable future. A fight with Jackson would be a fight with all one-thousand-plus pounds of the defensive and offensive lines.

Violet scanned the room, focusing on the kids she was truly concerned about: the mid-range players, the kids who'd signed up for the season in good faith. They didn't have a dog in this fight; they just wanted to play ball. Their football season was her responsibility.

Hacker might be willing to ruin the season for her, but she wasn't going to let him ruin it for these kids. Violet's gaze connected with Joaquin's. Everything she needed to say came to her in that moment.

"Congratulations," she said to the team in a calm, flat voice. "We won the first of ten games I intend to win during the regular season. Despite everything—" she paused, making eye contact with each boy involved in the sabotage "—we pushed through, and we won."

She paced across the front of the room, then stilled at the podium. "I'd like to offer you two choices." She held out one hand. "Be on this team. Go all in. Give your best to the Eagles and work together as one body to win and grow." Then she held out her other hand and said simply, "Or don't. You all signed up to play with Kessler. I'm not what you were expecting. If you don't want to play for me, quit now. No hard feelings, no looking back. Football is a tough sport, and no one should be on the field who doesn't want to be."

Her words wove through the players, like her dad's used to. Violet watched as each kid made a choice. Expressions shifted and lightened throughout the room. Carley twisted in her seat to see who might be wavering. Jackson sat up straighter, ready to pick up any slack that might come out of this night. Violet made eye contact with each kid, eliciting a commitment to the team.

Until her eyes landed on the back row.

Brayson stood. He glanced around to make sure some kids were still with him, then said, "Why should we be the ones to quit?"

The sentence seemed to reach out and grab her by the throat. Brayson could sense his advantage.

"You're not even from this town. You've never been a head coach before. You should be the one to leave, not us."

Violet narrowed her eyes but kept her breathing steady.

Never argue with a teenager. Never get angry.

Never, never quit.

"That's not going to happen."

"Fine." Brayson shrugged, imitating her calm response. He picked up his gear bag faltering only slightly as he said, "I can transfer schools. I'll play for the Bend Swarm."

A dark murmur washed through the room.

"Okay." Violet nodded. "That's not what I want for you, but if it's legal in the state of

Oregon to transfer schools and still play ball after the season has started, go for it."

Brayson paused. Violet refrained from smiling. Not everyone knew Oregon School Activities Association rules as well as she did.

"The Swarm." She gazed up at the acoustic ceiling tiles, as though trying to recall information. "They're coached by Richard Ombada, who used to play for the Rams."

"That's right." Brayson kept his eyes on his bag, trying to keep cool.

Never embarrass a player in front of his peers.

"And let's see, first string quarterback there is...the coach's son. I know he's been talking to Linfield about playing for them next year. Second string quarterback has already signed with Western Oregon University, so he's pretty good too."

Brayson looked up at her, color flooding his face. His eyes connected with hers and she saw someone trapped and angry and desperate. She was all too familiar with those feelings not to recognize them.

He threw his bag down. "You're ruining my senior season!"

She tightened her lips, not trusting herself to speak.

"Brayson, *you* are ruining your senior season," Ash's deep voice cut through the silence. "Coach Vi wasn't out there bungling the ball tonight. She wasn't claiming injury during practice."

"Then why don't you just kick me off the team?"

Violet shook her head, forcing herself to remain calm. "I'm not going to give you an out. I'm offering you a choice. Commit to the team or walk away."

ASH TURNED TO the exit, exhausted. How could so much have happened between four and nine o'clock? He glanced over at Violet, who was busy talking with CJ. Clueless to the drama around him, CJ was asking Violet for information on his twenty-eight seconds of playing time. Violet was patiently talking him through it.

She'd been a brilliant leader tonight.

And what had he done? Stood at the sidelines and watched as the team tried to sabotage her, then basically joined ranks with those boys when he questioned her decision in sending Jackson in as quarterback.

The fog of exhaustion rising through his brain made it difficult to think. Brayson had walked away after Violet's speech, but he hadn't quit. If Ash could figure out how to keep the first-string offensive players on the team, it would put Jackson out of Violet's sights for quarterback.

But he'd make that plan another day. Right now, he wanted to get back to the ranch where he could breathe. He gazed at Violet, who'd now spent significantly more time discussing CJ's brief stint on the field than he'd actually *had* on the field.

Ash wanted to talk to Violet. To say, *Thank you*, and *I'm sorry*, and *Please, treat Jackson differently than all your other players, because he's my son*. And if he could do all that while giving her a long hug?

Ash closed his eyes and pushed out any thoughts of folding Violet into his arms.

He could manage this feeling. Nine weeks left. Unless they made the playoffs.

Violet finally glanced up and gave him a brief smile, no vulnerability or connection implied. "Thanks, Ash. See you."

Ash's heart slumped, and even his head had trouble getting on board with the easy dismissal. After their roller coaster of a night, all she had was, *Thanks, Ash. See you?*

"See you Monday." He rolled his shoulders and headed over to where Jackson was still talking with his friends. Maybe Violet was as tired as he was.

"Time for Eighty Local?" Jackson asked.

Ash stopped. *Right*. It was a Friday night, after the game. Everyone would be at Eighty Local, and his son had thrown the winning touchdown. Even back when Ash was a teenager, long before Hunter bought what had been the Kwik Burger and renovated the old place, everyone had gathered there. At the time, the one restaurant in town was rundown and of suspect quality, and still he and his friends and the rest of the town would crowd in to rehash the game.

Ash tried very hard not to sigh. "Sure." He glanced back at Violet who was picking up papers and looking over her clipboards. "You want to run ahead with the guys, and I'll meet you there?"

"Yeah." Jackson looked past him to Violet. "Coach Vi, you coming?"

Violet looked truly stunned. "Um…coming where?"

"To Eighty Local. Outcrop tradition."

The color drained from her face. It was clear the last thing she wanted to do was walk into a public space in Outcrop right now. Ash was getting to know her well enough to understand that she wouldn't back down from a single responsibility.

But the look on her face suggested she'd do just about anything to get out of this one.

"Coach Vi probably has some planning to do—"

"Yes," she said, jumping on the excuse. "I've got a lot to wade through tonight. But thank you, Jackson."

Ash gazed at her, wondering if he should offer to help with the fake planning she claimed to have. She kept her expression neutral. Okay, so he wasn't invited to the imaginary work session.

The team filtered out of the room, and Ash managed to linger a little longer, putting up chairs, but Violet encouraged him to head over to Eighty Local.

"I've got this," she said, offering him a tired smile. She wanted to be alone, or more specifically, she didn't want him to be there.

"All right. Let me know if you need anything over the weekend."

"I've got a fully stocked kitchen, three bids for new helmets to go over and all the transportation forms from the school district to fill out. I should be good to go."

"Have fun with that," he joked.

"I will," she said, head bent over the podium, no humor in her voice.

Cold air washed over Ash as he stepped

out of the school. He pulled his Stetson lower on his brow and zipped up his jacket as he headed up the quiet streets to Main. Shops were closed for the night, with the exception of Eighty Local. Light spilled out the windows, illuminating the cheerful Friday night crowd. At the far end of the building the events center was starting to take shape, a monument to his brother's work ethic and ambition.

It was great to see his siblings doing so well. Clara and Piper's matchmaking business was more than just work for his sisters; it was their sacred mission on earth. Bowman had been named Firefighter of the Year, and despite a few hiccups along the way, he was beloved in this town for his willingness to risk all for the safety of others. And Hunter's restaurant was the town's hot spot.

Ash crossed the parking lot, his heart tugging him to the spot he'd first laid eyes on Violet. He hadn't wanted to make her angry tonight when he questioned putting Jackson in, but if it came down to Jackson's safety and anyone else's feelings, Jackson would win. Every time.

He glanced in the windows. Jackson sat at a table in the center of the room, his buddies all around him. Hunter was setting food in front of the boys, and if Ash knew his brother, he wasn't taking money for it.

In Ash's own days as Outcrop's quarterback, the scene had looked similar, but he'd been too serious of a young man to enjoy it. He'd seen himself more as the overworked engine of the team, rather than the star. That had always been his role. The responsible one, the doer, the fixer. The reliable leader, willing to make hard choices and put in long hours to get things done.

They were traits he'd been proud of, until they ruined his marriage.

Jackson looked up from his plate and laughed at something Aaron said. This was the kind of experience he wanted for his son. For that to happen, Outcrop needed a good coach. He had to help Violet out and get the team through this.

This town is small-minded and petty, she'd said. The generalization, as false as he wanted it to be, rang true in her experience. She'd only had contact with a small number of people, and a lot of them had been awful.

Ash pulled in a breath and reached for the door. The handle was cool in his palm, but warmth surrounded him the moment he opened the door and stepped inside.

"Coach Wallace!" Jet waved him over to

the counter where he, Clara and Maisy were clustered together. Hunter ran things on the other side of the counter, managing to serve a restaurant full of people while keeping up a conversation with his family. Ash crossed the room, acknowledging Jackson with a tap on the shoulder. Jackson gave him a quick, "Hi, Dad," then returned to rehashing the game. Ash hung his hat at the end of the counter.

"How 'bout my nephew!" Hunter crowed.

Ash nodded. "He did all right."

"All right? He saved this town from humiliating defeat by *Madras*." Hunter shuddered.

"He did. He stepped up. And I'm hoping Brayson and Gabe will come to their senses and step back *in* so he doesn't have to go through that again."

Jet, Clara, Maisy and Hunter all exchanged glances, like some kind of online geometry module. Then Jet cleared his throat and took another drink of his beer.

"Jackson didn't exactly look like he was suffering out there," Hunter noted.

"He was sacked five times."

"And came back swinging," Maisy said.

Ash shook his head at the young doctor, annoyed. "I thought you were the one who worried about everything."

She blushed, her pale skin lighting up red

as Ash referenced how concerned she got about Bowman. "I worry about everything that needs worrying about. Jackson was having the time of his life out there."

"No, the one we need to worry about is Coach Vi," Jet said.

"That's the truth."

"Seriously!" Clara said. "I couldn't believe Joe Hacker tonight." Jet slipped an arm around Clara and kissed the top of her head. "What's his issue?"

"There are a lot of issues," Jet told her. "Everyone's worried about Coach Kessler, and if Violet knows what happened to him, she's not talking. Hacker thought he was next in line for the head coaching position, and Violet's from out of town."

"*California*," Ash said, imitating Hacker's tone.

Clara's eyes narrowed. "We need a plan."

Maisy's face lit up. "I love a good plan."

Hunter set a basket of sweet potato fries in front of them, and the siblings and almost-siblings-in-law gathered around.

Ash pulled a napkin out of the dispenser and grabbed one of the pens by the register. He printed the facts across the top of the napkin. "I'm gonna start by saying she's a fantastic coach, smart and great with the players."

"Right," Jet concurred. "She's the GOAT."

"She's a goat?" Clara asked.

"Not a goat," Hunter said. "The GOAT. Greatest of all time. Do you know nothing about sports?"

"Literally nothing," Clara said proudly. "Okay, let's help people get to know how much Violet is a goat."

"The GOAT," Hunter grumbled.

"We could run a social media campaign," Clara suggested.

Ash gave her a dry look.

"You still don't have any social media accounts?" she accused.

"Forever and always uninterested."

Clara rolled her eyes.

"We need something more tangible," he said, continuing to scribble ideas on the napkin.

"I agree." Maisy glanced at his notes. "Social media is so malleable, plus it might spark arguments and an 'us-versus-them' mentality."

"You're totally right," Clara said. "We need irrefutable support for Violet that literally flies in Hacker's face."

"Messenger pigeons?" Hunter suggested.

Ash laughed, leaning in toward his family as they suggested ideas for supporting Violet. There was a funny feeling in his chest. He ran his palm over his heart, trying to understand what this thing was that felt good but also made him nervous.

He was having *fun*. For the first time in a long, long time, he had a cause to champion. Not a vague cause like "keep the family ranch profitable" which was complicated and overwhelming on the best days. Or Jackson's health and safety, which was forever unreachable because even when he'd made it through one day with his son happy and healthy, there was always tomorrow.

Getting the town to appreciate what they had in Coach Vi was completely within his grasp. And reaching that goal with the combined creativity of his family would be a hoot.

Ash wanted to help Violet. He wanted to show her this town wasn't small-minded and petty, and he wanted Hacker and his crew to realize how wrong they'd been. He wanted to do this for Coach Kessler too.

Ash pulled the napkin back toward him and glanced over the list. "What's everybody got going on this coming week? Because I've got an idea."

CHAPTER NINE

BY HER THIRD weekend in Outcrop, Violet
would have been happy to hole up in the little apartment she'd rented over the chocolate
shop on Main Street and not come out again
until practice on Monday afternoon. She had
absolutely no interest in getting raked over the
coals during her free time after getting raked
over the coals on the job.

Sadly, that would mean going without food
for twenty-four hours, and that just wasn't
happening.

She glanced out the window to see the sun
washing across the town for another glorious
Sunday morning in Outcrop. The weather, at
least, was agreeable. Practice continued to
be *dis*agreeable. But after another frustrating
week of defiance, her team had managed to
win their second game last Friday night. And
she still *had* a team. The boys were grumpy,
but they were there. All the boys but Brayson. He'd taken to calling in sick to practice

every day. He wasn't off the team, but he sure wasn't on it.

And what kind of kid intent on sabotage calls to let the coaches know he won't be there?

Ash was polite as ever, but definitely more reserved than he had been. He seemed distracted, muttering back and forth with Jet when they thought she didn't notice. It bothered her more than she wanted to admit. Obviously, there was no future for her with Ash, but in the short time she'd known him, he was the one thing she looked forward to. She had no idea why he was opposed to Jackson playing quarterback, but if it came down to it, she'd pick the team over Ash's concerns any day of the week. As coach, her job was to put the team before the desires of any one person, particularly a parent.

Yeah, it had been a tough first few weeks in Outcrop, and she was exhausted from being so tough in the face of it. When she got home from their second game on Friday night, she'd allowed herself to lock the door behind her and snuggle in with home-cooked meals. It wasn't exactly collapsing into the arms of a cowboy and letting him soothe all her concerns away, but it would have to do.

But by Sunday morning she was out of ingredients to cook, having gone through everything she'd bought from a big-box store in Redmond when she arrived. She had to brave the streets of Outcrop and go forage for fresh vegetables and pasta.

Violet took a deep breath and headed out the door. Steps ran down the side of the two-story brick building and let her out on Main Street. She glanced at her phone, where Google Maps was attempting to steer her in the direction of Manny's Groceries. Knowing her luck, the store was owned by Hacker, or Larsabal or some other guy who wanted her to quit. Would they even allow her in the store? If worse came to worst, she knew she was still welcome at Eighty Local, and her uncle sold snacks at OHTAF. Violet looked down at the little blue flashing dot symbolizing her on the digital map and started walking.

Keep your head up, she could hear her father saying. *Never let them see your fear.*

Violet reluctantly brought her gaze up from her phone, taking in the still, quiet morning. Something red caught her eye, and Violet turned reflexively.

Her feet stopped. Trying to make sense of what she was seeing was so consuming she literally couldn't walk at the same time.

I'm With Vi! exclaimed a red banner spanning the front of the chocolate shop. Violet stared at it: Outcrop Eagle red and white, an image of a soaring bird in one corner and Vi was definitely her name. One of the women from inside Three Sisters Chocolatier waved at her. Violet waved back uncertainly. The woman pointed to the corner of the big picture window. There were two helmet images, showing that the chocolate shop had donated money to buy new helmets for the team.

Wow. Nice to know she had the town chocolatier on her side. She could now add excellent chocolate to the list of foods available to her in Outcrop.

Violet gave her a thumbs-up and waved, then continued up Main. Maybe the chocolate ladies were supportive because Violet rented from them? That made sense. They didn't want to lose a quiet renter and committed customer.

But then half a block later, she came to a yarn shop with the same red sign out front, a hand-crocheted eagle hanging from one end. Her heart warmed. She was so grateful it was enough to make her want to start knitting. Where had they gotten the sign, and why, after everything else, did they choose to support her?

Violet turned slowly, scanning the quiet street. Red banners began to pop out at her everywhere. A store called Second Chance Cowgirl had one. The health clinic had two signs, and a hand-painted poster congratulating her on Friday's win. Her uncle's store had five banners, hanging at regular intervals along the front porch. Every single store in town displayed at least one football helmet denoting their donation, and most had several.

"Violet!"

She looked up to see Clara emerging from Eighty Local. Ash's sister was beautiful and cheerful, as always. Violet suspected she'd be just as gorgeous firing warning shots at a cougar in the emu pen at two in the morning.

"How much do you love these banners?" Clara asked. "Because they're literally my favorite."

"Are you behind all this?" Violet asked.

"We're behind *you*," she clarified. "Also, I made buttons." Clara reached into her bag and pulled out a red button with a picture of an emu squawking. The word bubble coming from its mouth read, I'm With Vi!

Violet laughed.

"These were my idea." Clara tapped the button. "Everything else is Ash."

Violet glanced back down the street. Ash?

He'd been to all these stores, garnering donations? She'd been at home sulking. Meanwhile, her favorite cowboy had been out rallying support for her.

Her heart twirled like a two-year-old in a princess dress. She tried to reprimand it, but like a two-year-old in a princess dress, it ignored her completely. "Ash did this?"

"I'm not totally sure he wanted you to know that, but yes. When Ash feels like something unjust is going down, he gets in there."

Violet nodded. This was about fair play and doing the right thing.

It isn't about me or any interest Ash might have in me personally, she told her heart.

Her heart disregarded this evidence, picked up a tiara and kept twirling.

"Good morning, Coach!" Jet emerged from Eighty Local and handed both Clara and Violet a coffee. "Hunter says this is his new invention, a maple cream latte with a dusting of…" Jet stared down at the drink, as though trying to remember the name of whatever had been dusted over the top.

Clara breathed in the scent. "Nutmeg," she finished for him.

Violet looked at the cup, then through the front window of Eighty Local. Hunter had the supportive banners hanging on the outside *and* inside of his restaurant.

A heavy pressure built at the back of Violet's eyes. She swallowed hard. "Thank you."

"Happy to help out where we can," Jet said.

She held up the coffee, gesturing toward the signs with it. "How did you get all this done?"

Clara shrugged. "We're a big family. And we're mad. Plus, I think you said something to Ash about this town being small-minded and petty, and he's not having that *at all*."

"Sounds like Ash." Violet chuckled, shaking her head. "My plan today had been to get a few groceries, then try to drum up donations from local stores for new helmets, but it looks like you beat me to it." She gestured to the helmet posters in the front windows.

"Oh, that was our dad. He's like, really excited about the helmets."

Violet took a sip of her coffee; a rich, fall-inspired beverage. It made her want to stay in Outcrop forever. That feeling, along with an inexplicable urge to meet Ash's parents, should have sent her straight back into her apartment.

Clara glanced up at Jet, and something passed between them. "Dad's also worried about Kessler. They're old friends. Like, *old* friends. Can you tell us anything?"

She hadn't heard from the legendary coach since he called her before entering the hospital. In her gut, she knew he needed to be shielded from the drama brewing in his absence. All she wanted him to hear about the situation was that they were winning games.

Violet let out a breath. "I can tell you he's in good hands."

Jet's jaw clenched, like he was holding back intense emotion. Clara ran a hand along his back. These two loved Kessler. Violet glanced around her. The rest of the town probably felt the same way. She wasn't just the new coach, but a living reminder that something was seriously amiss with a man they cared about.

Not that there was *any* excuse for sabotaging her team. But complex emotions were what they were, and accepting that helped her understand the situation.

"Keeping his team together and coaching a winning season is the best way we can support him right now," Violet said.

Jet nodded, keeping his eyes on the pavement. "You'll let me know if there's anything I can do?"

"Of course."

Violet heard a truck coming down Main.

The town was waking up. She was starting to feel more alive herself. The Wallaces had her back. She was here to advance her own career, but also to help out Coach Kessler. This was going to be okay, or at least now she felt like she had a fair shot at making it okay.

She drew her gaze from her coffee and looked first at Clara then at Jet. She was so grateful for both of them and was on the verge of telling them when the truck came to a screeching halt.

"Stop!" a deep, resonate voice called out from the truck. "I mean it. Whatever you're about to say, Clara, just keep it to yourself!"

ASH PULLED THE truck over in what had to be the worst parking job Outcrop had seen in a decade and hopped out, still yelling at his sister.

It was only then that he realized what he was doing.

His feet stilled, the last of his commands still echoing off the empty streets.

Objectively, he'd made an absolute fool of himself. He was running at Violet like she'd been juggling a hand grenade instead of chatting with his sister.

Or rather, chatting with his overly ambitious, matchmaking sister who attempted to set up everyone she'd ever met, whether they hired her to do so or not. And while he had absolutely no say over who Violet did or did not go out with, his body had reacted without one pulse from his frontal lobe.

And now he looked ridiculous.

"Good morning, bro," Clara said cheerfully. "What was it you wanted us to stop?"

Ash blew out a breath and turned back to close the door to the cab. He needed to slow down. This was difficult, made all the more so by the soft, pale blue sweater Violet was wearing.

"Good morning." He nodded to Violet. Her gaze caught his and, once again, his frontal lobe took a vacation and he let himself stare into her pretty eyes.

"Good morning," she said, then glanced back behind her. "It's a fantastic morning. Thanks to you all."

Ash smiled as he saw the red banners. "Town's coming around. I knew they would."

"They're coming around because of you and your family." She blinked back tears and gave him a wry smile. "I don't know how to begin to thank you."

"We're happy to help."

She nodded, one tear spilling out. Even though he knew she cried easily, that tear was all the thanks he'd ever need. It was definitely worth the late night of designing the posters and banner and subsequent days of drumming up support from local businesses. "You should see Manny's groceries. That place is plastered in red right now."

Violet's gaze dropped to her coffee, and a blush rose in her cheeks. How was she so incredibly beautiful? It didn't seem like it should be possible for a person to be this pretty.

"What needs to stop?" Clara chirped again. She was not going to let this drop. Ash sighed and turned on his youngest sibling.

"You know what it is. Stop it."

Clara widened her eyes in innocence, looking exactly like eight-year-old Clara trying to pass the blame for brawling with her brothers. "I have no idea why you would come crashing over to the side of the road hollering at us to stop." She took a sip of her coffee. "Unless you know something about this latte I don't."

He was in it now. Ash gestured at Violet. "Give her some time."

Clara got a devious grin on her face. No wonder she got along so well with Jet's emus.

"Violet has a lot going on right now."

"I'm aware of that."

"Are you? Because I saw how things went down with Maisy—"

Clara waved his concern away. "The whole reason I sent Maisy out with so many guys was because I needed her to realize Bowman was her perfect match. All those dates were secretly my way of setting her up with our brother."

Ash pulled his head back. "I set Maisy up with Bowman."

Clara reacted, a full body response of indignation. "You did not."

Ash put his hands on his hips and stared down his sister. "Yes, I did. I was supposed to run the kids' Cowboy Camp, and when I saw the Healthy Lives Institute had sent a young doctor interested in outdoor sports, I made Bowman do it. Then they fell in love, and now we're on the verge of having a doctor in the family. I don't have to tell you how that's gonna come in handy with Bowman. Now I don't have to have the credit for it, but don't pretend like you get the credit either."

Clara stared, confusion, then respect unfolding across her face.

"Awwww! Ash, that's the sweetest thing ever." Clara opened her arms to hug him, making things even worse. Ash kept his arms at his sides as his most dramatic sibling gave him a hug for doing something anyone with sense could have thought of. "You're a matchmaker."

"Wait," Violet interrupted the conversation, looking at Jet, then Ash for confirmation as she gestured to Clara. "You're worried she's gonna set me up?"

Worried wasn't quite the right word. He was drenched in nervous certainty that any minute now Clara would have every available man in a hundred-mile radius lining up to meet Violet.

"She has a habit of roping newcomers into her plans."

Violet laughed, a full, throaty laugh ringing through the quiet street. Like there was nothing as funny as dating someone from around here. Ash was simultaneously relieved and disappointed.

"I'm not sure it's *that* funny," Clara said, her eyes narrowing.

"No, I'm sorry," Violet apologized. "But Ash is right. I couldn't possibly fit a date into my schedule. Unless my date was interested in watching a film of our opposing teams and talking strategy."

Front porch. Violet tucked up under his arm. Clipboards strewn about as they planned for a Friday night game.

"I know," Clara defended herself, but it was clear from her tone this wasn't the answer she wanted. After a beat, she glanced up at Ash, her sly smile returning. "Although, football strategy sounds like a fun date."

Ash gave his sister the glower to end all glowers.

But then Violet glanced at him briefly, and Ash didn't feel at all like glowering anymore. The tight binding around his heart gave way, reminding him of the feeling he'd had in airborne training. It was absolute fear and freedom as he stood at the back of the plane, ready to jump and just hope whoever'd packed his parachute did it correctly.

Violet smiled apologetically before saying, "And I can't imagine I'll be in Outcrop for more than a season or two."

A rushing sensation filled Ash's ears as he realized he wasn't even carrying a parachute.

"You're leaving?" Jet asked.

"Eventually. Yes. My goal is to coach Division Three. I've got a long way to go."

"You…" Ash cleared his throat, then tried again, "You want to coach college ball?"

"That's always been my goal. I want to honor the chance my father gave me by going as far as I can in this sport." She glanced back down Main, then gestured to the red banners in the front of Eighty Local. "You three have gone a long way in helping me get through this first head coaching position."

Her *first* head coaching position. This was the smallest team she'd ever take on. They had her for one season, maybe two, then she'd be on to bigger and better things.

And Ash would be here. He might always remain her biggest fan, but there was no future in which the two of them sat on the porch swing and came up with strategies for Friday night games as they grew old together.

He had to get over this...whatever it was he was feeling for Violet. It wasn't love. The feeling he'd had for his ex-wife was more predictable. He'd known what he was looking for in a wife, and Kerri had checked all the boxes. Until she'd changed overnight, or rather changed while he was overseas. He'd gone from complete certainty in his marriage to no marriage at all in the course of an afternoon.

Ash shuddered against the wave of nausea accompanying the memory. Unthinking, he put an arm around Clara. He was home now, with his family and Jackson. Everyone was safe.

Clara and Piper probably had some word for what he was feeling, this uncontrollable, wild excitement every time Violet came near him. They talked a lot about love chemicals, and Ash guessed some trick of biology was behind this. He'd learned to overcome fear, hunger, stress and exhaustion in boot camp, and worse in the years his marriage disintegrated. Surely he could beat a few love chemicals.

VIOLET JOGGED UP the steps to OHTAF, feeling better than she had in weeks. The banners supporting her hung around the porch, creating a red frame for the pumpkins, dried stalks of corn and posters of a man who had to be the third Wallace brother and Firefighter of the Year.

The Wallaces were quite the family.

After running into them that morning, she'd made her way to Manny's Groceries, which was plastered in I'm With Vi! banners and helmet donation posters. "Manny" turned out to be Manuel Garcia Sr., and just as gregarious as his son. She'd had no problem procuring foodstuffs. And if she was still a little giddy because Ash had provided her with the exact help she didn't know she needed, she could let herself be giddy for one afternoon.

When her uncle had texted her with his

request, she'd responded positively, walking away from prepping a killer mac and cheese to head over to OHTAF. But now that she was here, the nervousness set in.

It's just a conversation. You'll be fine.

Violet pulled open the front door and glanced around her uncle's store. Solid wide-plank wooden flooring spanned the length of the large building. The open beams overhead held old advertisements for farm supplies, and were illuminated by the big multipaned windows. From where she stood by the entrance, she could see cattle feed, baby chicks, gardening supplies, fun socks, climbing gear, literary fiction and office supplies. And judging by the steady stream of customers heading up to the cash register, everything in this mish-mash of commerce was selling.

"There she is." Uncle Mel, who everyone else around here called Mr. Fareas, waved her over. "How's today?"

"Better than yesterday."

He nodded. "Can't argue with that." He glanced over her head, looking meaningfully at the banners in the front window. "You've got a friend there in Ash Wallace, don't you?"

Violet stiffened. Uncle Mel didn't need to be making any speculations about how friendly she was getting with anyone. "I hope I'm friends with everyone on my coaching staff."

"Since you've only got two men on staff, and one of them has spent the last week and a half talking you up around town, it shouldn't be too difficult."

"I'm grateful for Ash," she said, securing herself a spot in the understatement hall of fame.

"It's nice to have a champion rallying troops for the cause."

Violet pressed her lips together. Uncle Mel could be annoyingly observant. And while he wouldn't accuse her of favoritism, other parents most certainly would.

He gestured to a door at the back of the hardware department. "Are you ready for this?"

"Of course."

Uncle Mel chuckled. "You always were the toughest one in the family."

"You think?"

"Easily." Her uncle kept a perfectly straight face as he said, "Still nice to have Ash Wallace in your corner."

Great. Now she was imagining being in corners with Ash Wallace.

Uncle Mel pushed open the door into a packed storeroom. Aunt Rose sat at a desk in the corner, chatting quietly at the computer.

"Here she is," Uncle Mel announced. Aunt Rose stood and gestured for Violet to take her chair. Violet's nervous system reacted, sending fingers of apprehension through her.

A friendly, if somewhat weak voice rang through the computer's little speakers, "Let me get a look at this coach."

Uncle Mel gave her shoulder something between a pat and a push, and Violet sat down in front of the screen.

She'd seen pictures of Coach Kessler. The football office at school was filled with snapshots of a robust man in his fifties standing next to sweaty players, everyone happy about having won something. The man on the computer screen looked like his distant cousin. You could see the resemblance, but you wouldn't mistake one for the other. His face was thin and his skin sallow with the treatment.

Violet waved, faking a smile. "Hello, Coach."

"Back at you!" His smile was sincere, if shaky. "What's the report?"

"Two and O."

"That's what I like to hear."

She nodded, making brief eye contact with her uncle over the top of the computer.

"She's doing great!" Aunt Rose called.

"I don't doubt it."

"How are *you* doing?" Violet asked.

Osteosarcoma, a fast-growing bone cancer, had been found in his shin. He'd ignored the persistent ache and swelling, until his girlfriend finally convinced him to see a doctor. He'd been relocated to Oregon Health & Science University the same week, and they still didn't know if he'd ever leave the hospital. The treatment was aggressive, but so was the cancer. Osteosarcoma was a young person's disease, and his midlife body was not reacting well to the treatment.

He swatted away the question. "I'm fine."

Violet raised her brows. "And by fine, you mean you don't want to talk about it?"

"You catch on quick, just like your uncle. Tell me, how's Joaquin? Any chance the kid can take it to the next level?"

Violet respected his need to hear about something other than osteoblasts and cell counts, and filled him in on various athletes. She gave him a lengthy rundown on the linemen, then kept it as vague as possible when the problem players came up. Coach Kessler seemed to soak up her words, growing stronger as he heard about the team. Violet chastised herself for ever feeling nervous about this call. Kessler was a great guy, and her work here was giving him the space he needed to recover.

"Hacker giving you any trouble?" he asked abruptly.

Violet's gaze jumped to her uncle. He shook his head. Kessler didn't need to hear it. The only news she was going to give him was good news.

"Hacker?" Violet tilted her head and pretended to consider the name. "He was the old offensive coordinator, right?"

"Did he quit?" Kessler asked.

"I don't know the whole situation, but Ash Wallace took over for offense. And he's—"

"Ash? Ash stepped up?" A smile lit Kessler's face. "How'd you manage that?"

"I don't know?" Violet mugged a thoughtful expression. "He just jumped on board."

"You won't find anyone more solid than Ash. He was quarterback himself, back in the day."

She nodded. "He's still got a nice throw." *And a nice voice, and a nice face and a really nice habit of defending me to the community.*

"Listen up, Violet Fareas." Kessler leaned toward the screen, as though the computer were a recalcitrant sophomore in need of a pep talk. "I can't thank you enough for stepping up. Leaving the team at the start of the season was the hardest thing I've ever done. Knowing it's in your capable hands has allowed me to focus on getting better. I may never walk out of here, but whatever happens, I know my Eagles are in good hands."

He sat back. The manicured hand of a woman came to rest on his shoulder, and Violet could hear her saying something about it being time to rest. Kessler glanced up at the woman, love shining on his face.

Tears pricked the backs of her eyes at the intensity of their connection. She needed to provide this guy the time and space to heal. Giving her all to the team would alleviate his worries and let him focus on beating the cancer.

"I've got this." She placed both hands on the table next to the monitor and addressed the image. "The team is solid, and we're going to make it to the playoffs for you."

"If you can make it to the quarterfinals, I might be able to catch a game."

"Then we will make it to the quarterfinals." Violet let this promise sink in. She would do it for Kessler. "See you in the stands."

He gave a weak smile, intertwining his fingers with the woman's. "I like the sound of that."

Violet signed off. After a promise to join

her aunt and uncle for dinner after practice on Tuesday, Violet headed out, reinvigorated and determined to make this work. The Eagles were going to make it to the quarterfinals, and Coach Kessler would watch the game from the stands. She, Ash, Jet and a team of medical professionals at OHSU were going to make it happen.

She ducked out the door and jogged to the steps, then came to an abrupt halt.

Brayson stood on the sidewalk, hands in the pockets of his letterman's jacket, staring up at her banners. His face showed confusion, betrayal, frustration.

But under it all, he looked so young and sad.

Violet let out a breath. At Taft, she'd worked with a highly select group of students. If someone didn't walk the line, he was out. But in this case, she didn't want Brayson to leave the team. It wasn't just because he was a good player. She had the sense that deep down inside, he was a good kid.

Brayson dropped his gaze from the banner and saw her.

Violet looked over her shoulder, as though she were guilty of... What? Shopping without a list?

She lifted her chin. Her natural reaction would have been to deliver a glare, then stalk past him. But she sensed that wasn't what this seventeen-year-old needed right now.

"Hi, Brayson." She waved, giving him a polite smile.

Reflexively he started to wave back, then tucked his hand further into his pocket. He glanced across the street to where his dad was getting something out of his truck, then back at Violet. Finally his gaze dropped to the sidewalk, and he turned and walked away.

CHAPTER TEN

ASH TRIED TO show a little more restraint in parking this time. He pulled in at the high school, a chaste two spots down from Violet, and got out of his truck at a reasonable speed. She was nearby, juggling clipboards and other items for today's practice, but he wasn't going to rush her with help. He might not be able to control the sparks that lit up whenever they were together, but he *was* getting better at anticipating those sparks.

He just needed to keep a growth mindset about the whole situation. He couldn't control the sparks *yet*.

"Hey there!" Violet grinned at him, sunglasses slipping a little on her nose as she readjusted her stack. A breeze kicked up, stirring a few leaves on the sidewalk and blowing a lock of hair across her face. "Endurance day!"

And a man was supposed to be able to resist this?

Ash shook his head and forced himself to walk. He'd done a great job of keeping things professional with Violet so far, no matter what gossip Hacker and his friends continued to spread around town. "What's more fun than endurance day?"

"Right?" She glanced at his jacket as they headed to the practice field. "I like your button."

Ash looked down. Yes, he was wearing a button with his least-favorite bird on it. "My sister attached these to all the family outerwear."

"I love your sister." She kept her eyes ahead, a smile growing across her face. "This team is really coming together."

Ash glanced over at the high school, where kids were now streaming out of the building. "I know. You're doing an incredible job."

She passed the stack off to him and grabbed a hair band from her back pocket. Ash's heart dipped. It was always so sad when she pulled her hair back.

"I'm able to do my job because you're running interference with the town." She nodded in the direction of Main Street. Three weeks into the season, and three wins later, most people were starting to see that while they missed Kessler, they were lucky to have Violet. As new equipment began flowing in, most parents conveniently forgot they'd ever questioned her to begin with.

Most parents, but not all.

Brayson still hadn't returned to practice, and his crew continued to straddle the fence. Gabe, who only had so much allegiance to the rebellion, saw the opportunity to get in some playing time and took over as quarterback. He was erratic and nervous; some days he was on and others...not. Ash hoped to help him settle in the position. He didn't want Jackson to have to step in again and get sacked over and over. He knew the new helmets mitigated the chance of injury, but still. Jackson was a sophomore; he didn't need to have the weight of quarterback on his shoulders, or the risk.

Ash shook his head and refocused on Violet. "You do realize that even with my powers of persuasion, we're still on the practice field today."

Violet laughed. The band director had jumped in to claim more practice time on the football turf when Kessler disappeared. Ash had taken up the battle for Violet, but Mr. Katz was tenacious. The final decision was the band would practice their routine on the turf Wednesdays, bumping the football team to the practice field. The band really did seem to think the football game bookending their performances was a nuisance. Ash heard one flute player refer to the stadium as *the marching field*, as opposed to the football field.

"It's okay. Endurance is better on the grass than on Astroturf. More pull on the athlete."

As they walked up the small hill to the practice field, voices of their athletes floated on the fall breeze, mixed with the sounds of instruments warming up. Players came flowing out of the locker room. First it was the regular trickle, then the kids started running.

It probably wasn't because they knew endurance drills were on the docket.

Jet trotted up from the parking lot and joined them. "The guys seem excited today."

Ash was about to agree when he saw Jackson sprint out of the locker room. It wasn't his son's excited, this-is-going-to-be-awesome run. Jackson looked like Ash, when something was wrong.

Violet looked up at Ash in concern, then the three of them lengthened their strides and crested the hill.

The expansive green practice field was peppered in white, ringed with players. Ash stared at the field, unable to make sense of what he was seeing.

"Are those…forks?"

Violet sprinted to the field.

Hundreds of white plastic forks stuck up

out of the practice field. Kids were laughing, mostly out of discomfort, but some actually thought it was funny. Several had their phones out, filming the forks and Violet's reaction.

Violet spun around, glaring at the team. The laughter died down immediately.

"Who did this?"

The players silenced, looking at one another. The phones disappeared.

She took a step toward Soren. "Who. Did. This?"

Soren held his hands up, stuttering as he said, "I...I was in class."

Violet scanned the players. The implication was clear to Ash, although Violet didn't seem to realize it yet. These kids had *all* been in class. If they skipped, they wouldn't be allowed to practice.

This juvenile, destructive prank was the work of adults.

Ash was overwhelmed with the desire to fix this for Violet and put a fork in anyone who challenged her. He'd had it with those guys—underestimating Violet, making their boys sabotage her coaching, accusing him of cozying up to the coach to get playing time for his son.

He should have dealt with them head-on

weeks ago. Ash spun on his heel to go find Hacker, now.

Jet caught his shoulder. Ash tried to flinch off his hand, but Jet increased the pressure. "She needs you here."

"What's the endgame?" Violet asked her players. They stared back at her. "Because I'm *not* quitting. I don't care what kind of silverware or stunt you try next; I am *not* quitting. Today is endurance day, and you all have a lot to learn from me when it comes to sticking with something."

By now the assistant principal was on the scene, using her massive walkie-talkie to communicate with the campus supervisor. "I'm sorry, Coach Fareas. We're going to have to cancel practice today—"

"No," Violet snapped. "We meet the Swarm in less than two weeks. I don't care if we have to do our drills on the sidewalk or on someone's front lawn. We are not skipping one practice."

"Can we just get this cleared up?" Jet asked. "Each kid pulls up a bunch of forks, then we practice?"

The assistant principal shook her head. "We need to write up a report, and ideally whoever did this will be responsible for cleanup."

"Ideally whoever did this is gonna find a

way to reuse all these forks." Jet shook his head, disgusted. "Who uses single-use plastic for a prank?"

Only Jet Broughman was a good enough person to think that grown men who tried to sabotage a football practice would consider the environmental impact of their actions.

"Well, we need a field." Violet looked dangerously over to where the band was moving into formation. She really didn't get it. Mr. Katz was not a band director to tangle with.

Jackson stepped forward. "We can practice at our place."

Ash nodded his head, before the words fully set in. *Forty teenagers on the ranch, tearing up the lawn before Clara's wedding?*

Jackson looked up at him. "Right, Dad?" *Forty teenagers it was.*

"Right. Everyone, go get your gear. Text your parents and let them know what's happening. Figure out who you're going to catch a ride with."

"I can take two in my truck," Jet said.

"Jackson and I can take three more in ours."

Violet's eyes connected with his, a slow, determined smile spreading across her face. She nodded. "I've got room for three. Get your stuff and hustle. I want this practice moving in a half an hour." The players stared back, a little stunned. "Let's go!" Violet yelled. "Move it."

The kids turned and ran back to the locker rooms.

Violet stormed toward the parking lot, Ash and Jet trying to catch up. Ash was still tense, and furious, but he had a feeling this might turn out a whole lot differently than Hacker had expected.

VIOLET HAD TO ADMIT, being consumed by vengeful fury wasn't the worst when it came to inspiring a good endurance practice. She was in no mood to put up with anything, and the players picked up on that. She'd been pushed to her limits and kept coaching. They could push past their limits too.

If her saboteur had any idea what a good workout these kids were getting as a result of his actions, he'd be horrified. It wasn't a technique Violet looked forward to repeating, but it *was* effective.

"Step it up, Joaquin," she called as the running back took off. "Carley, you're up. Please keep in mind how much I hate it when Joaquin outruns you."

Carley grumbled something about not getting outrun by anyone, then took off.

Every kid was all in, even the boys who up

until now had been dragging their cleats. It was as though whoever had forked the field— and everyone had a pretty good sense of who it was—had stepped over a line. The team took it personally now.

"Jackson, let's go!" Jackson ran, putting on good speed. She had to get him off the line and into a position where he was handling the ball. She glanced up to see Ash watching his son. That man was going to have to accept her decision, even if he wasn't going to stand around being handsome and her personal hero all the time.

Violet let her emotions roll. She was mad, and everyone was going to see it today. Ash Wallace was an attractive man, and she was tired of pretending otherwise. She cared about these kids, even the ones making more work for her, and she was going to drag every one of them along on a winning season.

"Nice work, everybody. Let's line up and go again. And yes, Manuel, I'm talking about you. Even linemen need to know how to run."

"Coach Vi?" Violet looked up, startled. Jet ran over to her. "Ash and I had an idea. There are about three miles of running trails on this property." He pointed to a path receding into the woods. "To finish this up, we could have the kids race the path. Winners are next week's captains?"

She grinned. "Sounds like the perfect finish to practice."

He nodded. "This is turning out. Endurance day at Wallace Ranch might have to become an Eagles tradition."

Violet would be happy to have every practice, game, team meeting and even her morning coffee at Wallace Ranch, but Jet didn't need to hear about it. She redirected her attention to the running path. "Is it a loop?"

"No, there's a whole network of trails." Jet grinned. "It's a Clara thing—some trails for hooves, some for feet. Ash thought the two of you could lead them."

Violet frowned. She was in decent running shape, and Ash was definitely fit, but she wanted these kids running fast, emptying everything in the tank for their last exercise of the day. She wasn't in any shape to outrun a fit, motivated high school athlete.

Jet, as though reading her mind, pointed over her shoulder toward the stables.

Ash walked toward her, leading two of the glossy brown Canadian Horses. He glanced up and smiled, and her frustration disappeared. All that existed was an extremely good-looking man walking toward her with pretty horses. Her heart caught, then started beating hard, rushing in her ears as Ash came closer. Jet was saying something about not mentioning to Clara that they were taking horses on a running path, but Violet wasn't tracking it. She was entirely focused on the cowboy.

Ash stopped in front of her. She widened her eyes, questioning him. He grinned back and handed her the reins.

"This is Midnight."

Midnight dipped his head to sniff Violet's hair, and she giggled. Several players looked up at the sound, shocked to hear their coach giggle. Ash kept his eyes on her as he asked, "Have you ridden before?"

Violet couldn't remember anything she'd ever done before. Had she ridden a horse? It seemed likely.

"It's easy." The sunlight washed the brown from Ash's hazel eyes, leaving a woodsy green with a glint of humor for her. "And Midnight here's the sweetest horse in the herd."

Midnight pressed his nose into Violet's shoulder. She scratched the horse's mane, and it gave her a snort of approval.

"I think he likes you."

"Well, he's a sweetheart, or so I hear."

Ash grinned. "You up for this?"

"I'm up for it. I'm just not sure how to actually—" she gestured "—you know. Get up."

"Grab the saddle horn," Ash instructed. Violet grabbed the horn, then placed one foot in the stirrup.

"Try your other foot," Ash said. "That way you'll wind up facing forward."

Violet shook her head at her own ineptitude, then put her left foot in the stirrup. Ash placed his hands on either side of her waist to help her up. His strong fingers steadied her, and he began to lift. Unfortunately, rather than leaning toward the horse, Violet leaned straight into Ash, which was legitimately where she wanted to be. Then she overcorrected and sort of fell against the horse. Midnight, unperturbed, shook his mane and waited patiently for her to figure it out.

"Let's try it again," Ash said as she landed awkwardly on the ground.

He talked her through it this time, his deep voice setting off tremors in her belly. Ultimately, Violet managed to grip the saddle horn, put the correct foot in the stirrup and shore up all her focus to ignore Ash's hands on her waist. This time she landed on the saddle.

She gazed out across the field to find all her players staring at her.

"I'm feeling some serious Joan of Arc vibes," she said.

Ash gave her an appraising look. "Sounds about right to me."

Jet lined the kids up and gave them instructions as Ash explained the basics of driving a horse. Then he swung into the saddle, nudged his massive horse with his heels and the animal took off at a trot. Midnight followed while Jet got the players ready to race.

Endurance day at Wallace Ranch was *definitely* going to be a tradition as long as she was here.

"We'll stay together and head up through the aspen grove." Ash pointed to the trails ahead. "We'll get to the first turnoff and direct the players from there, then go ahead of them to the next intersection to keep them on the right path."

Violet nodded. On a normal day, she preferred to call the shots, but she didn't know what the shots were at Wallace Ranch, and this day had departed from normal a long time ago.

Delicate yellow leaves fluttered in the early evening breeze, filtering the light. The trail was well-kept; someone's feet had pounded the ground here for years.

"Do you run?" Violet asked.

"Sometimes. Most days I get enough exercise working with the horses." Violet glanced at his arms. Horses must be a real workout. "This is Clara's path. Running helps keep her centered."

He didn't offer any more information, but Violet got the sense there was more to the situation. The Wallaces seemed so perfect, but there might be more going on than she could see. And that was probably true of every family, even Joe Hacker's.

Especially Joe Hacker's family.

They pulled the horses up at a juncture to wait. Birds flittered between branches. It felt like she and Ash had moved into a quieter, softer world. The air was cool, with an earthy scent unraveling from the ground.

While there were the occasional fall leaves in southern California, the weather was remarkably steady year-round. Seasons were marked by Starbucks coffee drinks and the sports being played. Here, fall was more than just football.

Ash studied the reins in his hands, then glanced up at her. "What I can't quite figure out, Violet Fareas, is what you're doing here?"

"On a horse, in the middle of an endurance workout? That's got me flummoxed too."

Ash shook his head. "In Outcrop. With your

skills and knowledge, you could coach any-where. How'd you come to be here?"

He was so sincere in his question, she felt like she could finally admit the truth.

"I got myself into a real mess in California. Tangled up in a bad program."

He raised his brow, inviting her to say more.

"I worked for a bully named David Laur-rent. He needed me—my skills made his team successful." She drew in a deep breath. "To keep me there, he mocked my ambition, be-littled and threatened me. I felt pretty worth-less by the end."

A mix of anger and empathy flickered across his face. "I'm so sorry, Violet. You never should have had to put up with someone like that."

"But I did. I put up with it for five years."

He gazed at her, as though he understood her shame and frustration. "I know a little about getting stuck in a bad situation."

Violet appreciated the sentiment, but how could he possibly understand the self-loathing? She'd stayed in an impossible situation because leaving meant admitting defeat, admitting she'd been wrong to begin with.

He glanced down, turning the reins in his hands. "What finally made you leave?"

Her stomach dropped at the memory. She didn't want to talk about it, but he needed to know. "Someone started a rumor. About me and David." She watched his face as the implication of this sank in, then said, "It was probably David. Then this position opened up, and Outcrop seemed about as far away as possible. I jumped ship, and now I'm just trying to keep my head above the water."

Ash's eyes narrowed under his Stetson; his jaw tightened. "I hate guys like that."

"Thank you."

"I hate *that* guy."

"I do too." She glanced up and smiled at him. "But now I'm working with you and Jet."

He drew in a breath, and paused before asking her, "You're happy here?"

"Let's see. Some guy just wasted hours of his time forking the practice field—"

"With single-use plastic," Ash imitated Jet's complaint. She laughed, then stilled as she found herself gazing into Ash's eyes.

"But yeah, I'm happy." She warmed at the realization. She had a great team, and friends, and the support of Ash Wallace. She wasn't sure she'd ever been as content as she was right now. But she probably didn't need to let Ash know he was such a big part of that contentment. "You do know I live over a chocolate shop, right?"

Ash chuckled. "I've heard that."

"I can't leave Outcrop until I've tried every chocolate those ladies make."

He gazed at her. "Then I hope they keep coming up with new recipes."

An unfamiliar sound came rushing through the trees, something like a stampede of smack-talking cattle.

"Here they come," Ash said, subtly adjusting his reins and doing something with his leg to make his horse back up a few feet. Midnight, wonderful animal that he was, followed suit just in time. The players came rumbling up the path. Violet held out her palm for high fives, encouraging the kids as they pushed through the last task of the day. Ash directed them down the correct path, then the two of them took off on the horses to meet the boys at the next juncture. The exercise was so fun and effective, she felt like sending Joe Hacker a thank-you note.

The sun was setting, bathing the property in pink and gold when they all emerged from the trail system and raced down the home stretch. Behind the farmhouse, Jet waited at the finish line with a stopwatch. Soren and Joaquin were in the lead, with Carley not far behind. Kids were laughing, joking with each other, threatening to beat whoever was nearest. CJ put on surprising speed, and Manuel shouted encouragement while simultaneously cutting him off. But, as a group, they all made it across the finish line, falling into the soft grass, whooping and laughing as the sun set over the mountains behind them.

They had become a team.

Violet felt Ash's eyes on her. "Nice work, Coach," he said quietly.

She let the compliment soak in, but it couldn't quite settle until she admitted, "There is no way I could have done this without you."

ASH WAVED AS KIDS, exhausted and exhilarated, drifted toward their vehicles. Parents chatted with each other, pausing to thank him for hosting practice.

"I just provided the place. Thanks goes to Coach Vi."

Violet shook her head and started to contradict him, but she was interrupted by a muscular, tattooed woman.

"Brenn Theis, Carley and Aaron's mom," she stated, holding out a hand.

Violet shook. "I remember. Thanks for being flexible and picking the kids up out here today."

Brenn nodded. "I like the way you stuck with this, even after the stunt with the forks." She folded her arms over her chest. "Gotta admit I wasn't so sure about football. But I like the way you handle things."

Violet's eyes teared up a little. Ash could tell she was tired and very pleased with the way practice had gone. "Your kids are *amazing*. I don't know what I'd do without Carley and Aaron on this team."

Brenn nodded, the pride in her expression giving way to a shadow of regret. "I don't know what *I'll* do when they leave. They're both talking about college now."

"I went halfway across the country for college, then came home to coach with my dad," Violet said. "And there are so many ways to finance college or trade school, plenty of options for two smart, hardworking kids like Carley and Aaron."

Brenn chuckled. "Oh, I know. Coach Broughman gave me the full lesson on that one." She paused, looking down at her folded arms. "But what if they don't come back home? They'll be brain surgeons or astrophysicists and live in some big city. They're not even gonna remember their mom."

Violet, who really did cry at the drop of a hat, was now consoling Brenn as the tears ran down her face. She said all the right things, but Ash *understood*. Brenn Theis loved her kids and couldn't imagine her life without

them. He felt the same way about Jackson.
And while he would encourage him to reach
for every goal, he didn't want his son to be
hurt, or disappointed or experience the weight
of failure like he had in his own life.

Jackson approached, still grinning after the
tough workout. Ash didn't want his son to
leave or grow up. He wanted to freeze time
and stay Jackson's dad forever.

As though on cue, Brenn turned to Jackson.
"When are you going back in as quarterback?"

Jackson glanced at Violet. He was gunning
to handle the ball again but wasn't the type
of kid to push it.

Brenn nodded at Violet. "He's just like Ash
used to be out there. Cool and easy. Apple
doesn't fall far from the tree, does it?"

This particular apple looked up at him.
"Maybe we can practice some throws tomorrow?"

Ash nodded without meaning to. Violet
caught his eye, saying, "I think that's a great
idea."

Jackson stepped back and mimed a throw,
grinning.

"Looks like you too," Brenn commented.
"Except for those blue eyes. Those must have
come from Mom."

The land blurred around Ash at the mention of Jackson's mother. He could still see everything clearly, walking in the door of the simple tract house. He could hear the plaintive wailing. See the relief in those same blue eyes as Ash lifted Jackson into a hug. Feel his chubby hands as they pressed against Ash's face, patting to make sure he was really there.

He could still see the bland defiance on Kerri's face when she returned hours later.

Nausea washed through him. He placed a hand on Jackson's shoulder, anchoring himself. They were in Outcrop now, and Kerri was two thousand miles away. His son was a responsible young man, despite everything.

Jackson glanced down at the gravel drive, as though the blue eyes were a birth defect he was ashamed of. He didn't remember the early years, but Ash had prolonged Kerri's effect on Jackson by trying to fix an unfixable marriage.

"Thank you for your support," Violet said to Brenn. "It's been a time, and not all parents are as enthusiastic about my coaching as you are."

"Hacker's a piece of work," Brenn said, walking a few paces away. Then she turned back. "I'll be honest—the fact that he doesn't like you just makes me like you more."

Violet laughed, and Ash finally gave in and

let himself gaze at her. Beautiful, determined, smart, fun, kind. In a different life, he'd have pursued her with everything at his disposal. He'd have pulled out his guitar, written her songs, trained up a horse for only Violet to ride and asked her to accompany him on every ride.

But they didn't have that luxury. He had his son to raise. She would be out of Outcrop before the dishes had been cleared from the football awards banquet. All they had was this season, and they couldn't risk the scandal that would arise if the coach started dating the parent of one of her players.

"Hey, can you come over for family dinner Sunday?"

Ash pulled his gaze away from Violet and stared at his son who grinned as he issued the invitation. Also shocked, Violet began stuttering. "W-well, Sunday? I, um. Sunday I—"

"Every other Sunday, the whole family comes over for dinner," Jackson explained. "My uncle Bowman is back, and Aunt Piper is coming from Portland. It's fun."

Violet glanced up and locked eyes with Ash.

"We'd love to have you," Ash said.

Violet nodded. She looked nervous, but she was nodding. "You're sure? I'd hate to intrude."

"I bet we could play a game of football." Jackson glanced up at Ash for confirmation. "We have *a lot* of people in our family."

Jackson's steady pressure with the invitation found its mark. A spark lit her eyes. "If there's football involved, I'm in. What can I bring? Chocolates?"

CHAPTER ELEVEN

"ARE YOU GOING to set the table or stand around in everyone's way?" Ash asked.

Piper stepped in front of him, two hands full of silverware. "I was just planning on standing in *your* way. Getting in everyone's way is too ambitious for a Sunday."

Ash glowered at Piper. She kept her gaze on the silverware, humming to herself. As Ash stepped around her and back into the kitchen, she sighed. "Ah. So good to be home again," she said.

"You shush!" Clara commanded. "I've been missing you all week. Ash doesn't get to ruin you being home just because he's grumpy."

"I'm not grumpy," he called over his shoulder to the twins, pushing through the swinging door into the kitchen.

The farmhouse kitchen had never been big enough for the Wallace family and seemed to shrink as they got older. Everyone always crowded in here, despite the perfectly fine real estate in the living room. At the center of today's mayhem, as always, was Hunter.

"Hand me the olive oil," he said to no one in particular, holding out a hand. Jet passed him a bottle of canola, which Hunter eyed like it was WD-40. "Man, you have got to learn the difference between canola and olive oil before you marry my sister."

"We're getting married in two weeks." Jet picked up a piece of carrot Hunter had just sliced and popped it into his mouth.

"You can't learn the difference between two types of oil in fourteen days?"

"Got a few other things on my mind," Jet said, holding back a smile.

Maisy set the correct bottle in front of Hunter, although how he could see it through the blockade of vegetables he'd set up around himself, Ash didn't know. Hunter reached for it as Maisy, like metal shavings to a magnet, returned to Bowman.

Bowman slipped an arm around Maisy, grinning as he lifted her hand to look at the ring he'd given her when he came home after the Fallen Ridge fire. Mom explained the difference in oils to Jet as she set out some unnecessarily fancy crackers Piper had brought from Portland and the miniscule wedges of cheese Clara had contributed.

"Love, did I know the difference between olive oil and canola oil when we got married?" Dad asked, mock serious.

"I feel like the emphasis on culinary oil delineation is a modern phenomenon," Mom responded. "It's possible Jet and Clara could make it through the winter without having a clear understanding of the difference."

"I'm just saying." Hunter upended a bowl of sliced onions into the heated oil. "If Clara comes crawling into Eighty Local, half-starved because you can't make a decent vinaigrette for her, we're gonna have words."

Clara banged through the door from the dining room into the kitchen. "I am perfectly capable of feeding myself." She attached herself to Jet's side and beamed up at him. "Besides, what's the point of Eighty Local if your family members can't come crawling in looking for salad dressing?"

"The point of Eighty Local is having an ethically focused, sustainable restaurant at the heart of my community," Hunter said hotly.

"I thought the point was to work yourself to exhaustion," Piper quipped.

With Piper's entry there were now nine people crowded into the small kitchen, all arguing on top of one another and snacking on what was supposed to be dinner.

"Why is everyone in the kitchen?" Ash demanded.

The family silenced, glanced at him, then each other.

"Because it's the kitchen?" Mom guessed.

Dad put a sympathetic hand on his shoulder, saying, "Son. This is where the food is."

Ash was not going to shrug Dad's hand off his shoulder. He could, however, glare at his siblings.

"So, when Violet arrives, we're just going to ask her to scrunch into this tiny kitchen? Or maybe she'll sit in the living room alone."

Again, his family exchanged glances.

"You're not doing anything," Hunter pointed out. "You could go wait by the front door."

"But try not to start wagging your tail when she shows up," Piper advised.

"I'm trying to make sure you all get this done." He gestured to the melee of food, dishes and glassware.

Confused looks from his family members melted into barely concealed smiles.

Piper cleared her throat delicately. "Ash, are you...nervous?"

"No."

Piper's gaze connected with Clara's. Both were trying to keep a straight face.

"She's Jackson's coach," he defended himself. "This should be a nice meal."

Jet exchanged a look with Bowman, and that was too much. The guy wasn't even officially in the family, and he was nonverbally suggesting that Ash was nervous.

"What?" Ash asked him.

Jet held up his hands. "Nothing."

Ash did not like where this conversation, or lack of conversation, was going. He needed to gain control of the situation. "Jackson invited his coach to our family dinner." It was probably the twentieth time he'd explained that *Jackson* had issued the invitation, not him. "I don't want her to think we're some kind of socially aberrant clan that clumps in one room talking over each other."

"But we are a socially aberrant clan that clumps in one room talking over each other," Mom said.

"That's how we raised you," Dad joined in. "Your mom and I are thinking of writing a parenting book. *Social Aberrance for the Whole Family.*"

Ash glanced up at the ceiling, trying for patience.

Then Clara, the most empathetic of the bunch, tugged on his sleeve. "We're excited about Violet joining us." She smiled, and Ash dropped an arm around her. She was a good sister. "We're excited, and you're obviously super nervous—"

Ash pushed her away and tried to storm to the other side of the room. Unfortunately, there were far too many people in his way.

He *was* nervous. Violet always made him nervous, and he had to get his head in the game here. *Just make it through the next couple of hours and hope your family doesn't run her off.*

"We promise to be normal when she gets here," Hunter said.

Ash shook his head. His family was so far from normal they couldn't even see it from here. He glanced at Maisy. Maybe she could help.

Maisy smiled at him. "We could take her to see the thatching ants!"

"Great idea!" Dad said. "What guest doesn't want to see an ant colony before dinner?"

"No ants," Ash commanded.

Maisy mugged a sad expression.

"No ants!"

"Baby horse?" Bowman suggested.

Ash nodded. Violet hadn't met the month-old colt yet. Then he remembered that somehow the horse had been named Fresh Spinach and didn't want to have that explained.

"What if we just have a normal meal, like a normal family, and don't stand around in the kitchen all afternoon?"

"We can try," Hunter said, shaking his head.

"Jackson might have some ideas," Mom said.

Ash's blood seemed to reverse in his respiratory system, flooding his body with freshly chilled fluid.

"Let's *not* talk about this with Jackson."

"What, that you're nervous because his super gorgeous coach is coming to dinner?" Piper asked.

Ash glowered at her.

But yeah, that. Exactly.

It was bad enough that Violet probably knew how he felt; he didn't need Jackson in on the situation.

As though on cue, Jackson pushed in through the door from the living room. Piper slipped out before the door swung shut.

"Hey," he said, as though walking into an overcrowded kitchen filled with his entire family wasn't an issue. "What are you making?"

"Coq au vin," Hunter told him. Then he pointed at the two bottles in front of him. "Which of these is olive oil?"

Jackson tapped the correct bottle as he

headed over to Piper's outrageously expensive crackers and grabbed a handful.

"That's my nephew!" Hunter crowed.

"Don't eat too many of those," Ash told Jackson.

"I'm always hungry for coq au vin," Jackson defended himself.

"How is it our grandson knows what coq au vin is?" Mom asked Dad.

"Because he has such a great uncle," Hunter said, inspiring another round of bickering about which of the men in the kitchen was the best at uncle-ing.

Dad gave Ash a long look, as though he could see straight past his bluster to what felt like the twelve-year-old child inside him, still anxious for everything to go well. Below the din, Dad said, "I'm excited to meet her, son."

Ash's heart knocked up against his chest. Dad knew the type of terrible decisions Ash had made regarding women. One woman, anyway. It had been Dad who'd seen Ash's struggle and encouraged him to talk about it. Dad had driven to Salem to help Ash clean up the mess of his marriage and empty the house. It had been Dad's idea for Ash to take over the ranch, and under Dad's instruction that he'd learned to do it well.

At the time, Ash had thought his parents'

expressed desire to travel was just an excuse. But it turned out they really did want to see the world.

Ash just wanted to stay right here. And if he could keep his family where he could watch over them, too, he'd feel that much better.

The door flapped open, and Piper stuck her head in. "She's here!"

VIOLET HAD ALWAYS thought the Bend Swarm was a funny mascot. Like, what's so fierce about a cloud of bugs?

But here, actually being swarmed by the Wallace family, the mascot was starting to make a lot more sense. Her immediate family consisted of three people, who politely took turns talking to each other. In this family, talking seemed to be a competitive sport, with speed, timing and volume being finely honed skills among the siblings.

Violet had been nervous when she arrived. She'd been nervous since Jackson invited her. When she'd visualized the dinner, she'd imagined calm, controlled conversations, like politely asking Ash's mother about her interest in geography and having a nice chat about it. So far, Violet had seen the top of his mom's head, heard her laugh at something someone else said and that was about it.

A woman who looked a lot like Clara, if she were to dress like a chic city girl, stepped in front of her. "Okay, I am one hundred percent obsessed. Is it true you fired Joe Hacker at the first booster club meeting?"

Violet glanced up at Ash, standing solid and steady behind her. His calm strength always made her feel stronger and calmer too.

"He beat me to the punch and quit."

"Either way, fantastic. I could not have dealt with that mustache all season long."

Violet was about to respond when another sibling she hadn't met yet said, "What's wrong with a mustache?"

"Nothing is wrong with a well-groomed mustache. Joe Hacker looks like he's offering refuge to an angry bottle brush on his upper lip."

Violet laughed loudly, partly out of nervousness and partly because the image was spot-on. Then she snorted, and got more embarrassed, and laughed even harder. Right in the middle of the living room, and the middle of Ash's family.

"Okay, finally!" the sister proclaimed. "Someone who appreciates my humor. Also, Bowman, you need to shave. Like, right now."

A strong, steady hand ran down her back,

and Violet looked up into Ash's eyes. "Violet, this is my sister Piper. I'm sorry."

Piper immediately launched into Ash, but he placed two hands on Violet's shoulders and turned her toward his parents. "These are my folks, Bob and Lacy."

Violet, still red-faced and giggling a little, shook their hands.

"That's Bowman." He pointed to a handsome man who *could* use a shave, but his scruff didn't seem to be bothering Maisy in the least. Bowman nodded to her, pausing a moment before he said, "Welcome."

"Now," Ash glanced around at his family, "shall we sit here, in the living room? Violet, what can I get you to drink?"

Violet started to respond when Clara came out of the kitchen holding two glasses of white wine. She pressed one into Violet's hand and gave the other to Maisy, then said to Ash, "We're taking her to see the barn."

"I'll grab snacks!" Piper said.

Clara slipped her hand into Violet's and tugged. Violet glanced at Ash, who looked as helpless as she'd ever seen him, which included the time they'd agreed to let CJ give quarterback a try during drills. Then she was being pulled through a door into a kitchen, where Lacy snatched a bottle of wine from the fridge and Piper grabbed a plateful of cheese and crackers. The last she heard of Ash was a faint "Don't spoil your appetites!"

The women slowed to a stroll once they made it down the back steps.

"Sorry if that felt more like an abduction than you were expecting, but Ash gets super bossy when we have a guest," Clara said.

"And when we don't have a guest," Piper added.

"Ash is great," Maisy defended him.

"He is wonderful." Lacy gave a warning look to each of her daughters.

"Oh absolutely." Piper took a sip of wine. "But he was literally going to make us sit in the living room for a billion years until Hunter's done making his French chicken wine situation, and we never would have gotten to talk to you."

Lacy fell into step next to Violet. "The upside to being abducted at a family dinner is it sets the bar for appropriate behavior pretty low."

Violet laughed. It was true. She was no longer worried about breaking some unspoken family rule because there didn't seem to be any rules at all.

"Your place is beautiful," she said as they walked along the creamy crushed gravel drive, heading toward the big red barn. A tumble of pumpkins was clustered next to the door along with several bales of sweet-smelling hay.

"Thank you." Lacy nodded as she scanned the property. "It was a mess when we bought it. And was still pretty messy until Ash took over."

Piper shook her head seriously. "The mess wouldn't dare show its face with Ash around."

Violet grinned. "It must have been a lot to keep up with when you were teaching full-time."

Lacy shrugged. "Everything is a lot when you have five kids and are teaching full-time. We just did it. I don't mean to suggest it was easy, because it wasn't. But it all mattered to me: the kids, the horses, teaching. When you care about something, it stops being work and becomes a calling." She looked up at Violet. "I imagine coaching is like that for you."

"Exactly." Violet nodded, surprised by how Lacy had so clearly expressed Violet's own feelings.

"Those years were a lot of work, and kind of a blur, but I wouldn't change a thing." Lacy glanced at her daughters. "Even the hard things."

Clara slipped under her mom's arm and hugged her, but Piper shook her head. "Sorry,

Mom, I'm calling you out. You didn't love all of the hard things. Remember how mad you used to get when anyone would criticize your teaching?"

"Oh, well—"

"Yes!" Violet gestured more dramatically with both hands than she'd intended to. "Is there anything worse than being randomly criticized by people who don't know what they're talking about?"

"She gets it." Lacy pointed to Violet.

"Basically, anyone who has ever seen a football game thinks they can do my job."

"And anyone who has ever been in school thinks that not only could they teach, but that they'd do it right. Then the internet was invented halfway through my career, and suddenly everyone's an expert on the topic I have a master's degree in."

Violet laughed at Lacy's even more dramatic gestures. Then Lacy shook her head. "But honestly, most parents are doing the best they can with the resources they have. I had to remind myself of that again and again— people just want the best for their kids, and none of us know for sure what that is."

Violet let her words sink in. Most people really did want what was best for their kids.

Sometimes they had pretty warped ideas of what that was, but even Hacker loved his son.

They reached the barn, and Piper pushed open the bypass door with what looked like no effort at all. Her sophistication masked what Violet suspected were some mad farm-girl skills.

"This is where I'm going to marry your defensive coach," Clara said, striding over to a light switch.

As she flipped the switch, the barn was illuminated by hundreds of tiny sparkling white lights. They'd clearly spent hours sweeping out the corners and organizing the space. New bales of hay were stacked neatly along one side, and reclaimed barrels were set up with glass tabletops. Crates of mason jars, ready for flowers, or candles or whatever Clara had in mind were organized along a makeshift bar. It looked like a Pinterest board come to life.

"Wow. This is going to be gorgeous."

Piper wrapped an arm around her sister. "It's literally the most important wedding ever." Then she glanced at Maisy and said, "One of the two most important weddings ever."

A flush crept up Maisy's neck as she said, "Bowman and I are planning something simple at Fort Rock. Just family."

Violet suspected that *just family* around here would still be a serious party.

She wandered farther into the space. The room was enchanting. Violet could imagine Jet and Clara dancing at the center; she could see their friends and family looking on as these two good people started their lives together. Ash would be pacing the perimeter of the barn, making sure everything ran smoothly, keeping out of the limelight.

Although if that man were wearing a tux, she couldn't imagine anyone looking at anything else.

And now she was thinking about Ash, at a wedding, in a tuxedo.

"What about you, Violet?" Clara asked.

Violet startled. Had they been reading her thoughts? That would be just the sort of superpower the Wallaces would have and not tell anyone about.

"Um. I like big. If you're gonna have a wedding, you may as well go all in."

"Exactly!" Piper said. "When else do you have the dress, the outrageous cake and possibly the excuse to rent a French chateau?"

Violet laughed. She'd only known Piper for twenty minutes, but Violet could already tell she was exactly the type of person to pull off a wedding in an eighteenth-century chateau. "Do you want to get married in France?"

Piper's expression fell. She'd been supremely confident since the moment Violet met her, but the comment seemed to knock her to her knees.

The energy among the women changed immediately—it felt as though they wanted to comfort Piper but had been rebuffed too many times to try again. Piper dredged up a fake smile. "I don't think marriage is in the cards for me. Want to meet a baby horse?"

Clara gave Violet the exact right smile, saying *this is not your fault*, and *I'll take care of it*. Then she said, "He's adorable."

Violet paused for a beat, then said, "I'd love to. Every time I visit, the Wallace Ranch seems more amazing. Thank you for including me today and absorbing me into your family."

"Oh, absolutely," Clara said. "We're super glad you're here."

Piper's smile flashed again. "But *we* didn't technically invite you, Jackson did. And in terms of absorbing you into the family, that's all Ash."

How COULD ONE family be so loud? Or more to the point, why? Everyone was crammed around the dining table, which had barely been big enough back when there were only seven of them.

Three seats down, Violet was keeping up. He'd placed her between Jet and Jackson, thinking that would make her more comfortable. Unfortunately, Dad had been doing research on concussion prevention, so he was attempting to converse with Violet on this important topic from the far end of the table.

"What's different?" Piper asked Hunter, gesturing to her chicken.

"I'm glad you asked. This isn't chicken."

"What?" Piper dropped her fork. Their conversation escalated, something about Hunter sourcing pheasant for the restaurant, and wanting to try it out on the family first.

Ash gave up on any dreams of Violet thinking they were a nice, normal family and focused on what apparently wasn't chicken anymore. Hunter had made roasted potatoes, glazed carrots and a marinated, shredded cabbage salad to go with dinner. Mom had contributed homemade rolls, Ash's favorite, and together she and Hunter had set out dishes of pickled onions, pickled green beans, and various fruit preserves they canned together at the end of every summer.

Violet might find his family noisy, confusing and socially aberrant, but she did seem to be enjoying her meal.

"Two weeks!" Clara squealed. Ash wondered why she was so excited about the away game at Redmond, then realized she had to be talking about her wedding.

"Jet, you'll be gone for a week and a half?" Violet asked.

Ash had forgotten about this. *How are we going to handle things without Jet?*

"Yep." Jet nodded, grinning down at Clara. His words were simple but deeply powerful as he gazed at her and said, "I cannot wait to be married."

"Where are you going on your honeymoon?" Violet asked.

Ash was about to answer for them, since Jet had been yammering on about Paris for weeks, but Clara yelled, "Don't say it!"

She covered her ears, then Jet covered her ears as well, saying, "It's a surprise," to Violet.

Ash set his silverware down. "You haven't told Clara where you're going?"

"Nope!" Clara said with a big grin.

What is Jet thinking? Clara managed her anxiety well. But marriage was a huge step, and now they were throwing a mystery honeymoon into the mix?

"That's a terrible idea," he said.

"It's the idea we came up with," Clara said sharply. "And the idea we're going with, for *our* honeymoon."

"How do I not know this?" Ash demanded.

Mom reached out and rested a hand on his arm. "You've been very busy, Ash."

Ash didn't know how to react. He *had* been busy; football was taking up half his life. He was *allowing* it to take over, enjoying it even.

He was letting his family down as he got caught up in the drama of the team. He had to get his head back into what was important—his family and their well-being.

"Clara doesn't always do well with surprises," Ash reminded Jet.

Jet straightened his shoulders, and Ash amended his statement. "I know you would never do anything to upset Clara, but a surprise honeymoon?"

"Ash, I am completely looking forward to this. I'm fine," Clara told him.

"But what about when you get there?"

"I'm fine."

"But what if you don't have the things you need for the trip? You know how you get about having the right clothes."

"I'm packing for her," Piper said, clapping her hands.

Ash scanned his family's faces. *Why weren't they worried about this?*

Clara stood and walked to the head of the table, draping her arms around his neck in a hug. "You are a wonderful brother for thinking of me. But I promise you I'm ready. And if I'm not, and I lose it and other people witness me losing it, I'll still be with Jet."

Ash pulled Clara's arms tighter around his neck. He'd been away on deployment when she'd experienced her first major panic attacks. He hadn't been able to do anything to help, just sit in the barracks worrying about her.

He'd promised himself at the time he would make it up to her, and now he could make good on that promise. This wedding would be perfect, and he'd support her and Jet in any way he could as Clara adjusted to married life.

Jackson looked around the table, judging the mood like he did, then tactfully changed the subject. "We should pick the teams now."

Violet perked up. "For football?"

"Or a walk," Clara interjected. "We have some high-quality paths around here."

"But Coach Vi is with us," Jackson reminded her.

"You're right." Clara pulled her arms from

around Ash's neck and ruffled Jackson's hair. "Football it is. Who are the team captains?"

"Dad and Coach Vi," Jackson said. "I call Coach's team."

Ash's competitive streak kicked in. "Then I get Jet."

Violet sat up, scanning the table. "Hunter?"

"At your service," he said.

"Then I want Bowman. And Maisy." Ash wasn't sure Maisy knew the first thing about football, but she was among the most athletic people at the table.

"Okay," Violet glanced around the room. "Mr. Wallace?"

Dad stood and stretched. "I taught these kids everything they know about football."

"That's not even true," Mom said.

"No, but it sounds good. You gonna play for Ash?"

"Someone has to."

"Judge!" Piper called. "I call judging. I'm the football judge."

"Do you mean ref?" Violet asked.

"No, she means judge," Ash told her. "And if we can keep her from giving penalties for wearing the wrong shirt with a pair of pants, I'll call it good."

"Bowman was wearing two different types of camo at the same time," Piper clarified.

"Leaves and twigs on the bottom, something green and urban on the top. It was *not* okay."

Clara sighed and pushed in her chair. "I'll watch."

"Be on my team," Violet said.

"No, I'm bad. Literally the worst. Ask anyone."

Ash's heart warmed as Violet looped her arm through Clara's. "Sometimes the only skill you need is the ability to show up. Let me tell you about a kid named CJ."

THE WALLACES DID not mess around with the backyard football game.

To begin with, the "backyard" was the lush green field unfolding down to the pond that had served as the finish line to the team's three-mile run on endurance day. Irrigation ditches created a natural border, and Mrs. Wallace set up Tiki torches for goalposts. The air was crisp, but plenty warm. Warm enough that Ash shed his flannel shirt a few minutes into the game and played in a T-shirt and jeans. He was so distracting Violet could understand why some outfits deserved a penalty card.

The game started out politely enough, but when Ash picked off the pass made by his own son and scored, Violet could finally see these people for who they truly were. Cut-throat competitors. Chatty, goofy and loving, but serious competitors.

Ash, slightly out of breath and even better looking than normal, pushed his hair back as he strolled to the center of the field.

"That was my ball," she told him.

He smiled. "Then I appreciate your generosity in letting me score with it."

Violet shook her head. "I see how this goes down."

Ash grinned at her, holding her gaze. If he thought for one second he could just be handsome and make her want to hand the ball over, well...

Well...

Okay, that wasn't a terrible strategy. But now she was onto him.

"Let's go!" Jackson called.

Violet called the next play, a handoff from Jackson to Mr. Wallace, who was pretty fast. He made a lateral toss to Clara who bungled it impressively, but Jet gave her the time and space to get a hold of it. Piper looked the other way as her sister broke several rules, and Violet's team moved down the field.

Jackson scored, then Maisy scored twice in a row.

"That is one fast doctor," Violet commented.

"She's good at everything," Bowman said, giving his fiancée a quick kiss on the cheek. Then he launched into singing Queen's "We Are the Champions."

Violet spun on her heel to listen. Bowman, far and away the quietest of the entire pack, was singing, loudly, with perfect pitch, sounding just as good as Freddie Mercury.

"Wait until we break out the karaoke machine," Clara told her.

Violet nodded, then she pointed at Maisy. "I got my eye on you."

Maisy kept smiling as she moved back to the line of scrimmage. Violet studied the family, still not sure if this was tackle or touch football. They didn't tackle so much as grab someone and talk them into slowing down or giving up the ball. With their immediate family members, they were aggressive. At one point, Hunter held Bowman down and sat on him while handing the ball off to their dad. But they were less inclined to tackle Maisy, since she was newer to the group. It would follow they'd be even more hesitant to use any type of physical force to stop Violet.

Violet grinned.

"Jackson, why don't you take over as quarterback again." She tossed the ball to him, then sauntered over to where Jackson had been playing wide receiver.

Ash raised his brow at her.

"I don't think your mom's going to sack her only grandson."

"Then you don't know my mom."

Violet took her place. Jackson made an excellent throw, which Violet caught easily, then scored.

Her team cheered as she tossed the ball to Ash. As they lined up for the next play, he gave her a steady gaze, those hazel eyes trying to figure her out. She smiled back.

They quickly turned the ball, but Jet intercepted Jackson's next pass, which was apparently what he was famous for in this town. She really would have thought it would be the emus by this point.

They reassembled, and Violet scored again.

"Hey!" Piper yelled, not having a whistle. "That's a foul."

"There are no fouls in football," Hunter said.

"Whatever. That point doesn't count."

"Yes, it does." Violet was a little winded from the run, but she knew she hadn't broken any rules.

"Nope. You're too good. So, you only get to score once in a row."

"What?!"

Piper adjusted her sunglasses. "Seriously, have you seen yourself play this game? It's insane."

"The touchdown counts."

Piper raised her hands, like Violet was proving her point. "Love the competitive spirit, but no."

Violet turned around, appealing to the family. "Can she just make up the rules like this?"

"Also, Dad—" Piper pointed to his T-shirt "—we've had conversations about that shirt before."

"It's not so much that we allow her to make up the rules. She just does," Hunter said.

Ash looked extremely conflicted as he watched the interaction. Then he finally said, "Piper, lay off. Violet can score as much as she wants."

"No!" Piper gestured toward her. "She's too good. She could literally win against the whole family."

"Maybe not the *whole* family," Lacy said.

"It's not fair. She's super beautiful and a way better player than anyone else. She can't just run around being gorgeous and athletic. Why would I not call that?"

Violet paused. Flattery was a powerful weapon.

"What about her?" Violet pointed at Maisy. "She's beautiful and athletic."

"But she's literally going to get distracted the minute she sees an ant. Plus she doesn't care about winning. You?" Piper pointed a finger, then looked meaningfully at Ash. "You're a problem."

"You're a problem," Violet muttered.

"And you're snarky too! I seriously couldn't love you more. But no point. Sorry."

"Are we playing football or not?" Clara asked.

"*We're* playing football," Bowman muttered. "I don't know what you're playing…"

"Coach Vi, you go back in as quarterback." Jackson looked around at the assembled family as he negotiated the peace. "That seems fair. And if she scores, Aunt Piper, you have to let her."

"Fine." Piper studied her nails. "I'm not really sure why I'm the football judge if I'm just going to get overruled all the time."

Violet wasn't sure why she was the football judge either, but that was a different question.

Jackson trotted over and gave his aunt a one-armed hug. "You're a good judge."

Piper twisted her head, then accepted the compliment. "Okay, let's get back to it. There's a lemon raspberry torte and a whole bunch of chocolates in the house."

Violet reevaluated her strategy as she walked back to the field. Her team was going to win this game. How could she get others to score? And score subtly enough that Piper didn't call a foul, or a scratch or whatever other nonfootball, sport-like term she pulled out of her head.

She glanced at Piper. Piper crossed her arms.

As the game continued, Violet developed a grudging appreciation for Piper's seemingly random calls. Everyone played across their varying skill levels, yet everyone scored. Ash got called up for being too bossy, which he then tried to boss Piper into taking back. Violet couldn't remember laughing so hard. The sunshine and the adrenaline and the complete love this family had in being together was bewitching.

Ash seemed to shed years of worry as the game continued. He'd been tense when she first arrived but relaxed as the afternoon unfolded. Having his family together, in this beautiful space, he was completely present.

And so was she. For most of her life, Violet was focused on the next move, making it to the next level. The only time she felt present was when she was on the field. She'd worried for years about building the credibility to succeed, first as a player and now as a coach. She'd never taken any time to appreciate what she *had* achieved or enjoy the moment she was in.

All that said, she still intended to win the game.

"Last play!" Piper called, apropos of nothing.

The two teams were tied, and Ash had the ball. Violet suspected Piper was trying to leave the score even. It was the sort of thing someone who'd never played competitive sports would think was a good idea.

Ash had a nice throw. A classic combination of power and accuracy. Their go-to in this game was for Ash to throw the ball to Bowman, who caught it and lateralled to Maisy. Bob and Hunter were less inclined to tackle her, and she scored fairly easily.

The trick would be to intercept that ball. Fortunately, Violet was a former all-state cornerback.

She glanced at Jackson, who looked meaningfully at Bowman. He was thinking the same thing.

Ash launched the ball and Violet took off.

"Whoa there!" Ash called when he realized what was happening. Violet sprinted past Bowman and jumped up, catching the ball. She'd run three steps when a solid arm roped around her waist. Violet took another step, starting to laugh. Ash's other arm locked around her, but Violet kept moving. She was laughing so much it hurt.

"You are not getting away with this," he said, laughing with her. Violet leaned out of his arms, holding the ball as far from him as she could. Ash wrapped his right arm tighter around her waist, laughing harder as he reached for the ball.

"Clara!" Violet called.

Clara held her hands out awkwardly. Ash reached out to pin Violet's arms down, but not before she spilled the ball into Clara's hands.

Ash folded both arms around her, pulling her tight against him as they both laughed, gasping in air. Clara seemed surprised to have the ball but managed to keep a hold of it, slip between the Tiki torch goal posts and score.

"Yes!" Violet raised both arms in victory, then hugged the closest person to her. Which was Ash, the captain of the opposing team.

His grasp around her softened, becoming less of an attempted tackle and more of the sweetest hug imaginable. Violet leaned her head against his chest, as his hand slid down the back of her hair. In the warm safety of his arms, she could feel his breath, his pulse. Violet, who'd never really fit in anywhere, fit perfectly here.

Her heart reverberated in her ears, and she knew it was time to pull away. But she was so sheltered here. If the family was reacting to this show of affection, she had no idea. Joe Hacker and a flock of emus could be surrounding them at this moment, and she neither would have noticed nor cared.

Ash pulled in a deep breath. Keeping his hands on her shoulders, he pulled back to see her face. Her gaze connected with his, letting him know she didn't understand this any more than he did. For two people used to being in charge, it was unsettling.

Ash allowed questions to build in his eyes, and she was sorely tempted to answer them all with a kiss.

"Good winning, everybody!" Piper called out. "Dessert time!"

Ash nodded in agreement. They were confused, and any answers they came up with while in each other's arms were likely to lead to more confusion. The family started up the hill toward the farmhouse, the promise of lemon raspberry torte, chocolates and a rematch of the teams in a game of Trivial

Pursuit. They would leave these questions on the field.

But Ash kept one arm around her shoulders as they followed the family back to the house.

ASH LEANED AGAINST the molding at the entrance to the living room, watching Violet laugh with Mom as she walked to the door. He didn't want her to go, but the less he said the better at this point.

They'd come to an unspoken understanding about their feelings. What could he call it? Agreement? Acceptance? Truce?

He wouldn't get involved with anyone until Jackson was through college, at the earliest. She was likely moving on at the end of the season. Dating would open them up to even more criticism from the community. They couldn't go any further in this friendship, but it was still nice to know this was as hard for her as it was for him.

She glanced up at him over Clara's head and smiled.

And as fun.

"Okay, I should get home. Thank you for having me."

"When are we going to see you again?" Piper asked.

"At the wedding?" Jackson suggested, looking at his aunt and Jet to confirm this.

"Absolutely," Clara said, then smiled at Violet. "Did I tell you you're invited to the wedding?"

"Oh. You don't have to do that. I'm sure you already have your guest list."

"The guest list is literally everyone," Clara said.

"It is," Jet confirmed.

Ash watched Violet's eyes dart to the ground, then to him. She didn't know what to say. "You know, I…I don't know what I would wear. I should probably just—"

"Go shopping!" Piper said.

"Oh!" Clara grabbed Piper's arm. Piper immediately started clapping her hands.

"Makeover!" they both shouted at once.

"We'll take you to Second Chance Cowgirl," Clara said.

"Best store in the universe," Piper added. "Do you think Christy will be open anytime in the next few weeks?"

"She's coming home to help me with a few wedding things." Clara pointed to Violet's feet. "Could Vi pull off boots?"

"She could pull them off, but there might be better options."

"Oooh! Like a peep-toe ankle bootie?"

"That's what I was thinking!"

Violet's head spun between his sisters as they planned to decorate her for the wedding.

"Enough," Ash said. "She doesn't need a makeover."

"Of course, she doesn't *need* it," Piper said. "It's just super fun."

"I appreciate the offer—" Violet shifted her stance to take control of the situation "—but when would you have time?"

"There is always time for a makeover. Always," Clara said.

Violet glanced at him, like she sometimes did on the field when she wanted his opinion. Ash shook his head. This was a very bad idea.

"Please?" Clara asked. "As a wedding gift? I promise you'll still look like you."

Violet pressed her lips together as his sisters cajoled her into their plans, finally cutting them off with, "Okay! Pretty dress, new shoes, Second Chance Cowgirl. I'm in."

"You don't have to do this, Violet," Ash told her.

"It's okay," she said. "It can't be any worse than our upcoming game against the Swarm."

CHAPTER TWELVE

"HEY, COACH?"

Violet startled. She'd been deep in thought, going over her mental to-do list one last time before heading out to practice.

One: Prepare the team to meet the Bend Swarm on Friday night.

Two: Try not to look like you're falling for your offensive coach.

Three: Figure out how to convince that offensive coach that his son should be playing quarterback.

She looked up to see a nervous, recalcitrant kid hesitating in the doorway.

"Hello, Brayson Hacker."

The overhead lights buzzed, and the old radiator beneath the window clicked and wheezed as the heating system shut down for the night.

Brayson pulled in a deep breath. It took him a minute, but he finally said, "May I come back to the team?"

"Playing for the Swarm didn't work out?"

"I didn't—" He looked miserable but determined. "I'm not gonna play for the Swarm."

Violet hid a smile. *There's that Outcrop pride.*

"What's your dad have to say about your coming back?"

Brayson clenched his jaw. He meant to look tough, but the boy seemed so young and vulnerable. Violet made an educated guess.

"Does he know you're talking to me right now?"

Brayson shook his head.

Her heart went out to him.

She couldn't imagine the battle he was in for, getting Hacker to accept that he was returning to play for her team. Throughout all her struggles, she always had the support of her family. Brayson had gotten roped into his dad's ugly drama, but he had the strength to work his way out of it. She was impressed.

He wrestled with the next sentence. "I'm so sorry, Coach Vi. I shouldn't have…"

He let the sentence hang, but it was enough on its own. He just *shouldn't have*.

"Yeah. I know." She crossed her arms. "Gotta be honest, though—you weren't all in on the sabotage."

He looked up sharply. She waved a hand in front of her face. "I saw you helping Jackson readjust his grip on the ball. And am I right in suspecting you've been working on your throw?" Brayson reddened. "You gave it your best, but I could tell you really wanted to play ball."

He studied the floor, raising his brows in acknowledgment of her statement. "My behavior was inexcusable."

"True. But not unforgivable. I'm glad you're back."

Brayson nodded, then pushed forward. "What can I do to make up for it?"

He wanted penance, probation, some way to prove himself. For the most part Violet was a big fan of letting kids sit with their own bad choices. But in this case, she had an idea. Ash wasn't going to be happy about it. And while she wasn't in this position to make parents happy, Ash was…

Well, he was *Ash*.

But she was head coach, and she needed to do what was best for her team.

"I'd like to try Jackson at quarterback. He could use some help with his throws."

He locked his jaw and gave a solid nod. "I'm on it. I think he could be really good. That one night—" Brayson stopped speaking, which was a good call on his part. They didn't need to rehash the night he'd gotten himself benched for disrespect.

"I think he could be really good too."

Violet shifted the papers before her without purpose. Brayson had more to say, and he needed to say it without any prompting from her. Finally, he spoke. "Thanks for the second chance."

There it was. Violet looked up from her clipboard. "I'm happy we can try this again. But I should be clear, everyone deserves a second chance, but there will not be a third."

"Understood."

"Okay. Get out of here and go warm up. We meet the Swarm on Friday."

Brayson grinned, the first genuine, joyful smile she'd seen on the kid. "We're gonna kick some—"

"—three-point field goals," Violet finished for him.

He laughed, then looked at his feet. "Thanks, Coach Vi."

"I'm glad you're back."

He glanced up at her, as though evaluating her sincerity in the statement.

"I am," she reiterated. "Now go see if you can get a few throws in with Jackson before practice starts."

Brayson nodded, then bounded out of the room.

Violet returned her gaze to the podium,

but she couldn't see any of the papers she was shuffling. A heavy drop of water fell and warped the note she'd made in blue pen.

Because crying.

Solid footsteps entered the room. She grabbed the sides of the podium to keep from flying into the strong arms that she knew came with those footsteps. Ash must have been in the hallway. He would have heard the whole conversation.

Ash gave voice to what she was thinking. "Nice work."

"It felt like the right way to handle it."

He came closer, and she pressed her thumbs into the podium.

Self-reminder: Ash isn't here to suggest we hop in his truck, drive to Vegas and find an Elvis chapel.

She glanced up at him. He grinned at her.

Okay, he wasn't here to suggest an Elvis chapel, but that didn't necessarily mean he was averse to one.

"I don't know how you do it."

Violet wasn't really sure how she was doing this, either. After years of planning on being a head coach, she was finally here. Balancing competition with team values felt natural. The raw emotion and imperfections of the high school students didn't faze her. This team held a huge mix of ability, energy and focus. And managing it all felt like composing a score with over forty instruments, knowing how to help one blend in and another shine in a solo, while keeping everyone playing together. It felt incredible.

"My dad was a great coach."

Ash crossed his arms and leaned back against a desk, his legs stretched out before him. "I'm sure he was. But I doubt he ever had to deal with the fallout from Joe Hacker."

She laughed. "No. But there are overly invested parents everywhere."

"Even in California?"

"*Especially* in California."

Ash grinned at her. "Well, you had a great role model, but don't discount what you're able to do as a coach. My parents were two of the best teachers to come through this town, and their talent didn't rub off on me. It's all I can do to keep up with one teenager at home."

"Jackson is such a great kid."

Ash nodded, studying the floor. "Yeah. Despite my bungling, he's turned out okay."

Violet soaked in this rare moment of vulnerability in Ash. Since the day they'd met, he'd been supporting her, but he wasn't great about letting others help him. She waited a beat, then moved from behind the podium and leaned up against the desk next to him.

"Where is Jackson's mom?"

He let out a dry laugh. "I don't know. Not here."

The overhead lights buzzed, illuminating the room past all practicality. Why was it that high schools felt turning up the brightness would lead to more learning? The kids already felt scrutinized as it was.

Ash didn't seem any more comfortable in the spotlight than your average teen. He wasn't ready to tell her about his ex-wife. It hurt that he didn't trust her with his past, particularly after she'd spilled everything about her experience working for Laurent at Taft. But trust takes time, as her dad always said.

He cleared his throat. "I think he's doing okay, though. Absent mom, aggressively present aunts and uncles."

Violet bumped his shoulder with hers as she said, "He seems to be doing more than okay to me."

A smile flickered across his face, then Ash's gaze connected with hers. "I…uh, I heard you talking to Brayson about working with Jackson on his throws."

The quarterback issue hovered between them. Violet suppressed her instinct to fight him on this. It was going to take time for him to come around to Jackson as QB, and she needed to give him that time, as hard as that was.

She gestured to the window. Ash followed her gaze. Brayson and Jackson were passing the ball back and forth on the field, conversation shouted between them as Jackson tried to imitate Brayson's movement.

Ash watched the boys working together with a blank expression, then he nodded solemnly, not accepting Jackson practicing with the quarterback but not outright objecting either. "I'm glad Brayson's back. Now we've got a chance against the Swarm on Friday night."

ASH LEANED UP against the door as players drifted silently into the team room after the game on Friday night. As it turned out, a chance was all they had against the Swarm.

In the end, the massive, well-funded team was too much for them, even with Brayson playing a brilliant comeback game. It was the Eagles' first loss of the season, and a bitter one.

This group of kids—a third of whom had been ready to quit four weeks ago, and another third of whom hadn't even known they wanted to play until a large bird showed up on Club Day—could barely keep from crying.

And Manuel actually was crying.

Football: the home of big emotions.

Brayson stalked into the room and threw himself into a chair. "I hate the Swarm."

His teammates turned to stare at him. He seemed to be the only person who didn't remember he'd threatened to leave and join that very team.

"Me too," Jet grumbled. He had his arms crossed and was leaning up against a desk.

Ash watched Violet survey the room. She was beautiful, calm and perfectly in control. The team meetings were the easiest part of coaching for him because in these cases it made sense to stare at her. The rest of the time he felt like he needed horse blinders to keep his eyes on the players and off the coach.

She, and all the feelings she evoked, were still a mystery to him. A fun, exciting mystery, but baffling all the same. He just had to keep his priorities straight. Jackson came first, then his family, then his community. If all that was good, he'd let himself enjoy the confusion.

Presently, she continued to baffle as she was the only person in the room not on the verge of tears—which was saying something, given her ability to get choked up about something as mundane as an order of sweet potato fries. Even when the Swarm made their final touchdown, securing Bend's win over Outcrop, Violet was grinning. She saw something the rest of them couldn't, and he would really like to hear what it was.

Because if the dull pressure in his throat and behind his eyes was any indication, he was on the verge of crying himself.

"Jet, I'm so glad you mentioned that," Violet said. "You helped this team win against the Swarm once, right?"

"He's the Exterminator," Manuel said. "He's an Outcrop legend."

Jet shook his head. "It was one lucky catch."

"I've seen you play, Coach Broughman." Violet gave him a grin. "A guy doesn't hop up and catch like that out of luck. You do it because you've practiced."

She glanced at the morose team, then asked Jet, "Who else did what they'd practiced on the infamous night Outcrop beat the Swarm in the playoffs?"

Jet turned his Stetson in his hands as he answered. "Our line came together that night. That's why I was able to get open. It's part of the reason the score was so close in the first place." Jet thought back. "We had a couple of great running backs that year. They put us on the board early, so everybody felt like we could win. When I saw the ball coming, I knew if I could catch it, we still had a chance."

"So, for that catch, you were doing what you'd practiced with your team, to the best of your ability. And everyone else on the team was doing the same thing."

Jet smiled at her. "Exactly. The catch itself was no big deal."

She held up her index finger and gave it a sharp shake. "No, it was a great catch. We're still calling you the Exterminator. The name stands. My point is, your catch wasn't luck." She eyed the room, her gaze landing on Carley. "Carley made a great catch tonight. Who blocked for her?"

Jackson looked around, then lifted two fingers claiming the block.

"You kept a huge guy from taking her out. Brayson got in a good throw because Manuel made sure he was protected." She scanned the crowd and found Joaquin at the back. "Joaquin picked off the ball in the second quarter. Why were you able to do that?"

"Because I was there?"

"Exactly. Joaquin was in the same place he practiced being in drills. And he was able to get there because he's smart, fast and people were blocking for him. Then he scored."

Violet looked around the room, picking out other unseen moments of glory. She had an example for nearly every kid on the team doing something right.

"Who held their position on kickoff team perfectly and was ready for anything that came his way."

"Was it me?!" CJ asked.

"It was." Violet nodded, grinning. "And who noticed, and gave you a high five as you walked off the field?"

"Coach Wallace."

Violet turned her smile on Ash, and it was possible he blushed. "That's right." Her gaze held his, and Ash ballooned with pride at the patience he'd cultivated to congratulate a player on not completely messing up.

"Now, that's what I observed on our team. What can you tell me about the Swarm? Who runs the ball more than half the time?"

"Walker Larson," several boys groaned.

"Yep. Same guy, again and again. Now we know what to expect when Walker goes in." She looked at the defense. "Did anyone find a weakness in their line?"

"I did!" Manuel shouted. "Their big guy? He's kinda nervous."

"He seemed very nervous to me. So, he's your break. What did you notice about their two quarterbacks?"

On and on Violet went, soliciting useful information about how the Swarm worked, until she finally grinned at the team and asked, "Who's ready to take on the Swarm again, in playoffs?"

A massive cheer crowded the room, pushing at the doors and windows. Violet had seen what they couldn't—this was their best game of the season so far. And while they hadn't won, they'd learned what they needed to win next time.

Jackson stood and turned to the team, holding up both arms as he yelled, "Who's the best coach in the league?"

"Coach Vi!" came the resounding answer, as the kids jumped to their feet and applauded.

Violet faltered; a flush ran up her face. "Stop it," she commanded, waving their cheers away, but the players continued to applaud her.

She stared down at the podium, pushing an index finger against her tear ducts. "I mean it," she warned, laughing. "That's enough. Go to Eighty Local and shake down Hunter for free food."

The players gave a few last whoops, then

filtered out of the room, leaving only Ash and Violet.

"That was incredible," he told her.

Violet shrugged, then blinked and looked up at the ceiling. Ash took a step toward her.

"Are you finally crying?"

She shook her head, a tear slipping out. "No."

"You're crying."

"Um." She gave a little laugh and wiped another tear away. "I was just thinking about this film I saw as a child. A baby deer loses his mother. It was kinda sad. Sometimes the memory hits me."

Ash shook his head, continuing his advance toward her. "These kids love you."

She stared down at the podium. "I guess I kind of love them too." She pulled in a deep breath and raised her head, her eyes connecting with his. She gazed at him for a long moment, then said, "I love a lot of things about this town."

CHAPTER THIRTEEN

SECOND CHANCE COWGIRL was blissfully calm, notes of rose and cinnamon floating on the air, and everything was in perfect order.

Except for Violet.

She'd been a blubbering mess since the team meeting after the game on Friday. It wasn't so much that these kids appreciated her, although...*wow*. It was that she felt, for the first time, like she was in the right place. Coaching a high school team used all the skills she'd cultivated over the years and pushed her to learn new ones.

And the better she got at it, the better chance there was of her leaving at the end of the season for a larger team.

But she didn't have to think about leaving right now. She was in a beautiful store, with Ash's beautiful sisters, and what had to be the world's most beautiful fifty-year-old woman streaming toward her.

"Violet, I'm so happy to meet you." She took Violet's hands in hers and looked into her eyes. "I'm Christy Jones. I'm in love with Coach Kessler, and we can't thank you enough for what you've done."

Violet nodded and started to speak, but Christy cut her off. "I can, however, set you up with the perfect dress for Clara's wedding. Take your jacket off."

Violet laughed. "You're getting right down to business."

"We've got Clara for an hour, and I'm determined to have the right outfit before she has to leave."

Clara grabbed Violet's jacket, then swiveled her head around to stare. "Okay, seriously? Your arms."

"You have fabulous arms," Piper concurred. "We want zero sleeves involved in this outfit," she informed Christy.

"Agreed. Violet, how do you feel about a maxi dress?"

"For sure. Maxi dresses." She had no idea what a maxi dress was, but everyone seemed to like her answer. And while she was repeatedly asked how she felt about certain things, Violet got the sense that her opinion wasn't the most important one in the room. That was fine. After weeks of being in charge, it was blissful to have other people making the decisions.

"Try this," Christy said, pulling a lavender print dress from the rack.

"What size shoes do you wear?" Piper asked, scanning an incredible selection of vintage boots in the back.

"Eight," Violet called, stepping into the dressing room. "And I don't want to mess anything up, but I have to be able to walk in whatever we find."

She pulled the linen curtain closed behind her as Piper said, "One hundred percent in favor of being able to walk."

Violet slipped into the dress. It was more flowy than what she generally gravitated toward, but it might work. She opened the curtain tentatively to find the three women lined up, arms crossed over their chests.

"Nope," Piper declared.

"Absolutely not." Christy stepped forward. "You're far too fierce for this dress. I apologize for suggesting it. Try this."

The next dress was declared too boho. The next was too formal. The next was "too much," whatever that meant.

Through it all they exclaimed over parts of her body Violet had never thought much about. As an athlete, she appreciated her strength, but her curves sometimes got in the way. As a coach, her primary goal in terms of clothing was to look like she lived and breathed football, which wasn't too far off the mark. Occasionally, she'd dress up to go out with friends, but the years in San Diego had been isolating. She was out of practice getting dressed up.

These women lived as though every day were a chance to celebrate your body with a great outfit.

"You all take your clothing seriously," Violet finally said.

"Love rule number five—Look good, feel good," Clara said. "It's the last rule, but honestly it matters as much as anything. A person has to feel good in their own skin."

Piper said, "If you take time to care for yourself, it signals to others that *you* care about you, and they should too."

"And to be clear, it's different for everyone," Clara said. "It's not about fitting into society's unrealistic ideals—it's about celebrating your unique beauty and caring for your body."

"I can get on board with that." Violet glanced at the two sisters, then at Christy. "Dare I ask about the other love rules?"

"People rarely have to ask," Christy quipped.

Piper started speaking before Christy even finished the sentence. "Number one—Never waste time on someone who isn't into you."

"Number two—To find love, love yourself first," Clara said. "This is Hunter's problem."

Piper rolled her eyes and nodded in agreement. "The next is know your core values, and find someone who shares them."

"And then, know your love chemicals. Choose when, and with whom, to release them."

Violet furrowed her brow. "What are love chemicals?"

Clara got a devious smile on her face. "Love chemicals are the best. There are some, like pheromones, which are just your particular chemical makeup that will appeal to some people more than others. Have you ever been completely attracted to someone the first time you met them, and had no idea why?"

Um, yeah.

"There's nothing you can do about pheromones, but it's good to know they're out there. You do have control over your basics, like oxytocin and vasopressin. They make you feel attached to others and are released with touch."

"This is why you see older couples holding hands and acting like they're still high school sweethearts. Something as simple as palms touching can release attachment chemicals."

The feel of Ash's rough palm sliding against

hers the first time she'd shaken his hand came back to her. Could she blame wanting to marry a complete stranger on chemicals?

"But then there are the stealth chemicals." Clara grinned. "Like adrenaline."

"As in—" Violet pretended to run in place "—the same thing we release when we're exercising?"

"Or scared, or mad, or on a roller coaster," Piper said. "Basically, adrenaline makes anything you're feeling stronger. So if you like someone, you will like them more if adrenaline is involved. You probably experience it all the time. Like how well-functioning sports teams all care about each other and bond deeply. It's the adrenaline that makes the bond so powerful."

"But the reverse is also true," Clara said. "If you don't like someone, you'll like them even less after releasing adrenaline."

"So, my old boss down in San Diego?"

"Totally."

Piper looked at Clara and something passed between them. Piper grinned. "So imagine, you're coaching with a guy you *do* like."

"Maybe someone who can get kind of bossy but has an absolute heart of gold."

"And has literally the best son in the universe."

Violet turned to Christy in a desperate attempt to change the subject. "Do you have another dress for me?"

Christy held up her hands, as though powerless to stop them.

"A guy who breeds horses for a living and still wears the same Stetson his parents bought him when he turned seventeen."

"*Help me*," she mouthed to Christy.

Christy just shook her head and placed a soft, heavy jersey knit dress into her hands. Violet glanced down at the warm cinnamon color.

Clara kept chattering on about chemicals and her adorable oldest brother.

"I'm gonna try this on," Violet spoke over Clara. She ducked into the dressing room, but the linen curtain did nothing to block out their voices.

"I'm just saying adrenaline is like a litmus test for love, and if you still like a guy after endurance day—"

Violet hummed the Eagles fight song as she stepped into the ankle booties Piper had found, then slipped the dress over her head. The heavy fabric slid over her body easily. A wide neckline showed off her collarbones, and, yes, accentuated her strong arms. The dress was formfitting, but not tight, and fell to midcalf. It didn't show off her curves so much as partner with them to make her look…well…*good*.

Outside of the dressing room the sisters were still talking loudly about the possibility of Violet and one of her assistant coaches becoming closer through the magic of adrenaline. Like she needed any help finding Ash appealing.

Violet cautiously placed a hand on the curtain and drew it back. It didn't really matter what anyone else thought, she was buying this dress.

The three women looked up as she stepped out. A full-length mirror in the beautifully lit room greeted her along with stunned silence.

"She's a goddess," Clara finally said.

"Confirmed. Completely worshipable," Piper agreed.

Christy studied her for a moment, then brought a pair of dangling earrings from the case and held one up to her ear.

"I don't think I've ever looked this good in my entire life," Violet admitted.

Clara clapped her hands. "Yay! Best wedding present ever!"

Violet looked at her dryly. "You don't think you might receive something a little more useful than your nephew's coach in a nice dress?"

Piper smiled. "Every present will be the best present ever, and there is nothing wrong with hyperbole."

After choosing earrings and listening to a heated discussion between the sisters about how she should wear her hair, Violet slipped back into the dressing room. She turned and admired herself before the mirror one last time. She didn't want to take off the dress. It felt soft and cool on her skin; she felt beautiful.

Voices floated through the curtain.

"Okay, Ash is going to freak out."

"Right? He was all like, *Don't put Violet on the spot like this. She doesn't need a make-over.*"

Violet choked back a laugh. Piper's imitation of Ash was spot-on.

"Chances that he'll actually admit she's as beautiful in a dress as she is in a ball cap?"

"Saying it out loud? Zero chances. Because he's not going to be able to speak when he sees her."

Violet glanced back at herself in the mirror. *Would Ash like this dress?*

She looked over her shoulder at the back of it again. Then she flexed her arm. He was gonna like the dress.

But would he let himself like *her*? And what if he did? Where did Ash fit into her career goals?

Violet shook her head. She was putting the sled in front of the dogs here. Of all the things people would notice at the wedding, a football coach in what was admittedly a fantastic outfit wouldn't even register. This was Clara's day coming up. Violet was a minor blip in the lives of this little town, but hopefully a good one. And if Ash looked back on the season with a certain fondness, she'd be looking back that way too.

ASH READJUSTED HIS Stetson as he exited the stables.

Nothing to see here. No last-minute cleaning out of rafters done by a doting older brother so his sister's wedding would be flawless.

Ash strode past the gardener's cottage that Clara and Piper had fixed up into a little guest house a few years ago. Piper was staying there as they counted down to the big day, and there were so many ribbons and whatnot in there a person could barely get through the door.

Clara, Piper and their friends had beautified the big red barn to within an inch of its life. Fall blooming flowers were planted everywhere, and the leaves on the property were turning gold and red right on cue for the big day. Jet and Dad mapped out parking and set up signs. Bowman and Mom were helping Hunter with the food. Ash had given himself and Jackson the job of attending to the little details no one else would think of, as well as being on hand to deal with any unexpected crises. And since Jet was planning on bringing Clara's horse Shelby back for the wedding, and at least one emu, Ash could safely assume crises would arise.

His sister could be frustrating, and persistent beyond belief, but Ash was pretty sure no one worked as hard as Clara to bring love and joy into the world. This was the day to celebrate *her* joy, and Ash would work quietly to ensure it was perfect.

Car doors slammed. Ash looked up to see Clara and Piper loaded down with bags from Second Chance Cowgirl. He trotted up to the drive to help them.

"How'd it go?"

"How'd what go?" Piper asked. Ash rolled his eyes. Piper goggled her eyes at him.

"Super fun," Clara interrupted.

Piper charged up the steps. Most days it was pretty quiet on the ranch, with just Jackson and Ash in the house and Bowman and Hunter out in the bunkhouse. But with Mom and Dad home, and the entire, noisy family around getting ready for the wedding, the farmhouse seemed as busy as the big ant colony Maisy had found on the property.

"Sorry it's so frantic around here," Clara said. "You barely get finished with kids' camp, and then I take over the place."

"It's all good," Ash told her. It was more than good. He relaxed when his family was here. If he could physically see everyone, it meant they were all okay.

An autumn breeze brushed past, rustling the leaves of the oak branches stretching over the front lawn.

"I think the weather's gonna be perfect," he said, gesturing for Clara to take the path to the front steps ahead of him. "You sure you're okay doing the rehearsal on Friday morning, and having a rehearsal lunch rather than dinner?"

"Yes, absolutely. Plus, I'm actually coming to that football game. After all these years, I'm finally starting to get it."

"Better late than never."

Clara gazed up at him. "Ash." She took one deep breath, then two more. "Ash, Violet's really special."

He froze. Clara bugging him about a woman was nothing new. She'd been trying to set him up since he returned home from the National Guard. But her tone and expression were different this time. Ash opened his mouth to put a stop to whatever nonsense she was about to spew about love and relationships, but nothing came out.

"When I look for a match, I'm not just evaluating who's going to get along. Love is so much more complex than compatibility. I look for couples who will help each other grow."

"Violet's not going to fix me."

"I don't want you to be fixed. That's not what I mean. Jet will never 'fix' my anxiety. I will always have a predisposition for the intense thought patterns that can manifest in unhelpful behavior. But Jet's steady, unwavering love is like a balm when my anxious thoughts are too much." Clara placed her hand over his heart. "I don't know what Kerri did to hurt you. But I see the damage. It's like a broken bone that wasn't set correctly."

Ash started to push his sister's hand away, but she shook her head.

"Violet fills you up somehow. And I know you think you should just protect Jackson and be there for your family. Violet would make you even stronger. She wouldn't distract you, she would—"

"Clara, I can't—"

"She's not Kerri."

Ash stalked to the edge of the porch and gazed out across the land. He waited for his breathing to settle before speaking. "I know."

"You were so young when you married her."

Ash shook his head. "I was arrogant. I thought I knew what I was doing."

"You weren't arrogant, you were twenty-two."

"Same thing."

"Kerri didn't have any direction in her life. I don't think she ever will. You come from a family where the only thing holding any-one back is the need to sleep, and in Hunter's case even that doesn't have a huge effect. You aren't responsible for what she did."

Ash let his sister's words run through him. She was right. He was only responsible for what *he* did. He took the deployment. The plaintive wailing of four-year-old Jackson echoed in his ears, his son's panic at being stuck alone behind that locked door.

When he'd married Kerri, he'd known the US Armed Forces had a significantly higher divorce rate than the civilian population. They'd told him that in basic training, warned all of the recruits to think long and hard before committing. But Ash wasn't going to be a statistic. He knew how marriage worked. Hadn't he had the best role models growing up?

Jackson hadn't been planned, but Ash was thrilled when Kerri told him. His first thought had been, *Here we go!* He was ready—five kids, a farmhouse, his son playing for the Outcrop Eagles, just like he had. Ash knew it wouldn't always be easy, but it would be fantastic.

There was nothing about Kerri that suggested she'd handle parenthood well. She got distracted easily and wasn't good at sticking with tough situations. She blamed her unhappiness on others.

When Jackson arrived, Ash was completely taken with him. He could spend all day marveling as little fingers clasped around his dog tags, listening to the gurgling chuckle that erupted when Jackson shook the tags to hear them rattle. If his arguments with Kerri intensified, he blamed it on the lack of sleep. Things would get better once Jackson was sleeping through the night, once Jackson got older.

Ash assumed everyone else was as thrilled with his son as he was. When his parents kept offering to drive over and take Jackson for the day, Ash thought it was because they couldn't get enough of him, either. He couldn't see what they saw: a young couple floundering, in desperate need of help.

The National Guard was a good job, and Ash was good at it. Still, there wasn't a big paycheck at the end of the month. But overseas deployment? That paid. They needed the money, and Kerri said she had things covered at home. Ash could still remember how hard it had been to leave Jackson, and the sense of relief knowing he'd be away from Kerri for several months.

Then he returned on his first leave. It wasn't a surprise, but the flight got in early. He'd messaged Kerri. She knew he was coming home. Ash had wondered if she'd surprise him by telling him she'd found a job.

A friend's wife had dropped him off in front of the little house in Salem, and Ash could hear Jackson crying. He ran in, thinking his son was with a sitter, hoping to dry his tears with a big hug from Dad. But when he reached the front door, something felt off. Ash dropped his rucksack and ran into the house, ran toward the wailing to his son's bedroom. The door was locked. Jackson's sobs were rough, exhausted. Panic wracked him, blurring his vision. He turned the door handle with all his force, then dislodged it from the cheap plywood and ran into the room.

Jackson was alone.

Completely alone, locked in his room. He looked at Ash, relief filling his eyes but still bawling, chubby arms reaching for his dad. Ash dropped to his knees and gathered Jackson to his chest.

Daddy, Jackson said between sobs. *Daddy*. Patting his cheek to make sure he was still there. Ash clung to his son, fear slicing through him. Where was Kerri? What had happened?

But as he sat in the little room, cradling his son, he knew. Kerri had left a four-year-old home alone. He didn't know why, or for how long, or if it had ever happened before, but he knew with his entire being this wasn't an emergency. This was just Kerri.

Jackson clung to Ash, falling asleep in his arms. The weight of his son grew heavy, but Ash wouldn't set him down, he just gazed at the tear-streaked face.

Ash couldn't forgive himself for taking a deployment. He'd left his child when he had every indicator that Kerri wouldn't be able to handle things.

But what he did over the next few hours,

then years was worse. He tried to fix the situation, fix *her*.

Kerri had eventually come home. Ash had no idea how to engage in marital arguments. His parents had gotten along well, and when they disagreed they calmly worked things out until one of them made the other laugh, and they forgot they'd been fighting. He and Kerri disagreed so frequently he didn't know what to make of it. This argument spiraled to ugly depths, Kerri being furious that Ash blamed her for leaving their child alone. Ash understood logically that Kerri's abandonment was reprehensible, but somehow she made it his fault.

In the weeks, and months and years that unfolded after that day, Ash could have taken his son and walked away at any time.

He spent years, *wasted* years of his life trying to help her become someone she wasn't. She would leave him and Jackson, and they'd adjust. Then she'd come back. She'd ask for another chance. Ash spent money they didn't have on marriage counseling, then she wouldn't show up for their appointments. He kept trying to prove to himself that marrying Kerri, and working on their marriage, was the right thing to do, despite all evidence to the contrary.

Ash's military career faltered. He simply couldn't take a deployment. Jackson began to grow up. Kerri rolled in and out of their lives, leaving chaos in her wake. Ash continued to think he could fix the situation. A farmhouse and five kids…what a joke.

Then Dad had called one day and asked if he needed help. Ash didn't know what it was about his dad's tone that finally broke the dam he'd erected to hold everything in. The whole, messy story rolled out. Dad drove over to Salem that day. Ash could still see his father's expression—not disappointed, not surprised, just ready to help in any way possible. They sat on the sofa and hashed out a plan. Dad helped him fill out the divorce paperwork. Ash was granted an honorable discharge. Within a few days, he and Jackson were packed up and heading home.

And here Ash had hunkered down, protecting Jackson, trying to protect himself, for years. The light, easy feeling Violet now inspired in him didn't fit into the heavy world of order and discipline he'd created for himself.

He liked her, admired her, could barely keep his eyes off her. But if his eyes were on someone else, he might miss something going on with Jackson. Any energy he gave to Violet was energy that could go toward his family.

"I don't think this is the right time for us," he said simply. "I'm not ready."

Clara studied him, calling his bluff without saying a word. Then she patted her hand against his chest and grinned up at him. "You're not ready...*yet*."

CHAPTER FOURTEEN

AS VIOLET PLACED her peep-toe bootie on the white gravel drive at Wallace Ranch, she had one thought: *Outcrop, Oregon* loves *Jet and Clara*.

The whole town really was invited. She'd caught a ride with Uncle Mel and Aunt Rose, who shut down OHTAF for the afternoon to attend. The women from the chocolate shop had stuck a similar Gone Celebrating! sign in their front window and joined the caravan out to Wallace Ranch.

And it wasn't just people showing up for the wedding. A horse with ribbons braided through his mane walked out of a trailer like he was a guest.

Violet moved with the flow toward the even rows of white chairs set up next to the pond.

"We saved you a seat!"

Violet turned to see Maisy. The young doctor was beautiful in a bright sundress, with her short blonde hair and the dusting of freckles across her nose.

"Thanks."

"I've got to grab my hat. The Wallaces have enough pigment in their skin they can stay out in the bright sun all day. I get crispy after ten minutes in a light drizzle."

"I'll come with you." Violet followed Maisy. "I'm a little nervous I might get called out on my coaching in the middle of all this. Being in the shadow of the town doctor might make me less obvious."

Maisy gave her a frank appraisal. "Sorry, but you look too good to be in anyone's shadow. You really need to be more careful around Piper and Clara."

Violet laughed, following Maisy into the cool, dusky barn. The twinkle lights hadn't been turned on yet, and the vast space was illuminated with shafts of sunlight coming through the gaps in the structure. The wooden floor shone in the beams of light, along with mason jars filled with wildflowers. The space felt magical and sacred, like a physical manifestation of Jet and Clara's love.

That manifestation was interrupted by a deep voice at the far end of the barn. "You are going to walk out there, stand still, not eat anything. You got it? Then it's straight back into the pen with you."

Violet spun toward the voice.

Oh wow. Ash Wallace in a tuxedo. With an emu.

He wore the classic black suit with ease, a newer Stetson and clean boots reminding her that while he cleaned up well, this was still Ash. He strode confidently across the barn, emu in tow, ready to deal with whatever the world threw his way this afternoon.

Violet waved awkwardly in the dim light. "Hi, there."

Ash's head shot up. His confident gait halted and he stared. His eyes flickered over her face, across the dress, to her toes and back again. He opened his mouth to speak but nothing came out.

It was safe to say he'd noticed her new dress.

The bird, clearly as besotted with Ash as she was, wasn't happy with the lack of attention. The emu swiveled his head around to get in Ash's line of sight, and opened his beak in an emu grin. Ash pushed the bird's head away and kept gazing upon Violet, but Larry wasn't having it. Violet wanted to help, but she was far too taken by Ash in a tuxedo.

Maisy headed over and took the leash from Ash. "Let me help."

Ash relinquished the bird but still didn't speak.

"Hi," Violet finally said, managing a smile.

"Hi." Ash took a few steps toward her then came to a full stop. "You look beautiful."

Violet flushed, a little bit flustered and a little bit arrogant about how good she looked. She managed to refrain from flexing her biceps.

He glanced down at his boots and cleared his throat like he wanted to say more, but the words seemed to dry up the moment he met her eyes again. Violet bit her lip.

"Hey, we got a bird in here?" Violet glanced at the bypass door to see Jet, a huge smile on his face, gesturing toward Larry. "It's time to get started!"

A cheerful-looking man in thick glasses greeted Maisy and took the bird from her. Hunter popped his head into the barn. "Ash, let's go. If we don't get this wedding finished up in the next hour my marinade timing is going to be off."

Ash met Violet's eyes, a smile twisting his lips. "We wouldn't want their marriage getting off on the wrong foot, what with the marinade and all."

She nodded. "See you on the other side?"

His eyes ran over her dress once more and he nodded, then followed his brothers and the emu out the door.

Maisy settled a beautiful fawn-colored hat over her pale hair and led Violet to where a woman named Joanna Williams had saved them seats. Christy Jones leaned across Joanna and nodded approvingly at Violet's ensemble, then engaged FaceTime on her phone, presumably so Coach Kessler could watch the ceremony as well.

Ash picked up his guitar, strumming a simple tune as honored guests were escorted to the front by Manuel and Aaron. Jackson walked Lacy to her seat, then stood next to his uncles in front of an arbor decorated with sage, juniper and a whisper-thin swath of gossamer silk that shifted like the aspen leaves quivering on the hillside. Ash morphed the tune he'd been strumming into a new melody, and bridesmaids wearing copper silk dresses came down the aisle. Piper couldn't contain her smile, as though nothing in the world made her as happy as Clara finding love. Violet wondered again about her comment regarding marriage not being in the cards for her.

Ash's brow knit as he focused on the guitar, and the tune changed again. "Cowboy Take Me Away," by The Chicks rolled off the strings, floating over the crowd on the soft October breeze.

Clara entered with Mr. Wallace. She was stunning in a tulle gown embroidered with a subtle pattern of flowers. The dress was somehow classic, romantic and modern all at the same time, and Clara was ethereal. Violet glanced at Jet, who gazed at Clara like she was the only other soul on earth.

As the ceremony began, Violet let the fuzzy feeling in her belly wash over her as she watched Ash. He was still all cowboy, from his confident stance to the boots he wore with the tux. But he'd climbed into the suit for his sister, and that said something about his nature that she liked even more than the way he looked.

She was distracted when Bowman, the quietest of the Wallace siblings, took the microphone. Ash picked up his guitar again, and Violet leaned forward in anticipation. Bowman gave the crowd a brief smile, then launched into the 1960s classic "At Last." Ash's simple accompaniment gave the tune a country feel, but there was nothing simple or down home about Bowman's voice. It seemed to fill the entire basin between the Cascade and Rocky Mountain ranges.

A few minutes into the music, Violet realized she was holding Maisy's hand, tightly. She wasn't sure who had grabbed whose hand in this situation, but they were as close to swooning as two determined, professional women ever had been.

Bowman held the last note, and the audience could not keep it together. They started applauding, but Bowman held out a hand, indicating the show wasn't over yet. Ash plucked a few familiar, funky notes on his acoustic guitar. The groomsmen and bridesmaids began rhythmic clapping. Clara looked at Jet in question, and he shook his head, as though he was as confused as she was.

Then Bowman started singing again. He'd rewritten the words to "We Are Family," To celebrate Jet joining the Wallaces. The song was funny, and sweet and a heartfelt expression of how much the family appreciated Jet. The wedding attendants had choreographed basic dance moves, but Bowman let loose.

Violet gazed at Ash—solid, strong, practical Ash—as he sang silly lyrics with his siblings and danced, welcoming Jet into their family. He grinned at her, then winked.

At this point she and Maisy lost all composure. It was a minor miracle neither of them rushed the altar.

When the song ended, Jet grabbed Bowman, then the rest of the brothers and Jackson in a massive hug. Violet had picked up pieces of the story over the last few weeks and understood that Jet didn't have much of a family, but Bob and Lacy had been a major influence on him in high school. Violet leaned back in her seat to try to catch her breath. Maisy passed her a tissue because Violet, no surprise here, was crying.

Joanna leaned across her and asked Maisy, "Do you keep tissues on you just in case Bowman starts singing?"

Maisy gave her a wry smile from underneath her hat. "The tissues are part of a first aid kit I keep on hand for dealing with Bowman at all times."

Violet glanced back at the wedding party to see Bowman grinning at Maisy, a slightly off-center gap between his front teeth—exactly the type of guy on a date with whom you'd bring bandages and a suture kit.

The ceremony continued, with as much heart and beauty as she would have expected with Clara and Jet. As they said their vows, their love seemed to flow through the guests and out into the world, making everything else seem insignificant.

It was enough to make a woman think there might be some greater purpose to life than football. Or at least a comparable purpose.

"With the power vested in me," the pastor said, "I now pronounce you husband and wife."

Jet let out a whoop louder than anything Violet had ever heard on the field. He picked up Clara and spun her around, her brilliant laugh ringing out over their guests. Then he set her down and cradled her face in both his hands, as though she were the most precious thing on earth, and he kissed her.

The collective "Awwww!" was heard three counties over.

Violet had never been so grateful for waterproof mascara.

"WHAT A BEAUTIFUL COUPLE," said Mrs. Stamm, who was Ash's, and every other Wallace kid's, third grade teacher.

"Yes, ma'am. We're all happy to finally have Jet in the family." Ash tried not to be obvious about looking over her head toward the cake table where Violet had been pressed into service with a serrated knife and a stack of reclaimed, mismatched floral china cake plates.

He'd exchanged two awkward sentences with her since the ceremony. And after his complete immobilization when he'd first seen her, he was anxious to redeem himself with some decent conversation.

He was also anxious just to see her again.

But immediately after the ceremony, he was called off to deal with a grilling emergency. The emergency turned out to be named Larry, and it took Ash and Jet's friend Michael Williams twenty minutes to get the bird into a pen. From there, Ash helped get people served and seated, toasts made, music dealt with. But now that the first dance had happened and the cake was cut, he should get to spend at least a few minutes with Violet.

"I remember when Clara was eight," Mrs. Stamm continued. "That smile could melt your heart."

"Yep." A flash of cinnamon red caught Ash's eye as Violet took slices of cake to her aunt and uncle. "I'm gonna go check on—" Ash pointed vaguely in the direction of Violet "—things."

Ash stepped around Mrs. Stamm, then felt terrible because the woman had taught him long division, which couldn't have been easy. Fortunately, Bowman came over to introduce her to Maisy, and he was Mrs. Stamm's official favorite.

Ash had taken three steps toward Violet when an eight-year-old jumped directly into his path and pointed a finger at him. "You can't sell Spinach!"

Ash cleared his throat and tried to have patience with the fire chief's daughter. He crouched before her. "Spinach isn't going anywhere."

Josh Hanson caught up with his daughter and apologized, then asked Ash for his opinion on the county commissioner situation.

Ash wanted to be polite to Josh, but Violet was less than fifteen feet away now.

"Where have you been?" Piper materialized next to him. "I've been looking all over for you."

Ash sighed. It was hopeless. He'd never get to talk to Violet. She'd forever know him as the guy who couldn't speak whenever she wore a dress.

"Sorry, Josh, I need my brother. Miss Sammy, I'm home through Monday. Have your dad call and schedule a horseback riding lesson while I'm still here."

Piper grabbed his hand and pulled him away. "What have you even been doing all evening?"

"Whatever needs doing."

"Well, it's time for you to have some fun." Piper reached up, patted his cheek and planted him right in front of Violet.

All of his good intentions for making reasonable conversation flew right out the window.

How was she so beautiful?

Violet was similarly stunned but recovered faster.

"Hi."

"Hi…" Ash kicked around in his head for another word to go with the first one. Nothing came up.

"Have you had any cake?" she asked, holding out her slice.

"No." Her eyes were so pretty. Dark brown, with flecks of gold around the iris. Those eyes widened at him, and he realized he wasn't speaking, again. "Uh, how is it?"

The right side of her mouth quirked up. She held the plate with both hands in between them. "This isn't so much cake as an ode to chocolate."

Ash laughed. "Sounds like Clara."

She gestured with the cake to an empty barrel-table-thing. Ash followed her. Obviously, he followed her. She was a gorgeous, brilliant woman in a red dress carrying chocolate cake.

Violet pulled a couple of forks out of a vintage coffee tin on the table and handed him one. "I'm excited to try it. I've been serving for the last half hour, and in that time decided I'm going on an all-cake diet between now and playoffs."

One of Hunter's servers from Eighty Local walked by with a tray of champagne flutes, asking, "Prosecco or Pabst Blue Ribbon?"

"PBR, please," Violet said.

"Same. Thank you." Ash took two glasses of beer and set one before Violet. She touched the rim of her glass to his and the chime seemed like a switch, turning down the volume on everyone else in the barn and bringing Violet's voice into stereo.

Ash sank his fork into the cake, and Violet did the same. They each took a bite, eyes meeting over the slice as they swallowed.

"This is incredible."

Ash nodded. "I'm in on that all-cake idea."

She offered him a fist bump of agreement from across the table. "And who knew chocolate cake went so well with beer?"

They both dug in again. Things didn't get much better than cake, beer and Violet Fareas.

"Hey! It's my son's favorite coach!" a man said, approaching their table.

Violet startled, as though she too had forgotten the barn full of people.

"I'm Daniel, Joaquin's dad," he said, holding out a hand.

"So nice to meet you," she said. "Joaquin has come so far this season."

"He has. I attribute his improvement to a little talk I had with him at the beginning of the season."

Ash bristled to hear the man taking credit for Joaquin's growth—that credit belonged to Violet and Joaquin.

And maybe Ash deserved a little of the credit too? He *was* the offensive coach.

Violet just smiled. "Well, he's a great kid. I'm sure you're very proud."

"I am. I am. Now, I have some ideas about a new offense you might want to try."

Violet blinked. "You have ideas? About my offense."

She was trying so hard to be polite. Violet's offense was meticulously planned. When she solicited advice from Ash on which plays to run, it was after asking him to read about ten clipboards' worth of information.

Daniel reached into his pocket and pulled out his notes, moving to stand next to Violet. She widened her eyes at Ash. If she wanted to know what the correct protocol for turning down coaching advice at family weddings was, he didn't have anything.

"As you can see here, this is the offense the Patriots used in the Super Bowl—"

Violet closed her eyes, picked up her glass of PBR and drained it.

Ash dropped his hand on the piece of paper and somehow managed to fit his frame between the man and Violet. "Would you like to dance?"

Relief, and what looked like a healthy dose of humor, flashed in her eyes. Ash kept talking. "Because, the band won't be here too much longer..." he spitballed, trying to come up with a reasonable excuse, but knowing he was just making stuff up at this point. "My mom would be upset if any guests left without...dancing."

Violet grinned, slowly nodding.

Daniel looked from one of them to the other, baffled that the coach would choose dancing over his unsolicited advice.

"I'd hate to let your mom down." She picked up the notes and handed them to Ash. "Would you keep these for me so I can go over them later? Daniel, thank you for thinking of our team."

Ash grinned back at her as he folded the notes and put them into the pocket of his jacket. She slipped her hand into his, and everything, save her palm against his, disappeared.

If the dance floor was crowded. If people were speaking to him, if there were eight emus in a line dance, Ash had no idea. All there seemed to be anywhere was Violet.

He couldn't remember any of the reasons he had for not pursuing this incredible woman. Or had those just been excuses?

Ash pulled her to him, readjusting his right hand and letting his left rest at her waist. Music must have been dictating their movement, but all Ash could hear was a heartbeat.

She smiled at him, as if acknowledging the strange, sudden silence of the room, and how everything else had slipped out of focus. She placed her free hand on the lapel of his jacket.

Rather than broken, Ash felt porous, as though every brittle break in his heart had happened just so Violet could fill in these cracks and gaps. He felt strong and whole for the first time in years.

He looked into her eyes and saw the same feeling reflected back to him. It was freeing, and terrifying. Ash modified his hold on her hand, as though she could make this less frightening.

It was like airborne training, except rather than dropping and hoping for the best with the parachute, it felt as though he'd stepped out of the plane and could fly.

Some type of commotion was developing at the open bypass door. Ash wasn't inclined to deal with it, but the noise managed to pierce the focus he had on Violet. The slow song they'd been dancing to was over. He kept his hand at her waist, then followed her gaze to the door.

"Good-bye!" Clara called, her brilliant smile flashing. Jet waved.

Ash laced his fingers through Violet's so he didn't lose her this time, then pushed through the crowd. He wrapped a free arm around his youngest sister in a hug, then looked over her head at Jet. "You take care of each other," he instructed.

Jet nodded seriously, as Clara glanced at him, then Violet, with mischief in her eyes, muttering, "*You* take care of each other."

"Get out of here." Ash chuckled.

"Trying to!"

Clara gave him one last smile. Then Jet tugged at her hand, and they ran toward his old Chevy. Ash stood with Violet, his family and friends as they waved good-bye. Jet's truck bumped over the gravel drive and up the rise to Wallace Creek Road.

Ash was still holding Violet's hand. He glanced around the barn. Jackson was laughing with his friends. His parents were chatting with Mr. and Mrs. Fareas. Piper and

Maisy were arguing some point with Hunter and Bowman. Everyone was okay.

Maybe he could take a few more minutes to let himself be distracted?

Violet looked into his eyes, her beautiful smile shining up at him.

He grinned back, dropping his voice to a whisper as he asked, "What are we going to do?" He gestured between them. "About... this?"

The right side of her mouth curved up. "I honestly don't know."

Ash felt free, possibility sparking in his chest, setting ideas in motion he'd kept at bay for years.

"Dance?" he asked.

A blush rose in her cheeks, as her gaze met his. "I can't think of any better solution."

CHAPTER FIFTEEN

"THAT'S MY DAUGHTER!" Brenn Theis screamed from the stands. She thumped her fist against the ink on her chest then pointed at Carley. "That's my daughter!"

Carley, fresh off her second touchdown, pointed at her mom with the ball.

Aaron approached the stands and shouted, "Hey, Mom, you got another kid here. I held the block."

"Him too!" She pointed at Aaron. "And he's passing all his classes with As and Bs, so that's what's what, Outcrop!" Brenn gestured with both arms triumphantly, then sat down.

Violet glanced up at Ash. "I think Mrs. Theis is coming around to football."

His lips twisted in a smile. "She might be."

Carley came trotting back to the sidelines where she was summarily yelled at by forty extremely happy young men.

"That's how you win a game!" Violet said, holding both hands up for a high five. "That's how it's done!"

Carley returned the high five, then stood next to Violet. The last few seconds on the clock ticked down and the horn blew. Students and families came pouring out of the bleachers, engulfing the team on the field.

Their first playoff game was in the books.

"No meeting tonight," she yelled over the din. "We'll talk this out on Monday." Violet doubted more than three kids could hear her, but the message would spread.

Manuel slapped her hands, sending reverberations through her skeleton. The kid did not know his own strength.

"See you at Eighty Local?" Jackson asked.

"I'll be there in a few." Violet glanced into the stands where a recruiter from Lewis & Clark university in Portland was waiting to speak with her.

"You want a ride?" Ash asked.

She grinned at him. Where did rides stand in a friendship-with-sparks? It probably depended on how many smelly linemen were in the cab with them.

"I'll meet you there."

He raised his brow, as though he knew what she was thinking, then touched his fingers to the rim of his cap.

Violet watched him turn and exit the field, then let out a breath.

The last few weeks had been phenomenal. All the pieces she'd put in place for team cohesion throughout the season were paying off. They played together like a well-oiled machine. A happy, committed, winning machine.

Tonight, they'd beaten Redmond, and were heading into their second playoff game next week. It took all of Violet's self-control not to jump up and pump the air with her fist. Not because it was inappropriate for the situation, but because she'd done it at least twenty times in the last hour, and her shoulder was getting sore.

And Ash? Time spent with that man just got more fun by the minute. They weren't dating, unless running a practice for forty teenagers counted as a date. But they weren't... not dating. Still thoughtful of gossip, still unsure of the future, she and Ash were connected in a way that made her happier than she'd ever been in her life.

The field cleared, the massive crowd rumbling over to Eighty Local where Hunter would have tables and heaters set up out in the parking lot to accommodate everyone. Next year, when he had his events center open, it would come in handy for the overflow.

Violet stopped. *Next year?*

It wasn't the first time the thought had occurred to her. It wasn't even the first time in the last twenty minutes. *Next year.*

If she stayed, she'd never get to look Laurent in the eye and tell him she was coaching D III. She might, however, get to look in someone else's eyes.

"Coach Vi!" A man in a Lewis & Clark sweatshirt came down out of the stands. "I'm John McMannis."

"Hey! Welcome. You're here to talk about Brayson?"

"We can start there," he said. "This team is stout."

"Thank you." Violet inclined her head to accept the compliment.

"Your line is solid. Who's the big kid? Number 68?"

"Manuel. He's amazing. But before we dive in there, I'll let you know he has interest from Cornell University. And if the kid can make it to an Ivy, he's going."

"He's a scholar?"

"Manuel's very smart. Freakishly good SATs. Kid got a perfect score on the verbal section. Which, actually, as I'm saying it, shouldn't be much of a surprise."

"Well, if he wants to stay in Oregon, we could use a kid like him."

"I'll let him know."

"And was that a sophomore you sent in as quarterback in the fourth? Jackson Wallace?"

She paused, then nodded. "Yeah. Jackson."

"Where'd he learn to throw?"

Partially from his dad, who's still not comfortable with him playing quarterback...

Violet had been cautious about putting Jackson in, timing it carefully so Redmond's most aggressive linemen were on the bench, and the score was high enough he wouldn't feel too much pressure. Not that Jackson minded the pressure—it was Ash she was taking care of.

She shook her head. Time to move the conversation back to Brayson. She and Ash could cross the playing-in-college and playing-quarterback bridges with Jackson later. "Brayson's been working with him." Violet paused, then said, "Brayson has a good arm. And a four point. You should know, I sent video out to a number of schools."

"I'd expect nothing less. How's Brayson's team leadership?"

Violet considered her answer. "He had to make some tough decisions. In the end, he made good choices, and the experience, I think, has made him stronger."

John nodded. "I know a little bit about what happened."

"He came around. I think that says a lot about him. We all make mistakes. We don't all admit we were wrong and work to make things right again."

"It does say a lot about the kid. It also speaks volumes about you as a coach. You ever think about making a move?"

Violet looked up sharply. A month ago, the answer would have been a resounding yes.

But… Carley. CJ. A certain sophomore boy she sent in as quarterback in the fourth quarter. That sophomore's father, with worry and laugh lines around his hazel eyes.

But then there was *her* dad and all the sacrifices he'd made for her. She would be perfectly happy, more than happy; she'd thrive here as head coach of the Eagles. But her dad had done so much to help her develop as a player and a coach. She wanted to honor that by going as far as she could in the sport.

And David Laurent. It would feel so good to tell that jerk she was a Division III head coach.

But staying here might feel even better.

Violet pulled up a smile. "I'm always up for a conversation."

"Then I'm gonna talk to my boss, and we'll

get back to you about finding a time for that conversation."

Violet and John chatted further about Brayson and his prospects at Lewis & Clark. Then he shook her hand and headed out. Violet let out a deep breath. This was a night for celebration. She'd met her goal—a winning season and a spot in the playoffs. No matter what the future held, she had tonight in Outcrop.

ASH HAD BEEN craning his neck to look at the door since he sat down. After fifteen minutes, and a bad neck crick, Hunter made him change places with Jet so he could see the door more clearly. He grumbled as he moved, but he moved.

It was wonderful to be here with his whole family. Mom and Dad were still in the country. Piper was visiting from Portland. Bowman and Maisy had been leading cheers in the stands. Clara and Jet were safely home from Paris and full of stories. Jackson was with his friends a few tables away.

Ash glanced at the door again. Only one person was missing.

Finally, the bells hanging from the door rang, and a gorgeous coach arrived. All of Eighty Local burst into applause as Violet entered. Her beautiful smile shone as she scanned the restaurant. When her eyes hit him, she stopped looking.

Ash pulled out a chair next to him. Hunter set a batch of sweet potato fries in front of the open seat.

"Hunter, I don't know how you do it," Violet said. "Keeping this place running, building the events center, catering family weddings, reading my mind and knowing all I want in the world is a basket of these fries."

Hunter laughed, but Ash could sense the tension. He was barely doing it all but was determined to keep at it. "I've had two months to get to know your order."

Was it already November? The season had flown by.

He glanced over to where Jackson and his friends were laughing. Brayson stood next to their table, talking about the pass Jackson had made at the end of the game. Time was passing so quickly.

"How about that third quarter!" Clara said.

Jet readjusted his arm around Clara's shoulders and kissed the top of her head. Up until this season, Clara hadn't really gotten the whole four quarters concept. She'd referred to the *first and second act* of a football game and rarely had the patience to watch, either.

"I couldn't have been more proud," Violet said. "They worked together as one unit."

"Like an anthill!" Maisy said, exchanging a high five with Dad.

"Like a team," a voice from behind him said.

Ash and Violet turned around to see Coach Kessler, leaning heavily on Christy Jones's arm. He was thin and pale, but the spark in his eyes was still there.

"Coach!" Ash stood and, rather than the polite nod he'd perfected over the years, actually hugged the man.

"What's all this?" Coach's laugh morphed into a cough. "No one gets a hug from Ash Wallace."

Mom appeared, wrapping her arms around her old colleague. "You have some explaining to do."

"It's nothing." Kessler waved away her concern. "My shin turned on me. You can't trust your own bones these days." He focused on Violet. "Here she is, in the flesh. You've done a heck of a job, Coach Vi."

"Thank you. This is an amazing program." She stood and held out a hand. Kessler brushed it away and gave her a hug.

"Thank *you* for holding it together." Then

he looked at Jet and set a hand on Ash's arm. "Thanks to all of you."

Maisy pulled Christy aside and asked a series of questions while Mom and Dad pestered Coach about not calling. But the whole time Coach kept a hold of Ash's arm, like he wanted to say something to him.

"All right. You've had your outing," Christy finally said. "If you're going to be in any shape to sit through a game next week, you need to rest up."

Kessler pointed to Jet. "The Swarm! Don't let me down."

"We don't intend to," Jet said.

"Walk me to the door," Kessler commanded Ash.

It didn't matter how old either of them got, when Coach Kessler gave a direct order, Ash followed.

It took a while to get to the door, with all of Outcrop wanting to say hi, but when they got there, Kessler thumped him on the back. "I know you, Ash Wallace. You take your time making a commitment, but when you do, you're all in." He looked meaningfully back at Violet. "But take it from me, you don't have all the time in the world."

Ash glanced from Coach to Violet. *Was Coach telling him to bust a move?*

"Get in there, before she's poached by some other team."

Yeah, he definitely was.

Ash looked at Coach, trying to get more information out of him, but the discussion on Ash's love life ended as quickly as it had begun. Christy declared it time to leave. Dad and Mom walked Coach out to the parking lot, admonishing him for being so secretive about the cancer but still so happy to see he was okay.

Ash returned to the table, Coach's words rolling through his head like acrobats. He sat down to find Violet's brown eyes trained on him. In that moment, lost in her dark eyes, Ash Wallace gave up any pretense of not falling for this woman.

He glanced down at his hands folded on the table before him, then cleared his throat, trying to suppress a smile. "I remember you saying once you didn't have time to date during the season."

The right side of her mouth quirked up. "We had a conversation like that."

He nodded, a hot flush creeping up his neck. "I also remember you saying the only type of date you might have time for would be watching a film and making a plan for Friday night's game."

"I'm not sure I could resist an offer of film and strategy."

"A coach wouldn't want to date the parent of one of her players." Ash looked into her eyes, biting down on his bottom lip.

She flushed, eyes bright as she said, "It's not so much that she wouldn't *want* to. It would look bad to the community."

He looked back down at his hands. "But two coaches, planning strategy, on my front porch would be...?"

"Completely innocent."

Ash glanced up and held her gaze. "You busy tomorrow night?"

Violet slowly shook her head.

Ash grinned. "Six o'clock?"

She bit down on a smile. "Six o'clock. What should I bring?"

"You got any clipboards?"

Her laugh rang out, filling Eighty Local, and his heart. He still didn't know where this thing was going, but he sure couldn't wait to get there.

CHAPTER SIXTEEN

VIOLET CHANGED HER outfit fourteen times before finally heading out to Wallace Ranch—an impressive feat, given her limited wardrobe. She finally settled on a pair of jeans and a soft sweater, worn with the booties she'd bought for the wedding. Not that Ash would even notice her shoes. Or would he?

Maybe the shoes were too much.

Violet wanted to clobber her inner voice by the time she turned onto Wallace Creek Road. She was heading to a date with Ash Wallace, which had to be the best place anyone could possibly be heading. It was a big night.

Her first date in a long time.

They would come up with a plan to beat their nemesis.

She'd tell Ash about her decision to put Jackson in as Brayson's backup for quarterback. The conversation would take tact and understanding, not her strong suit. But Ash was worth honing these two traits.

Her car crested the ridge, and she saw Ash

waiting on the front porch, his guitar leaning up against the railing. She loved the guitar, and the porch. She loved the entire ranch.

And the man?

Violet gazed at him as she pulled up in front of the house. She'd never been in love. She loved her parents, many of her players. She loved the game of football.

Was this wild spinning feeling Ash set off in her love? Or was it just the by-product of adrenaline?

No, she'd been pumping out adrenaline next to men since she was fifteen, and none of her teammates or coworkers ever made her feel like this. A sweet, rushing freedom turning everything golden and beautiful.

Ash stood as she parked the car, then trotted down the steps to greet her. "What kind of load do we have today?" He held out his arms. Violet showed considerable restraint in not stepping into those arms.

"So many clipboards."

He grinned at her. "What is it with you and clipboards?"

"I like to think of them as individual, portable desks."

"Handy for a woman on the move."

Violet glanced up at him, wondering when the right time would be to tell him she might not be on the move anytime soon. She didn't want him to feel like he was the only reason she'd stay. If she ultimately decided to remain here, it would be for the Eagles. This team was the calling she'd been searching for. But she'd be lying if she didn't admit she was hoping for more than just a great team in a fantastic location.

She wasn't going to pressure Ash into any relationship. But given the look in his eyes, no pressure would be necessary.

He grinned at her. "You ready for this?"

Violet pulled in a deep breath. Yeah, she was ready.

"Let's do it."

IF THERE WERE words in the English language for what was happening with Violet, Ash hadn't learned them. But sitting on the porch together, planning football strategy, felt as close to heaven as anything he could imagine.

"So, you think that will hold Walker Larson." He studied the clipboard, trying not to be distracted by her pretty hands.

"It's the only thing I've seen work. And since it was only used on him once, by the kid from Madras, he's not expecting it."

"Good point. I wish we had another trick up our sleeves."

Violet nodded, then the right side of her mouth curved up. "Too bad we can't get Piper in as the football judge."

Ash laughed. "She is *not* OSAA approved."

Violet glanced out over the property to where they'd played football. "Your sisters are great. I've enjoyed getting to know them."

Ash settled back on the porch swing, his arm resting along the back, just over her shoulders. In the past they'd held hands, danced, his attempted tackle wound up being a hug that he wasn't ever going to forget. Could he settle his arm around her shoulders now?

Violet looked up at him. His breath got tangled up in his heartbeat, and he felt like the only way to solve this respiratory problem was to get closer to Violet.

Was this the time to kiss her?

It had been years since he'd dated. And even when he was dating, he didn't keep at it for very long. He had a list of traits he was looking for, and dating for him was more along the lines of fact-checking.

Violet made him want to write love songs.

She was laughter and challenge. The dream of dancing in the kitchen after washing up the dishes after a family meal.

It had been a long time since he'd dated, but he'd *never* felt like this.

Her gaze darted away. "Let's talk out our opening sequence. If Brayson's feeling good, I want to lean heavy on our passing game."

Ash wanted to kick himself for missing his chance to kiss her. But there was still time. They were in the first quarter of this date.

The front door banged open, and for once Ash wasn't compelled to remind his son to open the screen slowly.

"Hey, Coach."

Violet looked past Ash and waved. "Hi, Jackson. How are you?"

"Good. How's strategizing?"

Violet held up a clipboard full of the letters *X* and *O* and lots of little dotted lines.

Jackson nodded approvingly. "Let me know if I can help out."

"You sound like your dad," she said.

Jackson broke into a wide smile at the compliment. That one bright smile blinked away years of panic and worry. The kid was thriving, despite every mistake Ash made. His son was okay, and he was sitting on the porch with a beautiful woman planning strategy. This was the best day he, or anyone else, had ever had. How was it not making national news?

"I'm heading up to Grandma and Grandpa's for dinner." He indicated the apartment over the garage. Dinner with the grandparents had been Ash's idea. He and Violet had what he was calling a coaches' meeting, and this was a good opportunity for Jackson to spend some time with his grandparents before they took off for Indonesia in a few weeks, right?

Jackson, being his son, had said that sounded great.

But as the nephew of two matchmakers, he'd given Ash the side-eye while saying it.

Now Jackson was grinning as he trotted down the porch steps. "Have fun."

They both waved as Jackson walked away. Ash resettled his arm on the back of the porch swing, closer to Violet's shoulders.

"He's such a great kid," Violet said.

"He is. He was born that way."

She held up her thumb and forefinger, indicating an inch of space. "You might have had a tiny bit to do with it."

Ash placed his fingers over hers and shortened the gap. "A very tiny bit."

"You do realize parents are supposed to take credit for their kids' successes. That's why they invented Facebook."

Ash laughed.

"Truly. He's amazing. And he's grown as a leader on the team this season."

"He has," Ash agreed. "I'm glad to see him stepping up."

Violet redirected her gaze to the clipboard. "The scout from Lewis & Clark was asking about him."

"He was asking about Jackson?"

"Yeah. He told me to keep him apprised of his growth over the next few years."

"You sure he wasn't just being polite?"

Violet knit her brow. "Why would he bother being polite about a sophomore I put in for the fourth quarter? They were there to discuss Brayson."

Ash shifted. "Jackson doesn't want to play football in college."

Violet lifted her head, first staring straight ahead, then turning to look at him. "He doesn't?"

"I mean, he's never mentioned it."

"I rarely mention my desire to meet Joe Montana, but I still want to."

Ash chuckled, but he felt uncomfortable somehow. Why were these guys from Lewis & Clark talking about Jackson? Had Violet brought him up to them?

As though answering his question, Violet looked him straight in the eye and said, "He's solid. And honestly our best option for quarterback after Brayson."

He flinched, her words sloshing over him like an icy water trough.

"What?" she asked.

Ash tried to settle himself. "Nothing."

Violet kept her eyes on him, gauging his reaction, but clearly not in the mood to be swayed. "I may as well get it out there, then. I'm putting him in as backup quarterback for Brayson on Friday night."

ALL THE WARMTH and light she'd felt from Ash switched off with a clunk, like the darkening of a field after a game.

"Violet, we talked about this," he said, as though his words somehow put Jackson's position on the team into Oregon State law.

"*You* expressed your concerns about Jackson in the position." Ash tensed, but she kept going. "You said you didn't want him getting hurt out there, and neither do I. But did we as two coaches have a conversation about this? Because if we did, I'm pretty sure my word would be final."

"No, not as coaches, as…"

"As what?" she challenged, calling his bluff. Ash pulled his arm from the back of the porch swing and clasped his fingers together.

"I have to look at this as a parent not a coach."

Violet shook her head, shuffling one clipboard over another. "Ash, I'm sorry, but it's just really hard for me to understand your concerns here. What parent doesn't want his son playing quarterback?"

"The one who doesn't want his sixteen-year-old son getting pummeled on the field."

"He has a much greater chance of getting injured as an offensive tackle. You know that, right?"

Ash pressed his lips together, studying his hands. This was about more than Jackson's physical safety, but Ash didn't seem to trust her enough to tell her what was really going on.

"What is it?" she asked.

He turned to her, frustrated. "I don't want him to get hurt."

"This is football," she snapped. "You should have thought about that before signing the permission forms."

The blood washed out of his face. She'd hit too hard with that comment. Going on the offensive wasn't going to get him to open up.

Violet closed her eyes, trying to pull herself together. Her back was up, and she never responded well when she was angry. She had to choose the right words. She needed to listen. "I'm hurt that you don't think I have Jackson's best interests at heart. I love that kid."

Ash nodded, clearly trying to reel this back

in as well. "I know you do. You love all your players. But Jackson is my son."

"And Brayson is Hacker's son, and Carley is Brenn's daughter. Parents have a lot of feelings about this game—I get it."

"No, you don't get it." His glower, the one he'd used on anyone who challenged her this season, now turned on her. "You've never had kids. You've never been married. That's the problem."

Violet's chest tightened, making it impossible to breathe. She stood, moving to the edge of the porch as though physical distance from Ash could reset the conversation, take them back to her arrival.

But nothing was going to erase the real problem. He didn't trust her any more than any of the other parents who'd tried to get her to quit. He didn't respect her decisions any more than David Laurent had. She stared out at the darkening evening, anger amassing in her chest like the snowcap on the Cascade Mountains.

"You didn't even want to coach. You wanted to stay out of your son's way and let him have a football season." She turned around. "What you're doing right now is getting in the way."

She could see her words landing like darts, creating holes in his arguments. But Ash was not in the mood to back down. He stood and crossed his arms over his chest. "But I did coach, didn't I? As offensive coach, don't I get a say in who we put in as quarterback?"

"You can't have it both ways, Ash."

"But it *is* both ways."

"Fine, who goes in as second string?"

"Gabe—"

"Gabe is inconsistent, and he's not a team leader."

"I've been working with him—"

"And I appreciate that." Violet drew in a breath. Ash had been working with Gabe, tirelessly. The kid had gotten a lot better. But there were still other reasons to put Jackson in. "Gabe's a senior. We need to start developing next year's quarterback now, and in my eyes, next year's quarterback is Jackson."

This argument seemed to land. Ash glanced up at the apartment over the garage, then back at her.

Finally, he sat heavily on the porch swing, pinching the base of his ring finger. "You even gonna be here next year?"

Her lungs constricted, making her feel faint. She started to speak, then clamped her lips shut and turned away. He didn't think she'd consider staying? They'd never talked about what came next for the two of them, but he had to think there was some future, didn't he? All these feelings, the huge emotions she'd felt with Ash, were they nothing to him?

Maybe Joe Hacker had been right all along; Ash was just flirting with her to get what he wanted for his son on this team.

Violet shook her head, tried to get it together. She was overreacting. Ash was a good man. Unreasonable and frustrating right now, but good.

Violet picked up a clipboard and flipped over a couple of pages. Her voice came out small as she said, "I haven't signed a contract for another position next year."

"But you will, right? You came here to win, and you have. I've got more on the line with Jackson than just a winning season."

"This is *football*. We play to win. Are you seriously going to tell me now, after all this time, that you're not competitive?"

"I'm competitive. But I'm not willing to risk my son's safety for a win."

"What about Brayson's safety? What about Gabe's? What about Manuel, who at center is playing the most dangerous position out there?" She stepped closer. "Stop trying to pretend this is about anything other than you, just trying to shelter your son."

"Of course, I'm trying to shelter my son." Ash was exasperated, like this was the only point to any argument. "I will do everything in my power to protect Jackson."

"*Protect* and *shelter* are two vastly different words." She held his gaze, willing him to see this from her perspective. But it was only fear and doubt flickering in his eyes as he exhaled and ran a hand over his face.

All her hopes for a future with Ash, a future in Jackson's life, and with the Wallace family, washed out with that sigh. There was nothing here. Her chest felt hollow.

Violet clenched her jaw. She was not going to cry.

And the one surefire way to keep from crying was to let herself get mad.

"I don't understand how you can think for one second you're right, and I'm wrong."

"This isn't about you—it's about *my son*."

"Exactly. I can see something bigger for Jackson. And you're just holding him back."

Ash straightened, expanding his posture as his confidence in his argument shrank. Was he not looking at this clearly? Was he holding Jackson back? He tried a different tack.

"It's not just the injuries."

"Then what is it?" she cried, exasperated.

It was everything about quarterback: the stress, the pressure, the weight.

"I don't think he's ready for the position."

"And how do you get ready for the position?" Her voice shook. "You handled quarterback, why wouldn't your son?"

Ash hadn't handled quarterback; he'd borne it like all the other responsibilities of his life. Was it too much to want your kid to have fun, relaxed teenage memories? "What if he doesn't want the position?"

"He doesn't? He told you he doesn't want to play quarterback?" Violet glared at him. She was angry now, and Ash knew her well enough to know he'd stepped over the line. "Or maybe he doesn't want to upset you by admitting it. Maybe all this time Jackson has been protecting you."

The words rattled him. And the fact that Violet was probably right about this didn't make him feel one bit better.

"Why are you being so stubborn about this?" he demanded.

"Because I am stubborn. And I'm right. If you don't want to abide by my decisions, then pull your son off my team."

Her gaze connected with his as she laid down the threat. She blamed him for this, for pushing her too far, for questioning her decisions.

But they'd both gone too far. Whatever relationship they'd been weaving was delicate to begin with, like the soft, fluttering silk that hung from the wedding canopy. They'd taken their fragile bond and ripped it apart.

Why couldn't she understand that Jackson was the only non-negotiable?

Her eyes dropped, and she began picking up the clipboards. He stepped toward her. He couldn't take back what he'd said, but he could try to find some common ground, some clumsy stitching to repair their friendship. She turned her shoulder, blocking him. Her hands shook as she picked up her materials.

"You're no different than Joe Hacker. You think you know what's best for this team? Then next year you should apply for the job. But for right now, I'm the head coach. I make the decisions." Her arms were overly full, clipboards spilling off all sides. She tightened her grasp on them. "Jackson is going in as second-string quarterback against the Swarm on Friday night."

Ash turned his back, needing a second to get control of himself.

But a second was too long to ask. Violet strode down the steps, her car door slammed and gravel crunched as she pulled out of the drive. She didn't so much as tap the brakes; she just got away from him as quickly as possible. He covered his face with his hands, then pushed his fingers through his hair, keeping his hands on his head as he gulped in air.

Ash dropped into the porch swing, which was still warm from where she'd been sitting. Laughter spilled out of his parents' apartment over the garage. Ash glanced up to see his parents enjoying time with their grandson, their laughter seeming to mock his hopes for a life with Violet. And once Jackson graduated, he wouldn't have any kind of life at all.

CHAPTER SEVENTEEN

*JUST KEEP IT together through one last coaches
meeting.*

Violet glanced at Ash, leaning against a desk,
arms crossed as he kept his gaze out the window.

*Get through your coaches meeting, warm-
ups, team meeting.*

Then the most important game of the
season: the quarterfinal playoff against the
Swarm.

Violet forced her gaze onto Jet, who'd been
upbeat and cheerful ever since returning from
his honeymoon, and probably would be for
the rest of his life. He was going to have to
hold this all together because Violet was a
mess, and Ash was…well, she didn't know
what Ash was right now. He hadn't cracked a
smile all week. He barely looked at her aside
from a brisk apology before practice Monday.

*My behavior Saturday evening was un-
conscionable. I regret the way I handled our
conversation.* He'd pulled in a deep breath,

looked into her eyes and finished with, *Violet, I'm so sorry. I just don't want my son to have the pressure of quarterback.*

Then he'd walked away, not giving her time to say that she was sorry too. And as for her regrets, they just kept unfolding, one after the next.

She *knew* he didn't react logically where his son was concerned. She *knew* he was going to struggle with her decision to put Jackson in as quarterback. But where she could have considered Ash's feelings, and talked it out carefully, she'd just gotten her back up and picked a fight.

Then she'd compared him to Hacker. Could she have found a way to strike lower?

Actually yes, because what she was really doing was comparing him to Laurent.

It was *her* behavior that was unconscionable. Ash had a reason for letting his emotions get out of control—his son. She was just mad at an old boss.

Violet glanced up at the buzzing overhead lights of the team room, then faked the closest thing to a smile she could muster. "Okay, this might be our last coaches meeting." Violet passed a clipboard to each of them. "I have high hopes for tonight, but our goal was to make playoffs, and we did. If we get beaten by the Swarm tonight, they're a worthy opponent."

"I think we've got another win in us," Jet said.

Jet probably thought he could fly at the moment, but Violet was going to let that slide.

"I hope you're right." Her voice was calm, the way she'd spoken to them in the beginning, before they were all close friends. "But if we don't, let me take this moment to thank both of you. It's not an overstatement to say I could not have done this without you. You saved the team."

Ash finally looked at her. "You saved the team, Violet."

"Thank you. I feel good about my efforts," she said. "This has been a formative experience for me. But I couldn't have done it without your interference with the community and help on the field." She looked at Jet, then for the first time in a week, let her gaze connect with Ash's. "I would have failed without you."

He held her gaze and started to speak. Then he shook his head and looked out the window.

Violet blinked hard. *Just get through this.*

"Let's go over the lineup," she said.

Ash glanced down at the clipboard, then sharply back at Violet. "You've got Jackson on the line?"

"Yes. As you suggested. Gabe will be Brayson's backup for QB tonight."

Ash's brow knit. He swallowed, staring at the clipboard. Violet could at least make this a little easier for him.

"Look, I still think Jackson would make a great quarterback. But you're our offensive coordinator. I haven't questioned one suggestion Jet made on defense all season, and I shouldn't be questioning you, either." She forced out a chuckle. "I know how frustrating it can be to work with a head coach who doesn't listen."

"Violet, you—"

She met Ash's gaze as she cut him off, "I can get a little stubborn sometimes. You've been working with Gabe—you think he's ready. It's possible that you are right, and I am wrong."

A smile dusted across Ash's face, loosening the tight bandages around her heart as he said, "Or maybe it's the other way around?"

Ash loved his son. He was a good guy. Every piece of evidence pointed to a man who supported and cared for his family beyond all expectations. He had his reasons for not wanting Jackson to play quarterback, and she'd just plowed through with her own agenda.

The same way David Laurent used to dismiss her ideas when she was at Taft.

Jet, oblivious to the olive branch being passed back and forth, had his own concerns. "You've got CJ as receiver?"

"As a decoy," Violet explained.

"He's not gonna fool anyone."

"I know."

Jet shook his head. "It's like putting out a duck decoy for elk hunting."

"I've gotta put him somewhere. Plus, this is going to be CJ's great moment of the season. When he's old, he'll tell his grandchildren stories of the time he played wide receiver for the Outcrop Eagles the night we played the Swarm."

"The night we *beat* the Swarm," Jet clarified.

Violet gave him a tired smile, then nodded. "Sure. The night we beat the Swarm."

She shifted a few papers on her podium, desperately trying to hold back tears. There was a chance they could win, but she didn't feel the confidence in her bones. In all likelihood, this was her last game on the sidelines with Ash and Jet. She'd received other coaching offers, and Outcrop was only ever supposed to be a stopover for her. Her plan was unfolding just as she'd hoped, wasn't it?

Ash wanted to say more, but Violet had refocused on her pile of clipboards at the podium, lost in her own thoughts.

"Would you two mind getting team warm-ups started?" she asked. "I could use some time to focus."

"You got it, Coach." Jet headed out the door, ready to get this thing done. The guy would happily take out the Swarm on his own if OSAA rules would allow it.

Violet didn't acknowledge Ash as he remained behind.

Since the moment she'd stepped into this job, people had been questioning her decisions. And he, the one guy who should have been on her side, was the worst. There was so much he wanted to explain—about Kerri, and the past, and everything that led him to react like he did with Jackson. He wanted to thank her for keeping his son at defense. He wanted to flog himself for not trusting Jackson to do what he'd done in high school. But it all just congealed into a lump, blocking his throat.

Finally, he held up a hand. "See you out there?"

She nodded. "See you."

Ash exited the team room, his footsteps echoing down the empty hallway. He kept his head down, his hands in his pockets as he made his way to the exit toward the field. He pushed open the door and squinted into the setting sun.

"Excuse me." Ash turned to see an older couple, both wearing jeans and matching Outcrop Eagles sweatshirts. "We're looking for Coach Vi."

"She's busy right now." The couple seemed familiar, but he was pretty sure whoever they were, Violet didn't want anyone else's advice right now.

"If it's not too much trouble, would you let her know her parents are here?"

"My season ended last week, so we finally get to come up and see one of her games," the man said.

Ash's head jerked up, and he studied the couple, recognizing Violet in them—in her mom's dark wavy hair and bright smile and the glint of humor in her dad's eye. Ash would have recognized them anywhere. All of the missed possibilities flashed through him. These people could have been friends, maybe in-laws. They could have spent holidays in his home. Instead, they were just two people he would meet tonight and never see again.

Ash was overwhelmed with the random nature of the world, and the sadness of it all. He was overwhelmed, but he was still Ash, and his ingrained politeness overrode everything else. He walked down the steps and held out a hand.

"Mr. and Mrs. Fareas, it's nice to meet you. I'm Ash Wallace."

"Oh, Ash!" Mrs. Fareas held out her arms, enfolding him in a hug before he could respond. "I can't thank you enough."

Ash awkwardly took the hug. "It was my—"

His what? Duty? Pleasure?

"It was my honor to help out. Violet's an incredible coach."

Her parents beamed at each other. This wasn't late-breaking news, but they loved hearing it all the same.

"She told us all about the emu!" Mrs. Fareas peered around Ash toward the stadium. "Will it be here tonight?"

Another gentle reminder that no matter how bad things got, they could be worse.

Ash cleared his throat. "No, I don't think so."

Mr. Fareas held out his hand. "Violet said you've been an absolute hero this season. While I know she could have handled this on her own, it sounds like things would have gotten volatile without your help." His gaze connected with Ash's as they shook. "I will always be grateful for the support you gave my daughter this season."

The words swam around him. Violet was in her midthirties, and her dad still worried. He believed in her abilities but was glad when someone stepped in to help her out.

Ash studied the pavement between them, then looked up and asked, "Was it hard? Watching her play as a teenager? I understand it was your team, but—"

"It was horrifying," he said, with a big smile.

"Absolutely horrifying," her mom confirmed.

"She was just so tough out there, and fierce."

Ash imagined a teenage Violet, stalking out onto the field, alive with determination.

The image reminded him of his own son.

Maybe his fear wasn't entirely for Jackson; maybe it was for himself too. He was still scarred by the experience with Kerri. She'd hurt him, humiliated him, shaken his self-knowledge to the core. If he could rope himself and his son into that situation, what other bad choices was he capable of? He'd been using his son to shield his heart and excuse his indulgence in hunkering down behind his family.

He wasn't just afraid of Jackson getting hurt—he was afraid of Jackson growing up.

Then Violet had arrived at Eighty Local

with far more coaching manuals and clipboards than a human can juggle, and she'd cracked his charade wide open. He was exposed and uncertain. Ash ran a palm over his chest as he accepted the truth.

He was scared by everything he felt for Violet Fareas.

"Well, she's still pretty fierce," Ash said. "We're lucky to have her."

"How'd practice go this week?" Mr. Fareas asked. "We haven't talked to her since the last game."

Ash looked up. Okay, they hadn't heard from Violet since he was unconscionably rude and questioned her decisions. Which explained why they were being so nice right now.

"I'll let her tell you about it." Ash pointed over his shoulder. "I think Violet's in the team room. Let me run in and check, and if she is, I'll send her out."

He would send her out, just as soon as he said what he needed to.

"We don't want to bother her if she's getting ready."

"She'll want to see you."

Ash headed back into the building, heart racing. He paused at the open door to the team room. Violet's head was bent over the podium, her dark hair falling around her soft face, eyes unfocused.

She was so, so beautiful. And if he'd messed this up and lost all chances with her, he could own that. He wouldn't be happy about it, but he'd learn from it.

But he wasn't going to let this go without a fight.

"I HAVE SOMETHING I need to say to you."

Violet kept her eyes on the podium as confident footsteps brought Ash back into the room. It would have been nice to mourn the end of her sojourn in Outcrop, the end of this season and the end of her whatever it was with Ash alone, without a final raking over the coals.

But this was Outcrop.

Violet nodded, pulling in a breath. "Okay."

She made the mistake of looking at him. Jeans, boots and an old Outcrop Eagles sweatshirt from his own days as a player. How was it that after spending a lifetime with men who loved their expensive kicks and of-the-moment fade haircuts, she'd fallen for the guy in a pair of worn-in Wranglers?

He looked into her eyes, back at his hands, then his gaze ran across her face like it sometimes did when he couldn't seem to take his eyes off her. She was an expert at camouflaging herself to blend in with a football field, and yet he managed to look straight past all her armor.

"I got married when I was twenty-two, to a woman I never should have asked out on a second date. We got pregnant right away. Despite every sign that she wasn't a responsible mom, I took an overseas deployment. I did it for the money, and I did it because Kerri was hard to be around."

He took a deep breath and held out his hand, signaling to her that he needed to get this out.

"I came back to find out she'd been leaving Jackson home alone, for hours at a time, when he was as young as four. She'd lock him in his room, and he'd cry, and she'd just—" His voice cracked. He covered his eyes with one hand, like he could shield himself from the memory. "—take off."

He swallowed hard. Violet took a step toward him. He shook his head.

"That's not the worst of it. I kept trying with her. I couldn't believe that I, Ash Wallace, had made such a huge mistake and married the wrong woman. I kept trying. I spent *six years* of Jackson's childhood, fighting to turn her into someone she was never going to be. I kept both of us in a relationship with an unstable person because I didn't want to fail."

Violet blinked hard. She could imagine this strong, principled man working to keep his marriage together, and getting tangled deeper and deeper into a bad situation he never should have been in. She knew exactly how he felt.

"So when I think my son is in danger, I assume it's my fault. I assume that his pain is due to my negligence. I know I'm holding him back—I can feel it. I know I'm destroying—" he swallowed, gesturing between the two of them "—I know what I'm losing here."

Tears broke, and the strong cowboy let them roll. He gazed at her through his pain. "What I don't know is how to change. But, Violet, you have to believe me when I tell you how much I want to."

Violet moved toward him. Ash wiped the sleeve of his sweatshirt against his face, shaking his head slightly. "We've got a game, Vi."

"I know." She kept walking toward him. "But you don't get to come storming in, dropping apologies, and not let me say anything. *I'm* sorry. I'm so used to having to fight to be heard that I forget to listen. Your opinion matters to me, as a coach, as a parent—" Violet swallowed, closing her eyes to get the words out "—as a friend."

Her gaze met his, unleashing the rushing freedom Ash inspired in her.

"Since the moment we met, you've been supporting me. I should have listened and supported you with any concerns you had about Jackson." Violet reached out and took his hand, weaving her fingers through his. "But I want you to know that whatever happens—" she gestured between them with her free hand "—I've loved this."

A glimmer of a smile brushed his lips. Ash gave her hand a tug, pulling her closer. Violet tugged back and pulled him in a step.

Just as a really loud knock sounded at the outside door.

Ash dropped her hand. "Oh, man. I almost forgot. There are some folks here who want to talk to you."

Violet shook her head. Ash had poured his heart out; they were on the verge of the biggest game of the season, and possibly on the verge of something else, and he was suggesting she meet with someone?

He darted out of the room.

"Unless it's Joe Montana, I'm really not interested," she called after him.

"No, not *some* folks." His voice echoed

from the hallway as he headed to the outside door. "*Your* folks are here."

"Wait, my parents?" Violet ran after Ash, and collided with her mom as she came in the double doors.

Her mom's strong, soft embrace lifted every fear and worry from her chest. Dad blocked the overhead light as he put his arms around the two of them, and Violet was engulfed in the warm shelter of her family. Her parents' words of greeting and love filled her heart, strengthening her. Everything felt so right that when she looked up, she was surprised to find Ash wasn't there getting in on the hug.

Mom stepped back but kept a hand on her arm as she gave her a warm smile. "It looks like you're doing great!"

"Head Coach Violet Fareas." Dad beamed at her.

They were *so* proud. She didn't know where things stood with Ash or even if there *were* things with Ash anymore. But making her parents proud and repaying her dad for the sacrifice he'd made were the goals she'd come to Outcrop with.

"I've loved being a head coach." Violet faked a smile and floated out one of the options before her. "Currently, I have an offer to take over a larger team in Eugene and I'm talking with Lewis & Clark, which is exciting."

Her parents exchanged a long look. "You're thinking of leaving Outcrop?"

"Well, yeah. Maybe. That was always the plan."

"We thought the plan might have changed," Dad said.

"Dad, you sacrificed so much to have me on your team," Violet reminded him. "I want to do you proud and coach a college team in your honor."

Her parents had another quick, nonverbal exchange, then Dad asked, "What exactly did I sacrifice by having the all-state cornerback on my team? I'm not remembering a huge sacrifice."

Violet's heartbeat fumbled. Her stated reason for wanting to coach D III was always honoring her dad's sacrifice. *Getting back at my old boss* sounded petty.

"I don't want to sell my parenting short here, but any coach would have wanted you on their team. I did, however, take you to all those indie rock shows, and the screaming, angry band concert in LA." He shuddered.

"Yeah, no, thank you for putting up with the metal phase." Violet redirected the conversation to fit the narrative she'd cultivated, "I want to honor all the time and effort and energy you put into helping me develop as a player, so I'd get a chance to play in high school and college."

"Violet, *you* put in the time and energy. *I* was hanging out in the backyard playing my favorite game with my phenomenally talented daughter."

Violet faltered. "But, how cool would it be if you knew your inspiration helped me become a college coach?"

"If coaching college ball made you happy, it would be cool."

The right side of Mom's mouth quirked up. "If you like administrative details and directing a large staff, by all means, go for it. We support you in your goals."

"Personally, I chose to stay at the high school level because I love developing a team over the years, connecting with families, watching kids grow. And I got to coach *my daughter* on the team." Dad's eyes teared up a little. She didn't get her big emotions out of nowhere.

"You seem so happy here," Mom said. "Happier than you've been in years. According to your uncle Mel, you've made good friends, and your team is thriving."

Violet let her mom's words settle in her chest. She was happy. Still confused about Ash. Still salty about Hacker. But she felt alive, and like the opportunity to coach in this town was worth fighting for.

She looked up to see her mom giving her the raised-brow once-over. "But if you, my competitive daughter, are going for a college coaching position because you think outranking David Laurent will finally make that man realize he was wrong about you, that's not going to happen. You could be the head coach of the Green Bay Packers and Laurent will still be talking smack. He's a sad, unhappy man. You're a gifted athlete and coach, and that's always going to make him mad." Mom slipped her arm around Violet's shoulders. "And happiness really is the best revenge."

Wow. Okay. *Mom never was one to pull her punches.*

Could she stay here, even if things with Ash were, well, in ashes? There might be a future with her cowboy, but could she build her team here, even if she were certain there wasn't?

Her whole life, every major decision she made had been guided by football. No, scratch that, *all* her decisions had been guided by football. And as far as life guideposts went, football wasn't the worst. She'd make this decision based on her love of the sport, and everyone else could learn to live with it.

But right now, she had a team meeting to lead. She needed to inspire her players if they were going to exterminate the Swarm.

CHAPTER EIGHTEEN

MANUEL WAS ALWAYS the first to break through the paper banner as the Eagles raced onto the field. It was a point of pride, and Ash could respect that. Most games, by the time the large lineman came barreling through, there wasn't much of a banner left. But today Jackson was challenging Manuel for the break, which kicked in Brayson's competitive spirit, and he was faster than both of them. No one counted on Carley, who was not only fast but stealthy. She turned on the wheels and ripped through the banner first.

The crowd went wild.

Bend was less than forty minutes south of Outcrop, so the visitors' stands were packed. That explained the Tesla-choked parking lot and the massive glare coming off the Ray-Ban Aviator sunglasses across the field.

The Swarm's coach, a former NFL player, waved to Violet as she walked onto the field. She waved back. While Ash understood that Violet's wave to a competitor shouldn't fill him with jealousy, logic wasn't his strong suit this week.

But then she glanced at him as they neared the sidelines, a flush rising to her cheeks as she smiled. That one shy smile obliterated any other feelings. Ash was completely unaware of anything else as they lined up, listened to the anthem and moved through the coin toss.

Suddenly, the teams were squaring off. The whistle blew, and the game they'd been anticipating all season long started.

The kids had never played with such focus. Flowing on and off the field, each doing their utmost in the position they were asked to play.

But for every player they had, the Swarm had three. When a kid playing for the Eagles got tired, he dug deep and found another gear. When a player for the Swarm got tired, he took a rest, had some water and watched from the bench while someone just as good took his place on the field.

The Eagles were well coached. But so was the Swarm, who led twenty-one to twelve at halftime. Then, three plays into the third quarter, Brayson connected with Joaquin in the end zone, cutting the deficit to two points.

It wasn't until Brayson came trotting off the field that they noticed his limp.

"How's your knee?" Violet asked.

"Fine."

She raised her brows.

"It hurts," he admitted. "I just need to walk it off."

Violet pinned him with a look. Brayson raised his arms in innocence. "It's just a cramp in my quad. If I walk for a few minutes, I'll be fine."

Violet nodded reluctantly. "Go get some water. Gabe can take the next play."

Gabe sucked in a breath like he was diving into a freezing-cold lake, then headed in. Ash feared he wouldn't remember to exhale until he resurfaced.

"You can't breathe for him," Violet commented, coming to stand next to Ash.

He chuckled. "Sorry, just enjoying the fresh mountain air."

She laughed and glanced up at him, her gaze connecting with his. A ref's whistle blew, and they both turned to the field. Gabe had a false start, giving the team a five-yard penalty.

"Shake it off," she called, clapping her hands encouragingly.

Mr. Katz must have had the same idea, as the band began playing the Taylor Swift hit by the same name. Maisy, Clara and Joanna picked up the song and began leading the stands in singing.

"Just when I think this town can't get any weirder," Violet muttered.

Gabe tried his best to do as his coach and Ms. Swift instructed, but it wasn't any use. Violet sent Brayson back in after three plays.

With nine minutes left in the game, the Eagles were holding strong, just two points down at twenty-one to nineteen. Considering some of the blowouts the Swarm had this season, the Eagles were phenomenal. But the players didn't just want to do well. They wanted to win.

The ref's whistle blew, and Brayson caught the snap, then tucked the ball under his arm and started to run. Jackson and his friends held the line. Brayson had a clear lane, but he was moving slowly. Ash glanced at the kid's face, locked in a painful grimace as he gutted it out. The Swarm safety swooped in and barely had to tap him before he crumpled.

Maisy got to the quarterback before anyone else. When she looked up, Ash could read everything he needed to know on her face. Brayson wasn't going back in this season.

FANS APPLAUDED AS Brayson limped off the field with his coach under one arm and the town doctor under the other. Violet got him settled on a bench, and Maisy took over. These kids had given their all, and she knew they should all be satisfied with a close score.

They *should* be satisfied, but they wouldn't be.

Ash jogged toward her, face set. For half a second, she forgot they'd ever argued.

For half a second, she considered wrapping her arms around him.

"How's he doing?"

"He's out." Violet pressed her lips together. Saying it made it real. This kid, who had come so, so far this season, was done. He needed to save his knee for a lifetime of fun and adventure, not to mention Lewis & Clark University, and she wouldn't have it obliterated just so they could beat the Swarm.

She glanced at the visitors' stands. Why did all those parents have to look so smug?

"Okay." Ash nodded. "I think we should put Jackson in."

Violet had already taken three steps toward the sidelines when the sentence caught up with her. Jackson?

"Gabe's jumpy tonight. And when he starts on a downward spiral—"

Violet spun around. Ash gazed into her eyes; she could tell exactly how hard this was for him. He cleared his throat, then continued, "When Gabe starts on a downward spiral, he has a hard time shaking it off. Jackson does pretty well with this type of pressure."

Violet lifted her brow, questioning him.

He shrugged. "As your offensive coordinator, I think it's the best plan of action. But you should do what you want to do." He gave her the tiniest glimmer of a smile. "I'm not going to question your decisions on the field." His smile grew. "Ever again."

Violet gave herself a full three seconds to stare at Ash, then she stepped around him. "Jackson. You're in."

Jackson leaped onto the field like an emu escaping its pen.

The ref blew his whistle, and play resumed.

The score remained close. Outcrop edged ahead with a field goal; Bend responded with a touchdown and extra point. The Swarm had clearly studied Outcrop's game plan as much as Outcrop had the Swarm's. With forty-six seconds left in the fourth quarter, the Swarm was up thirty-one to twenty-seven. The Eagles had the ball and needed a touchdown, but the Swarm wasn't giving up a single inch of the field.

Violet called a time-out, and Carley stormed

over to the sidelines, furious as she pulled off her helmet. "They have three guys on me."

"I know," Violet said.

"I can't get any traction. Same with Joaquin. I *hate* the Swarm."

"That's a strong word," Ash admonished her.

"That's a fine word," Jet said, dropping a hand on Carley's shoulder.

Violet studied the field. They had less than a minute left in the game, and Carley was right. Their rival had figured out that if they could stop Carley and Joaquin, they could keep Outcrop from scoring.

"We need to try something new. Jackson, could you do a quick handoff to Soren, then fake a throw. If they fall for it, they'll focus on Carley and Joaquin, and Soren can at least move the ball down the field."

"Yes, Coach."

"Okay, let's do it."

"Wait!" A voice from outside the circle interrupted them. It was CJ. "I haven't been in yet this game."

Violet stared at her most enthusiastic, least coordinated player. She'd promised at the beginning of the season that she'd do her best to give everyone playing time every game. She didn't need to look at the stands to know that

CJ's parents, grandparents and various second and third cousins waited to watch.

"Okay. You're in for Devin."

"Yes!"

"Go, get in there. Let's finish this up." Violet glanced at the clock.

"It's not over yet," Jet said.

As they headed back out to the field, Jackson put his hand on CJ's back and said something to him. CJ beamed in response. Carley joined them as they jogged onto the field. Jackson motioned for everyone to huddle up.

But he didn't simply call the play, and it didn't look like a pep talk. Jackson seemed deadly serious as he spoke at length about... something.

Violet let out a sharp breath. They'd gone into this game knowing the Swarm was a worthy opponent. And if they went down in the second round of playoffs, they'd still have had an incredible season.

At the line, Jackson called the cadence and caught the long snap. His handoff to Soren was clean, but Soren seemed to fumble briefly, then cut right as Jackson pulled back to fake a pass.

The Swarm's defense picked up on the intention immediately, players running toward Soren as he started down the field.

The crowd gasped. Violet tore her eyes off what looked like the certain demise of Soren's run.

Then the ball was in the air.

She glanced back at Soren who still pretended to have the ball and kept running, distracting at least one of the tackles.

The ball flew to Carley, and two defenders were closing in as she leaped to catch it. CJ was inexplicably running toward her as well. Violet glanced at the clock. When they tackled her, they'd still have a few seconds left.

Carley landed lightly, ball in hands, just as the cornerback reached her. In the defender's grasp she made a lateral pass, tossing the ball gently, an underhand throw one might use to pass a Nerf ball to a child. And CJ, who no opposing coach, defensive back or tackle had paid one second of attention to all season long, was exactly where he was supposed to be. He caught that ball and ran.

It was a full second before the crowd caught on. CJ stood in the end zone, gripping the ball, looking around, as though checking to make sure he was in the right place.

Everyone in the stadium leaped to their feet and roared.

CJ's face lit up; he raised his arms in triumph as the entire team rushed him. Violet's vision blurred immediately; she opened her mouth to cheer, and a big messy sob choked out.

This cry was gonna get so ugly.

Solid, strong arms wrapped around her, pulling her head to Ash's chest. Violet sobbed in complete happiness and pride. He pulled her tighter against him. The horn buzzed, and a cheer went up through Outcrop that could probably be heard in New Mexico. Ash readjusted his arms around her, and Violet cried harder. She pressed her cheek against Ash's sweatshirt, breathing in his scent, knowing she'd have to get control of these messy emotions at some point but unwilling to think about when that had to happen.

"Coach Vi, up high!"

Violet took one, last deep breath of Ash Wallace before stepping back. She loved Manuel, and as center, he'd played an incredible game and deserved her attention. Violet turned around and began the Outcrop Defense high five sequence. Ash kept close, leaving a hand on her shoulder blades. She desperately wanted to ask him to keep his hand on her back forever.

"Party at the Broughman house!" Jet's voice came booming over the speakers.

Ash and Violet looked up to see Jet and

Clara standing in the press box, speaking into the microphone. "All Outcrop is invited to Broughman Ranch for a celebration."

"You're not going to try to grill again, are you?" Kessler heckled from the stands.

"Hunter Wallace is loading up his truck now with fare from Eighty Local, so you're all safe. But the party's on us. We beat the Swarm!"

A cheer rose through the stands. Violet looked up at Ash. If he offered her a ride tonight, she was taking it.

"Coach Vi?" It was John McMannis from Lewis & Clark, with two other men. "Congratulations." He held out a hand. Violet forced herself to turn toward him, to shake his hand. Out of the corner of her eye she saw Jackson run up to Ash.

"Give me just a second," Violet said to the recruiters, before turning back to Jackson. "*How* did you come up with that brilliant play?"

He looked at Ash, then at her. "It's the same play you used with Aunt Clara at the family game, remember? When you picked Dad's pass and we won." Jackson's smile grew brighter. "I wasn't sure if it would work, but you said we needed to try something new."

She pointed a finger at him. "You are good."

Jackson shrugged. "I had some great coaches."

She stared at her grinning quarterback and finally admitted to herself how much she wished she were more of a mom than a coach to this incredible kid.

"Coach Vi?" John McMannis interrupted her again. "If we could have a second of your time."

Ash held her gaze for a second, then nodded to the recruiters. "Looks like you've got some business to take care of."

She gave him a wry smile, then spoke to John. Ash's parents arrived, congratulating Jackson and replaying the highlights of the game.

The crowd moved around them like water, the waves of people separating her from Ash. Parents poured out of the stands, coming to find their players. As Violet watched families connecting with their kids, she understood how natural it was for parents to question her decisions from time to time—not because they didn't trust her, but because they needed more information to understand her process and allay their own fears.

And when she dug her heels in and got angry, that didn't facilitate a lot of understanding.

Violet glanced up to see Joe Hacker and Greg Larsabal heading toward her. She scanned the surrounding area for her parking lot cowboy, but Ash was now fifty yards away, talking with his family.

She squared her shoulders. Hacker and Larsabal stopped in front of her.

Time slowed dramatically. Everything they'd all wanted to say all season long seemed to back up the clock, weighing down the hands of time.

Finally, Joe Hacker's mustache twitched, and he met her eye. "Good game."

Violet gave him a nod. She dug deep, as deep as any of the Eagles had that evening, then cleared her throat and said, "Brayson held the team together out there. Your kid's an athlete." She glanced at Greg Larsabal. "Soren too."

"Good season," Larsabal grunted, then mumbled, "We didn't know things were so bad with Kessler." He shook his head and blew out a breath. "Cancer." He looked at Joe, then said to Violet, "It's good you could step in this season."

"My pleasure," she said, remembering her words to Brayson, *Everyone deserves a second chance.* Even these guys, as hard as it was going to be to give it to them.

"Greg! Joe!" Jet materialized between the two men. "Party at my house, let's go."

Clara smiled brightly up at Jet. "And we've got that thing for Joe, back at our place, don't we?"

"Oh yeah!" Jet turned to Joe Hacker. "We found some forks you left on the practice field. But don't worry, we collected them all and have them for you. Hunter says you're free to bring your own silverware into Eighty Local until you've used them all up." His bright grin suggested that Joe Hacker wasn't going to be welcome in Eighty Local without his own fork for a long, long time.

Clara's soft hand slipped into Violet's, and she tugged, still smiling at Hacker and Larsabal as she said, "Let's go, Violet! Larry's waiting in his pen to see you!"

CHAPTER NINETEEN

OF ALL TIMES *for there to be a traffic jam in*
Outcrop.

Certainly, everyone was excited about the
win, and eager to celebrate in Jet and Clara's
beautiful home with free food from Eighty
Local. But didn't anyone realize that Ash
needed to speak with Violet? He'd left her
on the sidelines with scouts from Lewis &
Clark. Who knew what they'd offered her.
The moon?

It was no less than she deserved.

It had taken a lifetime to get out of the
school parking lot, then the whole town had
felt the need to drive slowly while honking
their horns in celebration. And now, they had
completely choked Jet's long driveway with
their haphazard victory parking.

Fortunately, Ash knew the Broughman
property better than most.

He spun the wheel, truck tires bumping
up off the driveway and over the front pas-
ture. Ash parked next to the newly renovated

cabin, hopped out of his truck and started running. He could hear the party spilling out of the brightly lit house. The moon hung huge and cold in the sky. Ash hopped a fence and put on some speed.

He planned to walk in the house, politely ask Violet to speak alone and tell her everything he should have said the day he met her. *You are the most incredible woman. You make me stronger, better. I want to walk next to you for as long as you'll let me.*

A noise distracted Ash from his thoughts. Something massive was moving toward him, *running* toward him.

Something massive, covered in feathers and squawking loudly.

Ash cut right to avoid the emu, but Larry and six of his closest friends all turned and ran with him. Ash came to the gate, and if he wasn't exactly able to get it shut behind him, well, it wasn't the first time these emus had gotten out.

He sped across the moonlit patio and lunged for the kitchen door, closing it behind him before Larry and his friends could join the party.

Jackson sat on the counter, a basket of house-made tortilla chips in his hands, chatting with Hunter.

"What are you two doing in the kitchen?" Ash asked.

"Waiting for the rest of the family?" Hunter said with a wink to Jackson.

A soft bump sounded on the window over the sink. Ash looked past Hunter to see Larry grinning at him through the glass.

"Dad, did you let the emus out?"

Ash waved a hand, dismissing the massive birds. There was a lot to get done this evening, and it wasn't his fault that Jet's pet emus had no personal boundaries.

Before he moved forward with Violet, there was something he needed to clear up with his son.

"Jackson, do you want to play quarterback?"

Nephew and uncle exchanged another look.

"Yeah. Of course." His bright blue eyes lit up. "I love playing quarterback, just like you."

Ash closed his eyes briefly. "You sure? It's a lot of pressure."

Noise and laughter from the party filtered into the kitchen, mingling with the sound of Larry and company bumping their beaks against the back window, trying to join in.

"I can handle it, Dad."

Ash nodded. "Okay then. I'm sorry I didn't see that earlier. You just...you had a real different childhood than I wanted for you. I don't always know the best way to make up for that."

"Dad, you don't have to make up for anything."

"Kerri was…" Ash cleared his throat. "Kerri was difficult, for both of us. You didn't have an easy childhood."

"But think about what I *do* have," Jackson said, sounding a lot like his grandma. "I have our whole family, which is awesome. Bowman is Firefighter of the Year. And Jet's the Exterminator. Do you know how cool that is?"

Ash nodded. Both Jet and Bowman were local heroes in their own way. Hunter reached out and turned on the faucet, picking up a knife to wash.

"And Hunter, the guy who runs the best restaurant in central Oregon, or anywhere, is my uncle. Everyone's jealous." Hunter stopped washing the knife, listening in as Jackson spoke. "I mean, I don't want to say it gives me street cred because—" Jackson pointed in the general direction of Outcrop.

"Right. There aren't that many streets."

"And half of them aren't even paved. But Hunter's *my* uncle. How can you even think I don't have the best family in Outcrop?"

Ash nodded. "You did win the uncle lottery."

"And the aunt lottery, and the grandparent

lottery. And you. Some guys have Joe Hacker for a dad. I got you."

Ash studied the ceiling, wondering what would constitute an ugly cry. He glanced at his brother, who was focusing very hard on the window over the sink, also trying not to cry.

"So maybe, you could stop worrying about all of us for once and start thinking about yourself. You need to ask someone out for a second date."

Ash tried to glower at his son, but the flush rising up his neck made that difficult. He cleared his throat. "What do you... Do you know about...?"

"You and Coach Vi? It's obvious. And awesome. So go." He gestured to the living room with a chip, then ate it.

Ash didn't move. Jackson sighed. "Look, I'm not a great matchmaker, like my aunts. But I *have* been trying."

Ash furrowed his brow, questioning his son.

"*I* invited her over to dinner, *I* reminded Aunt Clara to invite her to the wedding. I thought I'd succeeded, but no, you two still have to think about it, or whatever."

"You've been trying to set me up with Coach Vi?"

"Obviously. She's the GOAT."

Ash studied the floor between them. "I may have messed up there. I'm not sure she's going to stay in Outcrop."

Jackson crossed his arms and gave a fledgling glower that would be fierce in about ten years. "You don't think you might be able to change her mind?"

Ash glanced behind him into the living room.

"Enough of this." Hunter took Ash by the shoulders and spun him in the direction of the living room. "If you let her get away, you'll forfeit any credibility you have as the responsible one in this family. She is smart, gorgeous and pretty much the only woman I've ever met strong enough to keep up with you."

"Seriously, Dad, get out there. That guy from Lewis & Clark is here, too, and he's not just interested in Brayson."

Ash stood at the threshold. What would happen if he succeeded? What would life be like if Violet stayed and this unpredictable, overwhelming feeling he had for her became part of his everyday life?

A loud thunk sounded against the back window. Larry grinned at him. Who was he kidding? Life was already unpredictable and overwhelming. With Violet, taking on that challenge was fun.

Ash stalked into the living room, as well as any man can stalk in a room packed wall to wall with people. Violet shone on the far side of the room, like she was surrounded by her own personal spotlight.

Someone yelled, "Speech!" and others joined in. Violet glanced at her parents, who nodded back and smiled.

Violet moved to the landing by the front door. "Thank you all for joining in the celebration tonight."

"Thank you for giving us something to celebrate!" Brenn Theis called, holding up a beer.

Violet teared up but managed to keep going. She spoke lovingly of her players, their work and commitment. CJ got almost as many minutes in the limelight as he'd played that season. Finally, she drew in a deep breath and wiped a tear from her eye. "It's been my pleasure to coach the Outcrop Eagles this year." She paused, looking around at the faces of her players. "And I have an announcement to make."

Then she looked at the recruiter from Lewis & Clark.

Ash could feel his blood pounding in his ears. He had to speak now.

"Regarding next season, I'm excited to announce—"

"Now hold up." Ash was surprised at how loud that came out. He cleared his throat and unsuccessfully tried to drop the volume. "Hold up."

The crowd parted like it had Violet's first day in Outcrop, only this time they were staring at him rather than her. Violet's deep brown eyes met his.

"I don't think you should be in such a rush to leave." He sent a stern look to the scouts from Lewis & Clark. "There's a lot to consider before you make a move."

Violet crossed her arms over her chest. "Such as?"

Ash glanced around the room. His eyes landed on Mr. and Mrs. Fareas, standing next to Violet's parents. He gestured in their direction. "There's your uncle and aunt. They're getting older." Mr. Fareas scowled at him. Ash was well aware he was shooting himself in the foot here as far as local commerce went, but he kept going. "They need someone around to call in case anything comes up… health-wise."

Mr. Fareas gave a disgusted snort. Any special treatment Ash had ever received at the OHTAF flew right out the window. Violet smiled at her uncle, then trained her eyes back on Ash. "Anything else I should consider?"

"Yep." Ash nodded, gesturing at three women near the fireplace. "There's Three Sisters Chocolatiers. I understand business is up since you came to town, and if you leave, well, what's that gonna do to the local economy?"

Violet reddened but kept her chin high. "I'm pretty sure they have a website I can order from."

"Okay then." Ash put his hands on his hips and studied the floor. "You really need to consider the team. Coach Kessler's recovering, but he's not coming back. He's earned a break, and you know he won't hand over the team to anyone who's not worthy of it. That's you. You're the only choice." Everyone cheered in agreement. Ash nodded, looking around the room. "You can't leave these kids without a coach."

"You make a good point, Wallace." She pinned him with her gaze. "Anything else?"

It was time for the truth.

"Then there's me. I haven't been pulling my weight around this town for a long time. But you show up and within a half an hour, I'm volunteering again. I haven't laughed much in the last few years. I haven't felt this good. But now that you're here…"

Her gaze connected with his. Memories of airborne training flooded him, his heart pounding at the back of the plane, the sharp bark of the noncommissioned officer, the rush of empty air beneath him.

The power of tugging one cord, then the grace and thrill of flying.

"Violet, I'm in love with you. I love everything about you. And…and I think you're… well, I think you like me too." He crossed his arms and looked down at his boots. Then he shook his head and met her gaze. "No, I think you *love* me. We work well together. We *are* well together. With you, everything is easier…it's more fun…it's…it's right." He gestured between them. "So, yeah. Us. That's my final argument. Stay here. Let's do this."

Ash wasn't sure how he'd made it to the front of the room, only that he was now standing very close to Violet. She gazed at him, and the right side of her mouth rose. "I was trying to tell everyone I've decided to stay to coach the Eagles next year, but if you want to keep convincing me, by all means, go ahead." She pressed her lips together in a smile, then said, "This is fun."

Ash placed his palm along her soft cheek,

like he'd wanted to do since the day he first saw her. She didn't step away. He moved closer, running his other hand around her waist. She grinned up at him.

Ash leaned toward her, and everything else vanished. Her hands wound through his hair, pulling him closer. Her lips touched his, and everything in his world that had been knocked out of place came into perfect order. He wrapped his arms more tightly around her, falling farther into her kiss: warm, sweet, safe, free.

Violet started to pull back. Ash locked his arms more tightly around her. This was *not* the time to be moving apart. Closer was the only thing that made sense; surely she got that. Noise rushed his ears. He glanced up and only then remembered they were *not* the only two people in the world.

Whistles, catcalls, cheers and the entire Eagles football team surrounded them. Ash looked at the players—a rowdy, imperfect bunch. His gaze locked with Jackson's, and his son gave him a thumbs-up. Ash readjusted his arms around Violet, easy but solid around her.

"You're gonna stay?"

"I am." Her pretty brown eyes looked up

into his. "But if you can think of any more arguments, I'm listening."

Ash leaned down to whisper in her ear. "I have a lot of arguments."

She grinned, dropping her voice as she asked, "How long before we're able to get out of here so I can hear them?"

Ash glanced at the players surrounding them, and at his community surrounding the players. Then, in one swift movement, he swept Violet off her feet.

"Sorry, kids. Coach Vi and I have some strategizing to do."

She wrapped her arms more securely around his neck. Ash closed his eyes briefly and cradled her closer. Loving Violet Fareas was the only game plan he needed.

EPILOGUE

"PIE SHOULD BE served directly after Thanksgiving dinner," Bowman said, appealing to everyone else at the table. "It's dessert, not a separate meal."

"No, pie should be served at least an hour after the meal, so you can make room for it." Clara had her hands on the table, ready to stand. "You eat Thanksgiving dinner, you take a nice walk or play a game, *then* you have pie."

"If you were worried about room for pie, maybe you shouldn't have eaten so much," Hunter told her.

"If we weren't supposed to eat so much, why did you make the food taste so good?" Piper shook her head. "This is literally your fault, Hunter."

Jackson, family peacemaker that he was, came up with what Violet thought was the best solution. "People who want to can eat pie now, then we'll play football. After that, we'll all have room for more pie. And the chocolates Coach Vi brought."

"I like the logic," her dad said, glancing at Ash. "Your son has it all figured out."

Dad was right—Jackson had a lot figured out. He'd stepped in as quarterback for the last game of the season. They lost that semifinal game and didn't make it to the state playoffs, but the game was close. Jackson and the other returning players were already talking about winning state next year.

And so was she.

It was incredible how easy it was to make the right decision when that decision turned out to be exactly what she wanted. All the years of struggle and frustration had landed her in this town, with this man. She was grateful for her difficult experience at Taft because it helped her become the woman who would thrive here.

"Do you want pie now?" Ash asked her.

Violet shook her head. "No, I don't want anything that's gonna slow me down for this rematch."

Ash nodded seriously. "You'll want a consolation prize after my team wins."

"No, I'll be hungry after picking your passes and scoring with them."

Ash drew her hands into his and gazed at her, his eyes warm and brilliant. Then he stood, tugging at her hand. "Come talk to me on the front porch for a second? I want to ask you about something."

"More strategy?" Piper asked.

"Something like that." Ash wound his fingers more tightly around Violet's. Her palm snuggled against his, right where it wanted to be.

Hunter shook his head, mock serious. "You two do a lot of 'planning' for a sport that's not even in season."

"'Eagles football never sleeps,'" Violet quoted Coach Kessler. She'd learned the best way to deal with Wallace sibling banter was to flip it right back on them. If conversation was a competitive sport around here, Violet was in training. But for the moment, her coach seemed to have other plans.

"Quit hassling her," Ash commanded. "She's not one of your sisters."

Hunter looked at Bowman, whose crooked grin spread across his face. Piper coughed dramatically, and Clara clapped her hands together. That got Ash talking, fast. "Hold up, here—"

But it was no use. Hunter spoke over him. "She's not one of my sisters...*yet*!"

Violet felt a sharp tug at her fingers as Ash stalked out of the room, taking her with him. His posture made him look annoyed, but Violet could detect a little smile playing around his lips.

Cold, crisp air surrounded them as the screen door clapped shut. The late November day was clear with the sun already edging toward the mountains, even though it wasn't quite four o'clock. The day before, Ash and his father had strung holiday lights along the farmhouse and outbuildings in anticipation of the upcoming season. Within the next month there would be a tree lighting, a big mistletoe festival at the ranch and the grand opening of Hunter's events center at Eighty Local. Violet knew, deep within her, that she belonged at all of it. She'd finally found her place.

Ash drew her next to him, into their own quiet world of sunset and porch swing. Violet settled under his arm, his body warming hers.

She snuggled closer to Ash, the very best place to be.

He gazed down at her, something new in his hazel eyes. Piper was right, there *had* been a lot of strategy sessions over the last month. Conversations about goals and values mingling with laughter and lots of time tucked up under his arm. At the end of each session, Violet came to the same conclusion: Ash Wallace was an incredible man. He wasn't without his faults, which was fortunate because neither was she. Together they created something stronger, more flexible and freeing.

Ash cleared his throat, like he wanted to say something but wasn't sure where to begin. Violet bit her lip, gazing at him. Speaking wasn't entirely necessary. Kissing, for instance, was another option. Ash searched her eyes for a long moment, then gave that strong, confident nod.

He reached into the pocket of his shirt and leaned his lips toward her ear. He hesitated there, and she could almost hear him smiling. His hand slipped over hers and something cool slid along her finger.

"Marry me," he whispered.

Violet looked up into his eyes, then down at her hand where a ring of diamonds circled her finger. She gazed up at Ash again, then back to the diamonds because...*wow*.

It was her turn to be speechless.

Ash looked into her eyes. "Will you?"

"Yes." She placed her hands on both sides of his face. "Yes! Absolutely. This is a fantastic idea!" It all hit her in that moment. They were going to be married. She would live in this house, at Wallace Ranch. She would be a part of this wonderful family.

She would be Jackson's stepmom.

She could strategize with Ash Wallace for the rest of her life.

"We're gonna get so married, other married people will look like they're on a first date. The institution of marriage isn't gonna know what hit it. We will crush this."

His face lit up. "You're in?"

"All in."

"Then let's do this!" He stood and pulled her to her feet, wrapped his arms around her, then dipped her in a kiss.

Ash Wallace kisses really were the best.

The screen door banged open, and Jackson spilled onto the porch—no coat, no sense that it was forty degrees out. "Did she say yes?"

"Of course, she said yes." Ash pulled her up, wrapping an arm around her waist.

"Coach Vi always makes the best decisions."

* * * * *

*Don't miss the next book in
Anna Grace's Love, Oregon miniseries,
coming December 2023
from Harlequin Heartwarming*